SHE FELT NO PAIN

LOU ALLIN

RendezVous
Crime

Cover design by Emma Dolan

Le Conseil des Arts du Canada | The Canada Council for the Arts

We acknowledge the support of the Canada Council for the Arts for our publishing program. We acknowledge the financial support of the Government of Canada through the Canada Book Fund for our publishing activities.

RendezVous Crime
an imprint of Napoleon & Company
Toronto, Ontario, Canada
www.napoleonandcompany.com

Printed in Canada

14 13 12 11 10   5 4 3 2 1

Library and Archives Canada Cataloguing in Publication

Allin, Lou, date-
          She felt no pain / Lou Allin.

(A Holly Martin mystery)
ISBN 978-1-926607-07-8

          I. Title. II. Series: Allin, Lou, date- . A Holly Martin mystery.

PS8551.L5564S54 2010   C813'.6   C2010-904969-1

To the Crime Writers of Canada,
forever fighting to keep their country's
best and brightest in the forefront.
And above all, to the Executive Board from 2009-2010.
United we stood.

PORPHYRIA'S LOVER

The rain set early in tonight,
The sullen wind was soon awake,
It tore the elm-tops down for spite,
And did its worst to vex the lake:
I listened with heart fit to break.
When glided in Porphyria; straight
She shut the cold out and the storm,
And kneeled and made the cheerless grate
Blaze up, and all the cottage warm;
Which done, she rose, and from her form
Withdrew the dripping cloak and shawl,
And laid her soiled gloves by, untied
Her hat and let the damp hair fall,
And, last, she sat down by my side
And called me. When no voice replied,
She put my arm about her waist,
And made her smooth white shoulder bare,
And all her yellow hair displaced,
And, stooping, made my cheek lie there,
And spread, o'er all, her yellow hair,
Murmuring how she loved me—she
Too weak, for all her heart's endeavour,
To set its struggling passion free
From pride, and vainer ties dissever,
And give herself to me forever.
But passion sometimes would prevail,
Nor could tonight's gay feast restrain
A sudden thought of one so pale
For love of her, and all in vain:

So, she was come through wind and rain.
Be sure I looked up at her eyes
Happy and proud; at last I knew
Porphyria worshiped me: surprise
Made my heart swell, and still it grew
While I debated what to do.
That moment she was mine, mine, fair,
Perfectly pure and good: I found
A thing to do, and all her hair
In one long yellow string I wound
Three times her little throat around,
And strangled her. No pain felt she;
I am quite sure she felt no pain.
As a shut bud that holds a bee,
I warily oped her lids: again
Laughed the blue eyes without a stain.
And I untightened next the tress
About her neck; her cheek once more
Blushed bright beneath my burning kiss:
I propped her head up as before,
Only, this time my shoulder bore
Her head, which droops upon it still:
The smiling rosy little head,
So glad it has its utmost will,
That all it scorned at once is fled,
And I, its love, am gained instead!
Porphyria's love: she guessed not how
Her darling one wish would be heard.
And thus we sit together now,
And all night long we have not stirred,
And yet God has not said a word!

Robert Browning

Prologue

He relaxed on the soft green bed of bracken and shaded his eyes against the sun dappling through the cedar and fir canopy. After all these years, it was sweet to be back on the shore without city stink and noise. Tonight was hot for the island, nearly 25°C and humid for a change, so he'd left his shelter under the bridge for the freedom of the open air. Old Bill was tight-assed about his friggin' rules, strong for his age, too. He rubbed his bristly jaw, still sore from exchanging blows. Why not take another shot before he left, cold-cock the bastard from behind? He laughed deep in his throat, then coughed up mucus. Damn allergies. If butts weren't free, he'd have trashed the fucking coffin nails. Time in the can had probably prolonged his life by twenty years. Now that was funny.

Low tide during the day again, common in summer. He had nearly forgotten how briny the ocean smelled, its seaweed heaped in snakelike coils along the beaches. Sand stretches to the horizon were his preference, not these rock shelves and cobble which twisted the foot. The wild coasts of British Columbia weren't the gleaming white strands of Malibu.

He took a last drag from his rollie and dropped it with a hiss into a beer can. The rainforest was sere, the moss beginning to fade and curl in the short dry season, but bug free, thanks to the salt air. If there was one place the homeless could survive the winters, it was here. Never too hot, never too cold. The perfect porridge.

Wasn't that what dear old Mom always said? He took a swig from a mickey of cheap Alberta rye, chased it with water and wiped his mouth on his sleeve. Tasted like turpentine, but it got the blood moving. The sandwiches the Holy Joe guy brought from down the road and the bottled juice had filled him up. Breakfast in bed in Canada's Caribbean. Come the rainy season, buy a snorkel.

Urban life offered opportunities for gain but too many hassles. Here you were golden if you knew the angles. A whispered question and a wink to the teens lounging at the logger's pole in Sooke, a trip behind some bushes, and a tiny bag of wonders. A bald eagle screed in the blue sky, circling for a tasty rodent gobbling its last seed. Try a poodle, he thought, recalling that stupid animal that had snapped at him down at the Inner Harbour. Home sweet home, though, thanks to the wallet he lifted from that idiot in the crush getting off the ferry. Three hundred in fifties. A cash advance at the first bank machine. With his shabby clothes and grizzled chin, too risky to use the credit cards at a store. He had sold the Visa card to a kid at Cormorant and Blanchard for forty dollars. Got clean clothes at the Salvation Army store and a backpack and camping gear. The Canadian Tire card he'd keep for a week or so. The guy might not cancel it right away.

Then he had hitched a ride west on Highway 14 with a Sleep Country trucker going to Port Renfrew, the end of the road. First stop, Sooke. The sleepy fishing village had changed in over thirty years, now had a McDonalds and an A&W. Funny seeing Judy there when he bought a burger. An ugly scene about the boy, too. A man now. Making big bucks in the diamond mines near Yellowknife. Maybe they'd have had a chance if... Screw it. She'd gained thirty pounds. Looked like a grandmother. Probably fucked like one, too. He'd thumbed on down to Fossil Bay.

When he'd seen that story in the *Toronto Sun*, he knew the man upstairs was looking out for him. Then the visit and some ready cash, but he couldn't stay at the house. The grief wasn't worth it. Until the big score in a week or two, for now he had the perfect hiding place for a piece of insurance. A tight and dry coffee can in a black garbage bag. He couldn't read it so well without reading glasses, which were for wimps, but he suspected its importance. He'd moved it under a nearby rotting log. What kind of weird game was this anyway? Kiddie junk and a dumb-ass list of names and dates. His grimy hands were starting to shake. Unable to prolong the moment, he took out his joy kit. Mixed the happy dust with water on the spoon. Held the lighter beneath until the crystals disappeared. No boiling. Don't want to lose any part of the pretty little ticket to heaven. Across the bay, from a cabin cruiser came the sonar beat of a boombox: "I feel the earth move." Whatever happened to the Seventies? Everyone was bald, fat, both or dead, including Elvis.

He snugged the rubber tubing around his arm, laughing as his body cooperated with a bulging vein. Born to shoot. A crust from a sore on one elbow was still pink, but he read no warning of infection. Soft beds and softer women on the way. The skags he'd met on the road were all bones and dry. Then he filled the syringe, tipped up and tapped to get the air out, plunged into the vein and pulled back with blood. Then back again until gone. Warm fire, like being in a hot tub. Cold water the first time taught a rough lesson. He breathed deeply. As he closed his eyes, he could still hear that other stupid song: "Stronger than Spain and France." Talk about a brain fart. What did it all mean, anyways, and who the hell gave a shit? He gasped, dimly aware that he wasn't getting enough oxygen. His nostrils were stuffed from the humidity. He tried short, shallow breaths. But everything was slowing down, like a wind-up clock. He dropped the syringe and clutched at his throat. Before he could telegraph his brain one last time, the bellows in his skinny chest hung limp, and his head lolled. An adventurous ant climbed aboard his hand and headed for a tasty piece of dried skin.

ONE

At six thirty, the morning sky was bleached-denim blue as wisps of fog circulated like cobwebs. RCMP Corporal Holly Martin headed down West Coast Road. After the wicked curves of the Shirley hill, pulled over at a small picnic park by the fire hall was an older Audi with B.C. plates. A tall woman bent over the motor, shook her head, and slammed the creaky hood. Then she pounded it with a fist and wiped her eyes with her sleeve, shoulders sagging.

Holly made a u-turn and stopped to help. Engine trouble en route to an important appointment? She got out of her cherry-red vintage Prelude as the woman looked up with a tear-streaked face. No one else was in the car.

"You all right, ma'am?" Holly asked, tipping back her billed cap. She wore a light blue shirt under her jacket, duty belt, and dark blue slacks with the traditional yellow stripe. Despite Hollywood films, the famous Mountie red-serge suit was for formal occasions only. No love lost on the stiff, short boots with a spit shine that had taken years, but they held up better than the running shoes she wore off duty.

The woman was dressed in beige slacks and a light sweater with a striped silk scarf. Summer was cool on the Vancouver Island coast overlooking the windy Strait of Juan de Fuca. "Officer?" she said and swallowed, looking at the sports car with a quizzical expression. "I—"

"Just on my way to work. Got car trouble?" Holly considered the Audi. Given the faded paint, it could have been ten years old, it could have been twenty. With the soft winters and salt-free roads, vehicles ran forever. "I'm afraid I'm no auto wizard. How about we call a tow? Shouldn't take long to get you to a mechanic. Do you use Dumont? Tri-City? Or maybe you're visiting."

The woman pressed her full lips together in frustration. "I think I'm out of gas. With all that's been happening, I forgot to fill up."

Holly nodded. It was among the most expensive spots in Canada, especially during tourist season, and gas had hit $1.55 a litre this week. The woman didn't look like the type to cadge a free gallon by playing the helpless female. "Easy enough, then. I keep a jerry can in the trunk. We'll head for a station in Sooke and have you on your way pronto. Are you in a hurry?"

The woman gave a grateful smile, faintly familiar with its honest expression on a heart-shaped face. Holly might have seen her buying groceries or banking. Context was key. The woman looked the same age as Holly's mother had the last time she'd seen her. Late forties plus, but very fit. Her gold Nike tennis shoes had well-earned scuffs. "My partner Shannon is at the Sooke Hospice. I hoped to get there before...I mean...oh God..." Her voice dwindled to a small sob.

Holly put a light hand of reassurance on her shoulder. "Ten minutes then. But lock your car." The coast had its share of opportunistic petty thieves who broke into vehicles left by trusting hikers on the famous Juan De Fuca trail, or even in town. It was nearly impossible to stop them, especially at night with few streetlights. A video camera left in sight could lead to a broken window and a thousand-dollar repair bill.

As they settled into the Prelude, the woman extended a

slender hand, deceptively strong. "I'm Marilyn Clavir. Thank you for your help." She touched a tissue to her soft grey eyes and cleared her throat.

"I'm always passing by the hospice. It's small, but we're lucky to have it, so far from the city." Why did Holly feel that she had to make conversation? Becoming a better listener was on her planning board. Right after doing one hundred crunches a day and training for a marathon.

"They do limited respite care now. A dedicated room was funded this year. Before that they merely coordinated efforts to help people stay at home as long as possible. Usually I ask a neighbour to stay at the house with her, but she was away, and yesterday I had to go to the mainland on urgent business. Then the nine p.m. ferry was cancelled due to engine trouble, so I got home around midnight." A groan of a sigh expressed Marilyn's frustration.

People loved to complain about the rising costs of the ferries along with the shrinking service, but an island with a bridge wasn't a real island. Holly nodded as she drove swiftly but prudently on the winding road, knowing that a logging truck was around every corner. Becoming another statistic wouldn't help. "I'm sorry to hear about your partner. What...happened?"

Marilyn leaned back in the seat, taking deep breaths to calm herself, one hand on her breastbone as she loosened the scarf. A small blue vein pulsed at the fragile skin of her throat. "Nothing that we haven't been expecting. She's had multiple sclerosis for a few years. It came on late, and it came on fast."

"Isn't that unusual? I thought it struck people by their twenties." Holly recalled a girl in her zoology class who had managed with arm crutches, a real hero who didn't suffer fools gladly.

"Canada has one of the highest rates in the world, and British Columbia leads the provinces. It may have something to do with lack of sunshine and Vitamin D. Women are twice as likely to contract it, so are people with northern European backgrounds. As for age, most cases begin between twenty and forty. And some have a more benign condition with little progress in symptoms." She spoke with a resigned authority.

"Haven't there been any medical advances in recent years?" Holly slowed to let the car ahead pull into the post office.

"It's ironic, but that discovery about a vascular connection may have some merit. Even so, the provincial government won't pay for some of the latest drugs. Nothing helped Shannon, not even a treatment we got in Seattle. She was in acute pain from the spasticity. It was heart-breaking." Marilyn pinched the bridge of her aquiline nose until the skin was white. "Listen to me going on, but it was all so crazy. You get desperate."

"The island is famous for alternative therapies. You must have tried them all," Holly said sympathetically. Canada's pot laws didn't punish discreet personal use, and the boost to the provincial economy from B.C. bud was legendary. But many saw cannabis as a gateway drug.

"Bee venom. Medical marijuana. Replacing mercury fillings. Each time the disappointment increased. Then a heart condition developed as one of the side effects. To think that I was so naïve as a child that I believed people could have only one health problem at a time." Marilyn shook her head in self-rebuke.

"That must have been hard for you. Could she walk?"

Marilyn's hands clasped each other in her lap, taut with tension. "That was the worst part. Shannon was a great hiker. We did all the island trails, from Tofino, throughout Strathcona, even up north and across in the Olympics. Then five years ago the unsteadiness started. Bothersome vision problems. She bluffed for awhile, tried to pretend that nothing was wrong. But the myelin connections weren't working. Then her job..." She paused for a moment as if to muster the will to continue. From a pocket she pulled a tissue and dabbed at her nose.

"What did she do?" *There Holly was using the past tense. Dehumanizing the sick.*

"She worked as a nurse in the O.R. at the General. That requires not only consummate training and skill but considerable stamina. Those who can do it are worth platinum for the profession. Every surgeon asked for her. Double shifts were common, and not for the money. But it was no use, not even a desk job was feasible. The Valium for seizures made her so groggy, too."

"Medical personnel are godlike to me. I can't imagine the stress. The highs must be wonderful, but the lows...you can't save everyone." Neither can the police, she thought, but we try, one little corner of the world at a time.

They slowed for the first traffic light as West Coast Road became Sooke Road at the town limits. At the hub of the small village of six thousand were Wiskers and Waggs Pet Store, the Stone Pipe Restaurant, a Petro-Canada and a convenience store. They passed competing strip malls before turning right heading for a small building shared by a pizza business and the hospice, an odd couple made odder by the bloom-filled boat advertising a florist. From east down the highway, flanked by evergreen hills on one side and the sweeping harbour on the other, shrieked the Doppler sound of an ambulance. Marilyn was twisting her scarf into a rag. Holly could hear it ripping like the tears in the woman's heart.

Raucous crows dueled for the prize of a McDonald's bag. Wrappers and cups spilled onto the gravel. The crafty birds seemed oblivious to the presence of cars, hopping out of reach at the last second. Down the highway berm on a quad rode a figure in workclothes, carrying a stick with a pick on the end.

The car had barely stopped when Marilyn snapped off her belt, jumped out and ran the few steps to the hospice, yanking the door open. The ambulance arrived and backed in. A man and a woman hustled a gurney with dispatch. Holly held the door for them, seeing a bright and cozy sitting room with a desk to the side. Bateman prints on the walls. A vase of carnations. A shadowed hallway led to the back of the building.

Holly could hear crying from the interior. "Shannon, darling. I'm so sorry. I thought that..." Marilyn said. This part of duty Holly dreaded, forced to take a ringside seat at an inevitable tragedy. It was her role to be supportive but not intrude, get the information required, make sure there was support and move on to the next crisis.

"Please, ma'am," came an official reply from the crew. "Allow us. We'll take her now." Then there was a "Damn!"

"Defib! Stat!" The female ET charged back into the hall and ran to the vehicle. She retrieved a cumbersome machine on wheels and hustled it up the wheelchair ramp.

From inside, yells and thumps ensued, along with a few swear words. A cry rent the air, a dreadful keening alive enough to have strength to die. Then all was silent. Along with the woman at the desk, Holly lowered her head in respect. Had Marilyn arrived only in time to say goodbye?

Despite the early hour, a small crowd was gathering, and someone had the temerity to peek into the front window. Constitutional walkers strolled the quiet streets, fueled in the summer by hoards of tourists stopping at Serious Coffee, McDonald's and A&W. With no movie theatres or other commercial entertainment other than a par-three golf course, there was little to do but enjoy the temperate weather and watch the boats and comical seals in Canada's southernmost harbour. Holly went out to supervise, waving off a young boy with a practiced gesture. "We have an emergency here. Please stand back and give the ETs room to work. That means you, son. Now hustle."

Then the door opened, and the gurney rolled by like a deliberately slow funeral cortege. The body was covered with a light blue blanket, except for an exposed hand with a simple gold ring. Marilyn walked alongside, holding the hand, pacing herself. Her eyes met those of the ETs, and she nodded as the gurney stopped. Her finger touched its soulmate's index twin in the briefest contact, the final movement in a dance from a bygone era but one in which the energy of life could no longer pass. Then she blinked, moved back, and the team closed the van doors with a gentle push. With no sirens or reason for haste, the vehicle tracked down the road toward Victoria.

Marilyn's head was bowed, a lonely character on an empty stage. "She just let go. The spark flickered out. I don't know how she kept going the last few months. Sheer will, I guess."

"I'm sorry for your loss," Holly said, stepping forward to offer support as the woman's knees threatened to buckle. Yet she didn't seem the fainting kind. "Should you be driving? May I call someone?"

Marilyn straightened and looked into the distance at the fog across the harbour as if watching her old life disappear into the mist. She had short, curly grey hair in a no-nonsense cut and a broad, intelligent brow. Make-up, if any, was subtle. At five-eight, she was Holly's height. Her voice became stronger and preternaturally calm, as if she were convincing herself. "Her spirit is fled, and she will bide. Funny, that's my grandmother's word, and I never knew what it meant until now. For all our feeble human efforts, deaths can't be orchestrated any better

11

than births. When I left her yesterday, she was cheerful, almost rallying. Perhaps she knew. Do you think so?"

"It's possible." Holly had seen only one person die. Her mentor Ben Rogers, shot by a frightened deaf boy whose air rifle turned out to be a .22. When she thought of Ben, she still saw the red pulse of his blood spreading on her lap while she screamed for help.

"Do you believe in an afterlife?"

Holly swallowed, afraid to give a wrong answer, as if there were one. How strange to be having such an intimate conversation with someone she barely knew. And yet it seemed natural. "I'm not...religious in a formal sense. Perhaps the concept is meant to help the living, like funerals for closure. Then again, so many have returned after describing that tunnel of light. I guess I'm saying that anything is possible." Her mother had told her that once, during a painful and undiagnosed tubal pregnancy, her late beloved father had appeared to her in a dream and told her to go immediately to the hospital. That had saved her life. Or had it been her own intuition for survival?

"There are some things we can't explain, aren't there? Beyond science." Marilyn looked over for a brief validation, and their eyes met and held.

Holly stood, arms at her sides in sad ceremony. Notifying the next of kin in serious accidents or worse yet, fatalities, was a duty every officer dreaded. As part of their training, they had been taught the proper words for empathy, respect and care. But no canned phrases ever seemed to fit the moments. "Sorry for your loss." #1 "My condolences." #2. It was like reliving the same nightmare, but she hoped she'd never be calcified against feeling. As if summoned, the sun sliced through the morning fog and backlit Marilyn's strong profile. She was inspecting her hand as if it belonged to a stranger, perhaps remembering that last touch. This was a delicate leave-taking of kindred spirits.

"We...still have to get gas for your car," she heard herself say, then bit her lip. She thought about the sad tasks awaiting the bereaved, the paperwork, the palpability. Why hurry? The dead had no timetable. "If you'd like to sit for awhile, can I buy you a coffee?" Did she sound like she was suggesting that the woman pull herself together?

Marilyn managed a smile which bathed Holly in its warmth. Dreamy philosophy gave way to brisk acceptance and a return to the living. "Strong black tea would be best, I think. You're kind to ask. I must be keeping you from your job."

"Not at all. This *is* my job." Holly shifted in the heavy Kevlar vest. A trickle of sweat was making its way down her spine. "Some people think that we're on permanent vacation at the Fossil Bay detachment. It's quiet as..." She stopped and swallowed, distracted by the swooping flight of a shrieking pigeon heading for a daily pile of grain left by the keeper of a convenience store. "As you can imagine."

Two savvy locals, by mutual agreement they gravitated towards an alley on a backstreet across from the Legion. Dave Evans, his world-class barista certificate proudly on the wall, ran Stick in the Mud coffeehouse as a proud artist. In the small but cozy nook with tempting aromas of house-roasted fair trade blends mingling with cinnamon and nutmeg from on-site baked goods, Marilyn took one of the leather armchairs. Stacks of the radical *Monday* magazine sat on a table. Local artists were represented by photos and colourful art on the walls. Holly returned with a VOS1N0, Dave's version of an Americano, named for their former postal code, and a chai. "There's some sugar if you need it and a warm Morning Glory muffin. Or you can take it for later." The trite words *you need to keep up your strength* drifted into her mind, and she batted them to a corner.

The nuances of a smile reached Marilyn's face. Two shy dimples made their way onto her careworn cheeks.

Holly said, "You look familiar, Marilyn. I've just moved back to the area after fourteen years. Sooke used to be a tiny fishing village with a few B&Bs. Now it's a bedroom community for Victoria."

"Most of that cookie-cutter development sprawl hasn't reached Fossil Bay. We...live at Serenity. That little cottage at the Sea Breeze Road corner."

Did the quaint custom of naming houses come from England by way of California? It seemed more prevalent on the coasts. "Right. Isn't that a massage therapy business?" Full of retirees and fitness addicts of a left-wing lean, the island offered every possible treatment from chiropractic to reiki to acupuncture to spiritual astrology. Health food stores were as popular as gas stations. If you were looking for ear-candling, you had a choice. Mud baths and seaweed applications along with hot rocks and raindrop therapy advertised relief from toxins and tension.

"Nothing fancy. I have a steady list of clients, mostly older folk who live in the neighbourhood and a few who come from Sooke. Shannon and I bought the place years ago when prices were comparatively low, before the boom. She had a small legacy from her parents."

Although this was hardly the time to talk money, Holly imagined that they had nearly tripled their investment. Real estate in the last five years had skyrocketed, and the Western Communities next to Victoria were catching up.

Marilyn seemed to be distracting herself with the balm of common conversation. But she was a careful observer. "And you...?" She squinted a bit to read the nameplate on the blue shirt beneath the jacket.

In the excitement, Holly hadn't even introduced herself. A flush of heat rose from her ears in the humid room as she spoke her name.

"You say you used to live here, Corporal Martin?"

"Please, just Holly is fine. My family and I lived in East Sooke when I was growing up. Then I went off to school, joined the force, and now in my third posting, I'm back home, or near enough. My father has a house on Otter Point Place." She didn't add that she was living there, nor that her mother wasn't with them, but she wondered if Marilyn would catch the implication. It embarrassed her to admit that she had no place of her own.

Marilyn sipped her tea. A healthy pink was returning to her face, though her eyes looked strained. People coped in a thousand different ways. Holly's shoulder radio squawked, and she grimaced. "Sorry, duty calls." She got up as all eyes followed her. "Pardon me," she added, speaking to the room. In the worldwide concept of "island time", cell phones or the equivalent seemed crass and intrusive. The rainforest by the sea was as far from Toronto's Bay Street as Carmel was from Wall Street.

A few honks sounded as traffic was building in the lock-step migration toward Victoria. A prominent crosswalk allowed a few souls to sprint over the road as a red and white Number 61 double-decker bus pulled in and started loading passengers. One man hooked his bicycle onto the front rack before hopping on, his backpack as large as a turtle shell. Holly answered her radio.

Ann Troy, desk jockey at the detachment, said, "I wondered where you were. We've had a call about panhandling at Bailey Bridge. Must be those homeless people who've moved in with the warm weather. Some tourist from Toronto didn't appreciate being hit up for change when he was stopping his Infiniti to admire the ocean." View spots were magnets to fresh arrivals from the urban mainland. If they didn't run off the road in slack-jawed amazement, they were likely to screech off onto the berm, flattening the sword fern. Jaded residents were used to seeing the ocean lapping at the front door and only wondered when a tsunami might knock. A sunny Sunday might be the one day they'd go to the beach unless they were surfers monitoring the happy convergence of high tide and gale-force winds.

TWO

On my way," Holly said. On the temperate south island with snow and freezing temperatures rare as walruses, the homeless lived in "paradise". The truth was that the brutal, uncompromising rains of winter made life equally problematic. Green moss or black mould grew on everything that didn't pulsate and much that did. In Sooke, with more population and resources, the homeless had a better support system. One of the churches served a weekly meal, the Salvation Army pitched in, and the Salvation Army provided cheap clothing, gear and blankets. People said with humanitarian pride that they knew their "street people" by name, and they were usually harmless, trundling bottles or cans for returns to the supermarkets and basking in July sunshine on the green near the BC Liquors.

She collected Marilyn, filled a jerry can with gas at the Petro-Canada and put it in the trunk, smiling off the woman's twenty-dollar bill. "Your tax dollars at work," she said with a grin.

Ten minutes later back at the Shirley turn, they filled the tank, and the engine started purring immediately. Once again, riding a wave of sorrow, Marilyn's lips quivered as she offered a departing wave of thanks. "Bless you."

Holly watched the dowager silver Audi make steady progress down the road, disappearing over a hill. Everyone handled grief differently, but Marilyn seemed to have a core as strong as the muscles common to her trade. Then Holly covered the next few kilometres to the detachment at tiny Fossil Bay. Set in a community of only a few hundred, the outlier post of three officers handled policing another fifty kilometres of blacktop west to Port Renfrew. From there a logging road looped back up to Lake Cowichan, home of yet another of the 126 detachments in British Columbia's E Division, the largest in Canada with over six thousand employees.

The white frame building with a cedar-shingle roof was a refurbished cottage with an entrance room, where Corporal Ann Troy and rookie Constable Chipper Knox Singh had their desks, filing cabinets and computers. Remaining were Holly's office, a lunchroom, a small bathroom, and dark and drear interrogation room. Suspicious of the black mould that lurked under the old linoleum, Holly hoped to update when the budget allowed. The furniture consisted of castoffs from larger detachments, with chipped corners and mummifying duct tape. Holly had made some progress in getting the rooms painted and put up a few landscape prints, but here was the equivalent of Fort Zinderneuf on a day off. Truth was that the post would probably be disbanded before it was remodelled.

Coming through the squeaky front door, she left her hat in the closet, where three sturdy black umbrellas were planted in a stand. With the rains of winter and spring over, they had now entered the dry season. The danger of forest fires replaced floods. Holly took a reusable plastic cup of water from the cooler and sipped. "Tell me more about the complaint, Ann. I checked Bailey Bridge last week. Just an old fire pit and a dozen beer bottles. Did our volunteers report anything recently?" A squad of retirees and youngsters on bicycles made their job easier by reporting suspicious vehicles and property damage. A small percentage of the citizens of Fossil Bay operated their homes as mere summer cottages, so the occasional break-in often went unnoticed.

Ann rose to stretch her aching back as the palsied arm of the wall clock shuddered to nine on the dot. Degenerative disc disease hastened by a daring rescue during a convenience-store robbery had forced her to give up an active career just as she had made corporal. Instead of heading up the detachment by replacing retiring Reg Wilkinson, she drove a desk. The RCMP tried to make accommodations for its staff, especially since they were moved from post to post after only a few years and subject to morale challenges. "Last week Sean Carter said he spotted the first...guest. When you came last fall, the homeless had already moved back to winter quarters in Sooke or Victoria. With that large parking area and the sheltered places under the high bridge, the Bailey fills up fast in the summer. Get used to the minor annoyances and an occasional fight. It helps to set down the rules right off the bat. That's what I di...used to do."

"Better than gang wars, I suppose." Holly felt questions worm themselves around her temple. The more she learned about her turf, the better. Proactive beat reactive. Trouble was easier to head off when anticipated, rather than fighting a defensive action. "But they don't have vehicles. Where do they get their food? They're not eating at Nan's, and the gas station carries mostly junk food and picnic supplies."

"Some have old bicycles. And it's easy to hitchhike on the island. People are more laid-back and trusting. Pick up simple groceries like bread, peanut butter, tuna, soup, stuff that can be eaten cold from the can. Pastor Pete does a sandwich run with the Helping Hands van weekdays on his way home to Jordan River. We'd rather he didn't, since it only makes it easier for them to stay. But try to tell him that." Ann spread her large hands in a gesture of helplessness.

"Enablement is a problem everywhere, and a tough call. Are they all drifters? What's the profile? Are drugs involved?" Ann and Chipper had come the year before Holly had arrived. As post leader, she was in the initial throes of trying to identify her team's strengths and build upon them. Rivalry did not belong in the cards. But if she'd been Ann, she would have had a tough time adjusting to being second in command, especially to a leader ten years younger.

"It's usually a pretty harmless group. At least they're not hanging around schools like in Victoria, moving in at night with sheets of plastic and sleeping bags, leaving needles and human waste behind. A few older regulars know how to work the resources. Some even have small pensions. Reg said that until a few years ago, there were full-time shacks at Sombrio Beach."

"That was in my time. Sort of an old hippie hangout. Malibu North. Everything changed when the Juan de Fuca and West Coast Trail system got going. The authorities cleaned house for the tourists." Holly leaned against the wall and folded her arms. "Sounds innocent enough. I don't want to come down too hard. Usually it's live and let live around here. But the panhandling complaint worries me. It was a man, I'm presuming. Was he particularly aggressive? Any charges possible?"

Ann plunged into a slim "in" pile on her desk and consulted a paper. "There was no contact. The guy backed off." She gave a bark of a laugh. "Wish you'd seen the complainant. About fifty, dressed head to toe in Tilley gear, hat that went through the guts of an elephant, jungle jacket, belt knife. Aluminum water bottle in a case around his shoulder."

Holly smiled at the picture. "No pith helmet?"

"Do knee socks and shorts count? You know the kind. He didn't feel that beggars belonged in his dream vacation spot.

He'd had enough of that sightseeing in Vancouver and Victoria. 'Are there no workhouses?' he asked. 'Then throw the bastards in jail.' I don't know how I kept my big mouth shut."

"We rarely enforce vagrancy laws out here, unless assault's involved," Holly said. "Sounds like a malcontent who expected Disneyworld."

They heard loud music coming from the parking lot as a car door slammed and bootsteps came toward the door. "Morning, ladies, I mean officers."

Constable Chirakumar (Chipper) Knox Singh gave them a winning smile as he entered. At over six feet in his light-blue custom-made turban, he was Bollywood handsome, a trim beard adding a few years to his boyish, café au lait face. Chipper had entered the force nearly twenty years after Baltej Singh Dhillon had become the first Sikh to wear the turban as a member of the RCMP. Nearly two hundred thousand disgruntled Canadians took the case all the way to the Supreme Court and lost in a landmark decision. The five symbols, including the turban and a symbolic wooden dagger, were becoming familiar to people in the land of multiculturalism. She suspected that he took some grief for his career, and that as they got to know each other, they'd swap stories. She remembered the *Playboy* cartoons and tampons taped to her rookie locker. It was a broad and dangerous path between waving the white flag and showing some ovaries, so to speak.

Chipper placed his hat in the closet, opened his jacket at the neck and took a seat at his desk, swinging around to face them, the lightest scent of sandalwood drifting their way. "The traffic's heating up out there, even with gas prices. Guess if you blew two hundred thousand dollars on a diesel RV, what's a few more bucks?" The provincial government's two-and-a-half-cent carbon tax, returned in a one-time, chump-change rebate, had seemed negligible when the oil prices soared and now was as irrelevant as a male mosquito.

Holly gave him a nod. In contrast to the more serious Ann, Chipper had at twenty-eight a sunny personality. The fact that he awarded her more respect than did many silverback males gave her confidence in their generation. Women had only been accepted into the force in officer positions in the late Seventies. One had recently climbed to the top in the B.C. forces. "Any contributions for our provincial coffers?"

"A Ducati motorcycle passed me where I was set up with the radar near French Beach. He was doing 150 kmh. Sweet ride, though." He kissed his long, tapered fingers and mimed a handlebar flourish. "Wish I could afford one. Dad would be fine with it, but I doubt Mom would agree." Chipper lived at home with his parents over their small store in Langford, closer to Victoria. Speaking of coddled, his mother still starched and ironed his shirts and made his lunch.

"You caught him before he could exit the gene pool, taking someone along, no doubt. Good job. The next all-you-can-eat pizza buffet is on me." The long and winding road to Port Renfrew attracted motorcycle runs every weekend, especially at the Gordon's Beach strip, where the speed limit rose to 80 kmh. She didn't look forward to scraping someone off the pavement on a hairpin turn where the highway had been patched one too many times. The latest cheap-fix method of smearing asphalt on the cracks not only crossed drivers' eyes but left slippery spots for even experienced riders.

"Back atcha, Guv," he said, suppressing a wink and knowing that she preferred it to *Ma'am*, which made her feel older than Ann.

Holly told him about the report on Bailey Bridge. Chipper nodded. "Reg told me that the place attracts in the summer. Last year they were pretty quiet, though. We had a cold, wet summer, so not many came out. This year, with the sunny days, they're back in business. I've only stopped by once. An older guy runs the show. He called me over to take in a teenager sloshed to the eyeballs at noon. We had a bulletin on the kid, turns out. A runaway from Nanaimo. Lucky he barfed before he got into the backseat." He steepled his hands in a prayer gesture.

"Guess we'd better schedule regular drive-bys," Holly said, making a mental note.

Chipper stuck out his lower lip and shook his head confidently. "I know that creek. Another month, and it will be dry stones. Everyone will have to move on."

"Problem solved, but I need to check it out. I'll take the car," Holly said. They were limited to an older Impala with a Sooke decal on top of the trunk for air identification, and an ancient Suburban for winter driving in the high hills where snow could lurk. Keeping it full of gas was like pouring water into a sand dune.

*　*　*

She drove east from the sheltered enclave of Fossil Bay. Still tenanted by many former loggers and fishermen, its grid of streets had attracted a new crowd. Spying lower prices west of Victoria, retired boomers from Ontario and points east bought its more modest houses and occasional doublewides. The old clapboard grade school from the turn of the century had been refurbished and took students from Otter Point. Shopping was marginal, only a gas station cum convenience store and Nan's restaurant. Recently a few home businesses had opened, a hair salon, dog kennels, wood salvagers, or personal services like Marilyn's.

Holly rolled past the unmarked town limits and headed to Bailey Bridge, only too aware of the hazards of gaping at the world-class scenery as a gravel truck rolled around the blind curve, taking the centre line under the laws of physics. She eased off the gas and felt her heart skip several beats.

At this time of year, Bailey Creek was one of the last still flowing in salmon country. It would be a different matter in spawning season. "The persistence of Nature," said romantic philosophers, but nothing seemed more brutal than battered cohos pushing their way up their natal creeks, flopping shadows of their former iridescence. Short of an emperor penguin wintering five months without food on ice floes with a lone egg incubating between his feet, their ritual sacrifices were heroic.

"Please protect our resource," the signs at each spawning creek asked. On one side was an entrance to a public beach accessible only at low tide, and on the other, Bailey Creek followed circuitous paths up into the hills. She left the Impala in the sandy lot and headed under the bridge. A generous hollow of concrete held an assortment of shelters on the alluvial plain. The campsite was self-limiting, as Chipper had indicated. But though the rains had ceased, the fruit was oncoming. The salmonberries were emerging, which would draw hungry bears, tired of their spring-grass feed and down for the summer roaming the temperate rainforest. Later would come thimbleberries and finally the hardy Himalayan blackberry with thumb-thick thorny branches.

A grizzled old man with a handsome carved walking stick bearing a fierce eagle on the handle levered his body from a tippy lawn chair and approached her. He wore cut-off jeans, a t-shirt and flip-flops. A healthy tan testified to days outdoors and a shiny metal peace sign hung around his neck, though his salt-and-pepper hair was cut military short. Aging draft dodger? His arms were lean and muscular, though he wore a knee brace. In one discordant note, his left eye, irritated and red, sported a purple bruise. "Morning, officer. Fine day, isn't it?"

She held out a hand and introduced herself, tucking her cap under her arm. "And you are, sir?"

"Bill Gorse. Formerly of Gorse and Broome."

This made her arch an eyebrow at mention of two of the island's most tenacious plants. "Sounds like an old family company." She wondered if he were joking, like the Dewey, Cheatham and Howe firm in the Click and Clack Tappet Brothers radio show across the pond in Washington State.

"Pshaw," he added, emphasizing the "p" as her father had when he was in his Gay Nineties period. His sigh was palpable and self-effacing. "It's a law firm. Still is, for those not partial to corporate ethics. My late father, the Major, and two brothers. I squandered my youth with the family compact, but my nose couldn't take it. When they started chasing the dollar by representing goddamn mining polluters up north, I said adios. Wrecked Muse Lake with their diesel spills and got off with a paltry five-thousand-dollar fine." He flicked at a midge, whirling in its vortex. "Couldn't stomach it. Anyhow, now that we know each other, what can I do you for?"

A lawyer with principles. So much for the jokes sending them to the bottom of the sea to poison the sharks. Why didn't he pursue the prosecutorial side? Perhaps he was a true maverick and regarded the law itself as an ass. "There was a report of panhandling here."

He gave an unimpressed cackle then coughed into his hand.

"Thought you were into something serious. This is yee-haw land, not the prissy streets of Victoria." The local area was notoriously casual, the home of bearded Santas driving ancient Westphalias, llama and alpaca shepherds, and small organic farms. The elderly ladies in Sooke and Fossil Bay had mid-afternoon coffee at home instead of tiffin at the Empress Hotel with the blue-rinsed bluebloods. Unless they worked in the city, few people in the Western Communities went to Victoria without a shopping mission.

Holly gave an apologetic shrug. "It was reported, Mr. Gorse. I have to check it out. What's the story?" So far he'd been the only person she'd seen, but the gear indicated signs of others. She tried for concerned, not intrusive.

He tapped his chest, a few curly grey pelt hairs peeking from his v-neck. "Listen. I'm the old fart boss around here. I try to make a few rules so's we don't get into each other's faces too much. No stealing. Can the noise after ten. Pick up after yourself. Don't shit where you live, in every sense of the word. Not much different from that guy's book about kindergarten rules."

Suppressing a smile at the candor, Holly saw a neat pile of crushed beer cans in a clear plastic bag. "What about drinking or drugs?"

"Hell, drinking's legal last I heard."

"Not on the street. We have open-container laws."

He planted his feet and folded his arms. "We're not bothering anybody, not about to take a piss against a building. This is where we live. And it's public land, belongs to the people. Doesn't say 'no camping,' does it? Be reasonable."

Holly shifted her feet, feeling like a bully. She glanced at her watch. According to the schedule, she had this sunny afternoon off for a change. With the small population, the three-man post kept hours only between eight a.m. and six p.m. Any emergencies were routed to Sooke, a detachment of fourteen with round-the-clock service. "You're being a wee bit evasive about the drug question. Do I take that as a yes?"

His lined face grew sober and he scratched at his ear, where a silver loop dangled, giving him a pirate look. "I can't see that you have probable cause for a search, and I wouldn't be surprised if you turned up some wacky tobaccy. Personal use only. Hard drugs I don't tolerate." It was a cliché that the law in Canada ignored pot smoking, but Holly held up a placatory hand and adjusted her posture to official, not combative. She didn't want this to escalate. No needles or paraphernalia were in view, and no children would be hanging around under Bill's watch. "No worries, then. If you're not bothering anyone, stay as long as you want. But let's get to my reason for coming, the panhandling complaint." She arched an eyebrow in a 60-40 serious look.

Bill sat down with a grunt on an overturned blue recycling box and flexed his knee. "I'll tell you straight. Any guy around here pulling any of that crap answers to me. I don't want problems with the law. We mind our own business. That one asking tourists for money like some bridge troll, I told him to quit it. Next morning he showed up with a camcorder. Said he won it in a card game at the Legion, the liar. It was a high-end Sony."

Her interest was piqued. One strand led to another in law and society's tangled webs. She gave a light laugh. "Nobody gambles with camcorders. Probably he stole it. Is he around?"

"Went to hock it, ask me."

Holly frowned as possibilities tumbled through her mind. "It's too far to Victoria. More likely he sold it to a kid on the street, or for nothing at a junk shop. What's his name?" She took out her notebook.

"Says he's Derek Dunn. I don't ask for IDs. Hell, sometimes

27

I change my own middle name. Dick used to be an ordinary handle. Now..." He reached down for a bottle of an over-the-counter painkiller, shook out a few, and showed her one. When she blinked, he washed it down with water from a plastic jug.

Dating a fresh page, she wrote down the name and got a brief description, including a shortened right index finger which Derek said had been cut in a table-saw accident. "Thanks for the information. I'll check on it. For the record, how many...people are staying here now?" She could see at least four makeshift tents of tarps, branches, and plastic sheeting, more for privacy than rain protection, since it was dry under the bridge. All she could smell was the briny tang of the ocean. Where did they take their garbage? And where did they do their business? In the woods? She'd peed on her shoe in the bush more than once. If it were a crime to drop trou in the deep and dark, ninety per cent of the province would be in jail.

He said, "Varies a bit, more on weekends. I draw the line. Should have been a social worker. If a kid tells me he's been abused, I know where to send him. A youngster didn't even start shaving came last week. Said his parents were okay with his travelling, but I sent him packing. So...there's three, counting Joel Hall." He nudged a thumb toward a sleeping pad on cardboard beside the concrete bridge support. "Haven't seen him since last night when we had a bit of an altercation. Could be he's found a lady friend with a soft bed. He's past fifty but a charmer when he wants to be. You want to hitch into town, any guy with a pickup will stop."

Holly gave the scene a final scan. Recently a surprising legal decision had cities scrambling. When the B.C. Supreme Court ruled that since the number of shelter beds was "insufficient" for the area's needs, the homeless had earned the right to erect tents and sleep overnight in parks. Officials were outraged, since they had just spent tens of thousands cleaning up a camp hidden deep in the dense bush of Mill Hill Park, a wild green space in a millionaire community. The next week, a number of homeless people in Victoria had pitched camp in legendary Beacon Hill Park, managing to squash rare flowers. In a renewed game of push and shove, the city responded by counter-ruling that no fires would be tolerated and that tents had to be taken down by seven each morning. The issue of impromptu bathrooms went unmentioned. In the moral outrage and confusion that followed, suddenly another forty-five shelter beds materialized. Out here, far from civilization and away from most eyes, things were different. As long as they kept relatively out of sight, cleaned up their mess, and remained peaceful, people were left alone. They weren't displacing lawn bowlers or frightening carriage horses in front of the legislature.

"Thanks...Bill. I appreciate your honesty and sense of responsibility," she said, shaking his hand. "But there is one final important thing." Timing was critical in policing, and she had learned this technique from her father's *Columbo* tapes.

His light green eyes crinkled in suspicion. "What's that, officer?"

"The dry season is well underway. You've seen those signs prohibiting open burning. Even in provincial parks, fires aren't allowed. We may be rainforest, but the undergrowth gets like tinder. A cigarette butt tossed out a car window can do it. And with those winds off the strait..." She gestured to a colourful para-sailor skittering down the bay.

He gave a cooperative nod. "I hear you. But we gotta boil our water, like for coffee. We don't want to get sick. It's hard to haul plastic gallons around. We don't exactly get deliveries from Culligan."

"Understandable. Just keep it under the bridge and very small. Leave plenty of clear space around." As cars whizzed overhead, she looked up at the noisy belly of the bridge. "Sparks won't travel far under here. A small propane stove would be easier for cooking, though." She wondered about the black eye but didn't want to press her advantage. Men were more likely to let the hormones surge. Women had their ranks among the homeless, but they wouldn't strand themselves so far from services and safety. Even so, in Vancouver during a savage winter, a woman had burned to death trying to light candles for warmth under her overturned shopping cart.

She left him with a card. "Not that you have a cell phone handy, but any problems or questions, we know each other now." "Have a good day" wasn't a phrase she could tolerate. "Glad we could talk" made more sense.

*   *   *

Her shift over, Holly continued east, passing Gordon's Beach, a thin strip of land with a dozen tiny properties on limpet lots, from tumbledown shacks to half-million-dollar Hobbit houses with rounded doors, mullioned windows, and driftwood sculptures. The Beach Box. Four hundred thousand dollars worth of cute. She turned up from West Coast Road onto Otter Point Road then turned left again, climbing into the hills. In the nineteenth century, nearly every acre of the island had lain under timber-company rule, one western god of commerce. Then came the settlers with their agriculture. Only twenty years ago, the street had been farmland, parcelled off in lots of a third of an acre. One bonus was that everyone on the dead-end road knew everyone else's business. When the police blotter in the weekly *Sooke News*

Mirror listed action, Otter Point Place never made the Hall of Shame. She passed a llama farm, a pottery, and several B&Bs before slowing as two horses clopped down the narrow verge, their young riders wearing equestrian helmets. Some kind soul usually arrived with a shovel and biffed the road apples into the berry hedges as fertilizer.

At a time when she had recently tasted independence in her seven years with the force, Holly found herself living at home, a modern reality for which she made no apologies. With housing prices skyrocketing, few rental opportunities, and relocation every three or four years, she had little choice but to move in with her father. Paying him a nominal fee for bed and board eased her conscience. As well, she mowed the lawn and took out the recyclables and garbage. He cooked. She cleaned. Fair trade.

She parked next to his sassy blue Smart Car in the driveway of the white-sided villa. Except for its cedar-shingle roof, it would be more at home in the Aegean than overlooking the Strait of Juan de Fuca. The mighty peaks of the Olympics faced her, snowpack still spilling from the uppermost ranges like vanilla ice cream onto the purple peaks below. From eleven to seventeen kilometres wide, the strait was a living creature whose face changed with the prevailing winds. In summer, with the warmer water, fog banks began the morning, first on one side then the other, clearing to blue skies in the afternoon. "It must be June. I can't see the street," her father joked.

Floppy-leaved banana plants nearly seven feet high grew by the house. An irrepressible and stinky kiwi climbed its hairy way to the front deck. In the side yard next to a vacant lot overgrown with alders and the occasional bigleaf maple, muscular canes of Himalayan blackberries began to snake over the fence. A hot tub with a gazebo and purple and pink clematis vines completed the spa image, but summer was not its time, rather an icy January when a few snowflakes melted on your head as steam rose around you.

The family hadn't always lived here. It had been her father's surprise as she entered high school to move them from dark, secluded East Sooke to this sunny hillside. But it hadn't helped the rocky marriage. What had brought Bonnie Rice and Norman Martin together in university hadn't lasted the decades as their personalities diverged with a vengeance. Bonnie had been gone ten long years. The tiny holly bush she had planted for her daughter by the kitchen window now bore eight feet of shiny, prickly leaves, awaiting its star turn before Christmas. Did its growth seem like a reproach to them both?

Holly let herself in and was immediately greeted by a black-and-white forty-pound jumping jack, a streak of "paint" down his face. "Hello, Shogun," she said to the two-year-old border collie, his gay tail held high and his soft muzzle shovelling her hand. As a rescue, he'd been Hogan then Logan, answering to anything as long as he wasn't called late for dinner. The dog gave her father a focus other than his consuming research. He had taught Popular Culture at the University of Victoria for the last thirty years and had published countless journal articles as well as a book on Victorian children's board games.

Shucking off her boots in the foyer, she took the circular oak staircase to the master suite he'd given her, retaining for himself the other two bedrooms and bathroom. Or was it because he didn't want to remember the king-sized marriage bed and its six-piece matching cherry furniture? At first she felt awkward lying where her parents had once slept like knight and lady on a tomb, but sometimes when Shogun and his jittery feet joined her in the night, she welcomed its space. A small balcony gave the house's best view, though all of the front rooms, including the kitchen, overlooked the water.

"Bye, bye, Miss American Pie," drifted from the CD player in the solarium. She searched her memory, the quiz games she'd played with her father. Now he was in the Seventies, one of the best periods for food, television and music. He submerged himself in the decade he was teaching. Last fall it had been the Fifties, too far removed from her mind set. She took off her duty belt, placed the Glock in a drawer and put on shorts and t-shirt. Free from the Kevlar corset, she flexed her shoulders.

In the kitchen, she saw her father gazing out the window across the strait to Washington. Though no individual houses were in sight at such a distance, she felt mirrored by the Americans. The population was smaller, and a great chunk of the land was protected in the Olympic National Park by a country which had greater foresight. Across Puget Sound lay the shopping and airline metropolis of Seattle. Waves were bobbing the fishing boats on this sunny day. Great loads of shrimp, halibut and salmon would fill the nets. Far out, a container ship headed out to sea. She picked up the field glasses and read "Hanjin".

"What's up, old pal?" she asked. Norman Martin, never Norm, turned his cool, azure-eyed gaze to her. He topped six feet, and he was slim, his silvery blond hair trim and smooth. Lately she thought she'd imagined a slight stoop, though the adjective *courtly* fit him well. He scorned bad language and tsked at her occasional "fuck". Social-services lawyer Bonnie had cursed like a trooper at the unfairness that life dealt those who sought her aid. "Your father can't help it if he lives in an ivory tower where it's so quiet that you can hear yourself age," she had told Holly. "I hope you choose to live in the real world and make a difference."

"I'm glad you're back early. I have instructions about dinner."

Norman ruffled the silky fur of the animal, its flagging tail knocking from side to side and its feet dancing in anticipation of a walk.

"Are you going somewhere?" Though he'd taken one summer course for the extra money, recently he'd been going to dog agility shows and had begun training Shogun. Much of this was a result of his new friendship with a lady up the hill on Randy's Place. Madeleine Hamza, Swiss-Swede and the divorcée of a mysterious Egyptian engineer-millionaire, was allowing him to use the expensive agility equipment on her lawn. "I live alone. My dogs are my life," she had said when they'd first met.

The friendship was a healthy sign. Holly wondered if her father had been involved with anyone during his years alone. What about the departmental secretary who baked him blackberry pies on his birthday? He'd never filed for divorce or even probated her mother's will, to her knowledge. Did he, like Holly, believe she was dead? He never said as much but ran an ad at intervals in the *Times Colonist* seeking information. If anything had developed, he never mentioned it. Any avenues she might pursue with her connections to solve the mystery of Bonnie's disappearance had best be kept to herself until she was certain. In the months she'd been home, she hadn't found out much.

"Maddie and I are off to Wiffen Spit to cut broom," he said, brandishing a shiny pair of expensive secateurs, a Christmas gift from her, and fastening it into a leather holster on his belt. "Fifteen of us are going. Some red hat society she belongs to. We have to cut these pernicious bushes before the flowering is over. Root and branch. Do or die!" He referred to a showy but invasive plant of the pea family. Since being brought across the oceans by homesick Scots in the nineteenth century, it had elbowed out local favourites with its atomic tangerine blossoms, prolific seeds and woody stems. The sentimental favourites of Garry oak meadows were in particular peril. A yearly campaign run by zealots as serious as crusaders called for its eradication on the prized curvilinear finger of land which sheltered Sooke Harbour. Dog walkers loved the Spit and appreciated the free poop bags at the brass-gated entrance.

Dressed in a tie-dyed rainbow shirt he'd made himself, baggy knee-length khaki shorts, and his prized Vietnam War sandals with tire-tread soles, Norman primed a shoulder pack with a thermos and packages of peanut-butter crackers. "Dinner's all ready, so you needn't worry. This period is a cinch. Convenience is in, but weird food fads haven't arrived. I'm planning a quiche with tuna. The crust is baked. Coleslaw's in the fridge. It's a winner in every decade, bottled dressing or that boiled version I make for the Oughts period. Cabbage is versatile because it keeps."

She laughed but ignored the real-man quiche joke. "Our ancestors thrived on it," she replied. The hobbyhorse of the popular culture themes grounded him. Only sixty, he'd never retire unless they closed the university.

"And later we'll watch the first year of the *Mary Tyler Moore Show*."

"Surely not the entire year." Once the sitcoms started rolling, she couldn't shake the theme song from her head. "You're going to make it after all." The Minneapolis skyline. Why couldn't he just watch hockey and drink beer like a normal Canadian man?

"Keep it up, and I'll play *The Partridge Family*." He glanced at the dog. "Maddie's bringing a backpack for Shogun so he can carry a few jerky treats. It'll be a good time to teach him the down-and-stay command."

A toot from a black Kia SUV sounded in the drive, and Shogun erupted in the signature deep-throated barking which had earned him his latest name. Down the hill he charged as Bentley, a venerable Corgi and dog of the day from Madeleine's four-pack, urged him on from the vehicle. The feisty woman waved a medieval metal claw apparatus, which Holly recognized from Home Hardware as a Pullerbear. This was all-out war.

The late afternoon passed quietly as Holly basked on the deck while a swallow swooped back and forth, building a nest in the small birdhouse swinging from the oak. Clearly, she needed to get a library card. Her father's current reading selections covered the patio table. *The Exorcist. Jonathan Livingston Seagull. Watership Down. Fear of Flying?* Shaking her head, she went inside to the bookshelf and chose L.R. Wright's *The Suspect,* the first and only Canadian mystery hardcover to win the coveted American Edgar award. In high school, she'd given a book report on it. Now she was living the life of an RCMP officer.

Life had changed when her mother had disappeared. Holly had been committed to a career in botany at UBC. Then she had switched to criminal justice, completed her degree, and joined the force. After the six months of training at the Depot in Winnipeg, she'd been mentored in The Pas, then posted to Port Hardy up island, and finally to Fossil Bay when she made corporal. It was close to her home but not enough to disqualify her, since the force didn't want officers working in their own neighbourhoods. The Fossil Bay detachment had only been activated ten years before to monitor the road west to Port Renfrew. Domestic disputes, speeders, drunk drivers and teens with six-packs led the docket. In the summer, car break-ins increased at parks along the Juan de Fuca Trail. Overnight hikers were advised to use the seasonal shuttle buses.

She cracked open the book and was immediately drawn to the unconventional plot of the concise and imaginative novel.

In a quirky but daring twist, the murderer was known from the beginning and shared the point of view. The denouement was simply a cat-and-mouse game involving maddening clues and the question of motivation. The more she worked at her trade, the more Holly wanted to know why, not just how. But if she wanted to play detective, she'd have to move to a larger post.

An hour later, she went inside for a dry cider, sipping it on the deck. Though the view was panoramic, it was far from quiet. Secondary growth aspen and maple on the slopes below separated her from West Coast Road, but in a bandshell effect, the traffic noises revealed the critical artery. The guttural roar of a motorcycle gearing up for the change from sixty to eighty kmh blended with the shriek of jake brakes on a truck heading the other way. The single-lane road, the only east-west connection, was a worrisome fact for those who saw development as inevitable.

As she closed the book, leaving a few tempting chapters, she heard a car crunch gravel. The KIA, packed with dog crates for Madeleine's brood, raced up the slope, skidding to a dusty stop at the back porch. Holly waved and called, but the limber little woman, her flyaway reddish hair blowing in the breeze, hurried to Norman's side. She opened the door, then stood, hands on her hips with a worried frown. Holly left the porch and came around to the back deck as Shogun leaped out, backpack swinging. Her father was crouched in the front seat, his lean face contorted. In reflex, she put her hand on her chest in panic. Surely not a heart attack. He never talked much about his health. Her family had skated free of illness, pure luck that she'd taken for granted. Had fortune changed her mind?

"Dad, what happened?" She considered the car, pristine and uncrumpled, windshield intact. Not an accident, then. Nor something so serious as to call an ambulance or drive straight to

Victoria General. "Did you fall?" The elevated spit embracing Canada's southernmost port used sharp rip-rap for its breakwater and could be dangerous if they had left the gravel path to uproot the stubborn broom. She searched his knobby knees for signs of damage. Not a mark.

"Oooooo," he said with an undisguised wail, wincing as Holly and Madeleine helped him from the car, each putting an arm under his and heaving at the count of three. "It's just a wrench. I did it one year starting the damn mower. That's why I gave you that job, Holly." With a bitter laugh, he turtled forward.

"Enough self-diagnosis. Let's get you inside," Holly said.

For a woman in her late fifties, the wiry Madeleine had muscles from her daily clear-cut hikes with her pack. They maneuvered him with difficulty up the winding Tara stairs to his bedroom. Norman was soon safely tucked in with a very large rum. Straight up. No ice.

"Hot pack or cold?" Holly asked, her first-aid course a dim memory. Tossing a mental coin, they set up a heating pad.

Sipping an orange juice, Madeleine sat on the deck with Holly as they tried to wind down. From past the greenbelt, their neighbour's time-challenged rooster announced his superiority. "This type of injury is not serious, since it's merely muscular, but it can last several days, and you know your father. He is very stubborn and independent." Madeleine's charming accent replaced *th* with *z*.

"I'm no caregiver. What am I going to do with him?" Holly was thanking the gods that he had class only twice a week. And what about that quiche? Stress was giving her an appetite.

Madeleine pursed her lips together. "Men are very stubborn, but at heart they are babies with pain. It might be a good idea if he got a massage. Or two. And as soon as possible."

"I'm not sure he'll agree. They're expensive," Holly said. Norman could squeeze a loonie until it laid an egg.

To his egalitarian credit, he'd always cooked for the family. Once he had sprained his ankle and couldn't get off the couch. Her mother, whose motto was "Suffer in Silence", had clashed swords with him about his meal plans, by default her responsibility. "For Christ's sake, can't you make an exception? One frozen pizza or a TV dinner isn't going to kill us." A small-time lawyer turned full-time advocate for women's rights on the island, aboriginals in particular thanks to her Coastal Salish heritage, Bonnie spent much of her time travelling the province in her battered Bronco, snacking on fruit, nuts, cheese and bread. Meals were an inconvenience she often forgot. Rather than watch her parents continue to bicker, Holly had stepped in at fourteen and made the meat loaf, mashed potatoes and carrot coins for his Forties feast.

Holly saw concern but a no-nonsense approach in Madeleine's glacial Scandinavian eyes, more than a passing resemblance to an older Garbo. She was proving to be a good friend to the older man. Whenever Holly had called on Sundays before her return, he'd been having a "quiet dinner", presumably alone. Now not only did he have Shogun, but he was laughing again, chatting on the phone with Madeleine like a teenager. "Odd timing, but I met a masseuse this week," Holly said. Had Fate stepped in to lend a hand?

*   *   *

At ten the next morning, Chipper was doing mental calculations about how long it would take before he could afford an apartment and a sharp new silver Mustang convertible. His salary was bumping up big-time this year, but he had a ton of student loans. Living on the Prairies had been so cheap. True, his basement bachelor suite had been small, and the oil furnace woke him when it kicked in during cold winter nights. There wasn't anything in a hundred miles to spend money on anyway. It would take him hours to drive to Regina, see a show and go to a club. Then on Sunday he'd have to return to work.

At Bailey Creek, Chipper slowed as a man waved him over. He pulled to a stop in the parking lot and got out, making sure the doors were locked. Kids liked to peek into the windows at the shotgun on the console. He adjusted his duty belt to ride easily on his slim hips.

The man was drinking a can of soda. Watching from a nearby van was a young family.

"Yes, sir. What can I do for you?" he asked with a friendly smile. Maybe the guy merely needed directions.

"There's a body in the bush."

"A body…" He could hardly push saliva past his Adam's apple as he answered three notes above his usual range.

THREE

Officer, are they poisonous? We didn't know what else to do. We were hiking on the beach a few miles west. Darn cellphone dead as a doornail. Who could have thought? Telus told us no problem anywhere in Canada. We drove back at top speed then realized we had no clue where the nearest hospital was. Then we saw your flag flying and pulled in. Can you call 911?"

The gasping woman, clearly a tourist in her giant sunhat, light summer dress and clogs, stood in the detachment office, eyes wild with fear. Behind her, a man held a two-year-old in a Hello, Kitty jumpsuit, happily gurgling with a soother. The baby's colour was good, and it seemed to be enjoying the action.

Holly considered the pale-pink heart-shaped berries nearly crushed in the woman's sweaty hand. "No problem. These are salal. Quite edible even if they're not ripe. They were a staple in the native diet. My dog thrives on them." It was hard not to smile. A tour guide in darkest Kazakhstan.

Worry lines relaxed on the woman's round face as she dropped them into a wastebasket. She patted her chest and leaned on the desk for support. "We figured those others, the yellow ones, and the tiny blackberries, were fine. But I didn't recognize these. Dakota was toddling around and grabbed some before I could do anything. You know how kids put everything in their mouths."

"I told you so, honey. Just look at him." The man bounced

the baby in the air until laughter bubbled out of the tiny, bow-shaped mouth. "Women."

"The yellow ones are salmonberries. We have thimbleberries arriving, sort of a light reddish peach colour. You can't go wrong with the raspberry and blackberry families. The first pull off clean, the others have a core. But avoid anything else as a general rule, and that includes mushrooms, though they're scarce this time of year." Holly led the woman to a wall poster of edible and poisonous British Columbia plants, pointing out baneberries, along with the dangers of deadly nightshade.

"Should we be on the lookout for snakes too? We saw a striped one."

Holly laughed in spite of herself. About time she got to play ranger, a job she had trained for. "We're as safe as Ireland. But don't touch any rough-skinned newts. That's a cute little lizard with an orange belly. Even skin contact is dangerous."

"Thank you so much. We're enjoying the island. Is it always this cold, though? We had to buy sweatshirts." The woman gave a mock shiver and a friendly grin.

Holly pointed to a map. "We're temperate rainforest. By definition that means cool, but this summer's unusual. Go up island away from the winds if you want more heat. The Cowichan Valley is called the Warmlands for good reason."

Suddenly self-conscious about her unnecessary panic, the woman brushed hair from her brow. "We're from the San Joaquin Valley in California, and it's an inferno down there. What a relief to escape the smoke."

*   *   *

After the family left, Ann took a large sip of green tea, wincing at its bitterness. Recently she had changed from half-moon reading glasses to contacts, which cut the age difference between the corporals. Today she even wore a pastel lipstick and a bit of powder. The short cut of her sleek brown hair suited her. A new exercise regimen with a dose of yoga had smoothed pain seams from her face.

But Holly knew that she had her bad moments. The former supervisor had told Holly never to call Ann after supper, when she might be mixing alcohol and painkillers. Many people with similar injuries took advantage of disability pensions. Ann soldiered on and never made excuses.

As Holly returned minutes later from a bathroom break, a call came in on the radio. Ann listened carefully. "It's Chipper," she said, picking up a pen and notepad and asking a few questions. "He's down at Bailey Bridge. They've found a body."

"A drowning?" Holly asked. Summer wasn't a period of intense storms, but unwary tourists were caught in the occasional riptide or rogue wave. Ocean swimming was bitter cold. Even the surfers and parakiters wore wetsuits. She hoped it wasn't a child. No one had been reported missing, but this was prime boating season. Recently two people had perished in quiet Sooke Harbour. Alcohol was often the guilty third party.

"Not this time. Up the hill beside the creek. Must be one of those drifters camping under the bridge."

"Was it a fall? A fight?" Maybe she should have tried to get the men to relocate. Such a narrow line between proactiveness and bullying. This wouldn't look good if headquarters got sticky about her loose protocol on public lands. "You told him what?" she heard her superiors ask.

"Going by the scene, Chipper suspects drugs." Fatal overdoses had doubled on the island last year, but were still much lower than Vancouver. Addicts ran a calculated risk. Lower population, less chance of getting damaged goods.

"I don't understand. Bill said..." Her voice trailed off. What about that fresh shiner? Maybe he was the victim. But he'd said he never trucked with hard drugs, and she'd watched him carefully for signs of nervousness. Steady as Sir, the giant rock on Muir Beach.

"Who's Bill?"

"Bill Gorse. An older man I met down there. Resident peace-keeper, he fancies himself. Sets strict rules for drinking and drugs. He mentioned a couple other men, but they weren't around." Derek Dunn, was that the name? Had he come back from selling that camcorder? And what about Joel Hall?

She arrived at the scene ten minutes later. Chipper gave her a wave and came over with several notebook pages. This wasn't the first body they'd found, but she hoped never to be so callous as to be unmoved by death. It was her job to protect, but if too late for that, to serve in the ceremonial offices with every possible dignity. Even so, death had its hierarchy. Traffic fatalities were on the bottom of her list. Mangled remains which demanded a strong stomach and a gentle hand for survivors. What might she find here?

Chipper was out of breath, and a sheen of sweat covered his brow, perhaps from climbing up and down the path beside the creek. "Ann said that the ambulance should arrive any minute. Boone, too," he said. Boone Mason was their local coroner. British Columbia had an idiosyncratic system, dating back a century, employing thirty-two full-time and seventy-five part-time people on an ad hoc basis. Anyone with a strong medical, law enforcement or legal background could certify a death. Recommendations to prevent future accidents were also within purview of the mandate. It was Boone's call to request a Medical Examiner for an autopsy in case of a suspicious death. He had been a private investigator in Vancouver before a knee blew on him. He lived with his deaf cat in a spacious doublewide in a nearby trailer park.

Holly paused in the theatre of her responsibilities, looking at Act One, Scene One. A family of four stood by their loaded Grand Caravan with a dusty Ontario: Yours to Discover plate and a moulded plastic gear carrier open on top. The little girl of around seven was crying, her face buried in her mother's lap. An older boy sat looking at a small metal tag glinting in the sun while his father read a road map. Hapless tourists, or they wouldn't be stopping here at high tide when the beach was inaccessible. Perhaps they were admiring the distant rollers or counting the many fishing boats peppering the bay. The first of over two hundred cruise ships had entered the strait over a month ago.

Chipper held up his notebook, printed in his usual meticulous style. "I've got all the names. Plates, home numbers. Driver's license ID, the works. Plus I made a preliminary outline of the scene. Though my drawing's not—"

"Where *is* the body? And what are those people doing hanging around here? Are they witnesses?" Holly asked quietly. A cold trickle was making its way down her spine like mercury falling in a thermometer. She felt a twitch of annoyance at Chipper's priorities. How secure was the scene? Normally he loved stringing yellow tape.

"B-b-but *they* found the victim. Farther up the creek." He pointed up a path half hidden by leafy salal.

"Surely not the kids. They look pretty young for long hikes."

"They were geocaching."

"Geo...what?" The *geo* she got, but was it catching or cashing?

Chipper grinned at being a step ahead. He spelled the word. "I just heard of it. Apparently it's a game with an Internet site. You need a GPS."

"For kids? Sounds sophisticated, not to mention expensive." Then again, what did she know about the costs of raising a family? It sounded cheaper than outfitting a couple of boys for hockey.

"Maybe ten years ago. Now even Canadian Tire carries units at a reasonable price. Then you go online and search for treasures according to their coordinates."

"Treasures...what kind of—" Were people leaving valuables in the bush? Clueless townies fumbling around in the hinterlands surrounded by the perils of nature was an ugly picture. It didn't take much to get lost in thick and mountainous terrain with a disorienting canopy hiding the direction of the sun. Even in small East Sooke Park, a missing hiker had been forced to spend the night.

Chipper gave a small frown with his tilde-shaped brows, turning his back on the family and lowering his voice. "Not *real* treasures. Cheap little stuff that kids like. A pin, a toy, a balloon, a stick-on tattoo. When you find the cache, you can take something and leave something. Write in the logbook. It's actually pretty cool."

Holly observed the family from a distance, keeping her voice low. "What's that metal thing the boy has? Please don't tell me he found it at the site."

He made an effort not to laugh in what should be a sober moment and put a hand on her forearm. "Relax, Holly. It's called a travel bug. They brought it from Ontario to place in a cache. They're numbered so you can track them all over the world. It's like a parallel universe, another dimension."

She was getting distracted by the details, verging on short-tempered being left out of the loop. Death and games had no business interacting. "Okay. Sorry. Humour me and slow down. Does this have anything to do with the body? Was the *victim* geo...caching?"

"No sweat on that. The vic...the man looks like a regular here at the bridge. The game explains why this family was in the area, that's all. Good thing they weren't farther back, because a cougar and cubs were reported in the bush along Tugwell Creek, and bears are always around." Black bears, not grizzlies. The smaller brother was much less dangerous, both in size and temperament.

She nodded, flexing her shoulders, reminding herself that being in charge carried stress as well as prestige. "I need to talk to them. They probably want to get on with their vacation. Meanwhile, don't let anyone else pull in to admire the view. Say you're conducting an investigation." Number ten in the one hundred useful ambiguous phrases for law enforcement.

"I can put up neon cones or crime-scene tape. There's some in the trunk."

Chipper was a by-the-book man, but this time she didn't agree. "Then everyone will stop to gawk. Be firm, but try not to provoke interest. 'Investigation' could mean anything. Vandalism. Stolen goods."

He made his face as bland as a pail of chocolate milk. "Okay, Guv."

After tossing him a wry look, she walked over to the family and introduced herself. Frank and Chrissy Jones were from Sudbury.

"Mr. Jones, can you take me to..." She mouthed "the body" so as not to alarm the children.

He gave her a blink and a subtle nod. "You guys stay here. I'm going with the officer. Mom will give you a drink. And kids, I'm real proud of you. Remember that helping the police is important."

If only all parents thought like that. Holly knew the value of an upbringing stressing the right attitude. Some wouldn't turn in their child if he torched a school.

As Chrissy handed out juice boxes from a cooler, Frank led Holly up a narrow path by the stream into the rainforest.

Spared from the axe, giant red cedars and Douglas fir sent their branches up to three hundred feet into the air. Bigleaf maples were festooned with grandfather-beard mosses. In the dry weather, the forest colour had lost some of its lustre, and banana slugs napped in the moist patches under leafmould. Horse droppings showed where a few locals exercised their animals. Every now and then they passed a massive barkless stump with two deep holes six feet up the butt. These were cut for springboards, a pioneer practice which boosted up the axe- or saw-man to spare him the thickness. Before power tools, a ten-foot-diameter tree had taken a day to cut. Now the monsters, if any were left, were felled in minutes by a chainsaw. Whimsical people put piles of cobblestones in these holes, turning the stumps into wooden goblins. Moss asserted its dominion, and an occasional red huckleberry grew on top like a natural flower pot. The British navy had been cutting masts on the island before Confederation. A tree eight hundred years old would have been alive at the time of the Crusades. Now heli-logging was tracking the last giants into formerly unreachable corridors. Joni Mitchell was right about a tree museum. If Holly had been Minister of Forests, she'd ban taking anything over three feet in diameter.

"How far is it?" she asked, beginning to flag at his manly pace but too proud to show it. From the looks of his strong and sinewy legs, the Boston Marathon shirt he wore was well-earned.

Frank had a pleasant voice. "Only another five minutes."

"Are these caches always located in out-of-the-way places?"

"The object of caching is to offer a challenge, but without bushwhacking where kids might get lost. The cache is never in plain sight, though. Logs are good, big rocks."

"And you get the coordinates online?" When she looked at nature, she saw a different world. The heavy ground cover of salal, blackberries and huckleberries. A spaghetti plant, aka goatsbeard, dropped its fragile strands. The hard brown-and-cream carapace of a shelf fungus jutted from a dead aspen. "Can't be easy to get a satellite reading with the thick canopy."

Frank nodded. His head was nearly shaved. A cyclist, too, perhaps. The van had a rear carrier with a lightweight racing model. "It was easier in Victoria. Royal Roads campus had several. There was even a pub tour for grownups. We're going west and heading around Lake Cowichan on the loop. But here sometimes you *can't* get a fix. So you're told to walk so many paces." He showed her a print-off. People had related their experiences. They had names like Moss Troopers. Island Rovers. Virtual Dogs.

"And these caches look like..." Asking questions was her job. It wasn't prudent to pretend to know everything. Listening was a primary tactic of interrogation.

"This is wet country. Generally a waterproof container is used. Tupperware works best, but sometimes only a big coffee can in a garbage bag." He used his hands to approximate the size and shape.

"Sounds like fun for kids. Parents, too."

Frank nodded, brushing a spider web from his face. "Much healthier than sitting at a mindless video game. This gets the whole family outside. And while they're in the car, they're planning ahead." They had come about three hundred feet along the winding, narrow path. On one side a steep bank led to the rocky creek. High tide backed into the freshwater streams. "Over there," Frank said. He stood down by a mossy log in a small clearing, watching his feet lest they trample evidence. Like most of the world, he had probably seen his share of forensics shows.

Gesturing to him to stay put, Holly walked up to the body, looking from side to side at the surroundings and stepping carefully. With shaggy brown hair streaked grey at the temples, the man looked younger than Bill, but his skin was weathered from outdoor living. He wore faded, ripped jeans, a plain sweatshirt with one sleeve rolled up and scuffed runners. Lying on a comfortable bed of bracken, he had one hand over his head in an almost demure posture as if to shield himself from sun. Her eyebrow lifted as she scanned the area, creating a mental grid. "Make haste slowly," Ben had advised, quoting her the Latin like the good Catholic boy he'd been at fifteen when he'd nearly entered the priesthood. "What you do often can't be undone." She was not the coroner, but merely here to secure the scene, whatever Boone might decide about an autopsy.

At first sight, it seemed like a slam dunk. Near the body was a classic collection of drug paraphernalia, a clear bag with white-powder residue, spoon, plastic lighter, a water bottle and a faded plastic pencil case stamped "007" with the original Sean Connery in action mode with his Walther PPK. *What a strange collectible for a loner.* His hairy arms wore an embroidery of needle marks. Lab tests would probably reveal an overdose. Was this the man Bill had said he hadn't seen recently? Or the panhandler? And speaking of Bill, where was he?

The equipment was a HIV/AIDS minefield. It would have to be carefully removed. Nearby was a rolled-up sleeping bag and a small backpack, both of which looked new. She blinked as a tiger lily lifted its orange Turks head to a shaft of sun, before a cloud shadowed the path. Then came the pad of heavy feet and heavier breathing.

"Christ on a cupcake, are you trying to kill an old man, making me haul butt up here? Why not just put a gun to my head?" a gruff voice with a hint of humour asked. It was Boone, his stomach surrounded by suspenders and broken-down brogues on his feet. His teeth clamped an empty corn-cob pipe in homage to his former addiction. A battered leather doctor's bag dropped onto the ground. He rooted through it and snapped on a pair of latex gloves.

Holly turned to Frank and introduced them. "Thanks for your cooperation, Mr. Jones. You and your family can leave now. We have your contact numbers if any questions arise. It was a sad introduction to the island for you."

Frank gave a quick nod. "Glad I could help. Almost went into police work myself, but the wife would have divorced me. It's duller but safer being a math teacher."

"Good luck up at Cowichan. There's a record-breaking Sitka Spruce just off the road near Harris Creek. It's on the tourist maps."

As Frank jogged off, Holly took a log for a seat and watched Boone do his job. Easier on the eyes and nose than an autopsy but not half as interesting.

He gave a series of hmms as he completed a mental checklist. "No blood, no apparent wounds. Eyes are getting cloudy. Rigor's just set in, and liver mortis indicates this is where he died," he said, having moved the body and loosened the clothes to check underneath. "A bit of bruising on his knuckles. Right hand. Might not mean anything."

Judging by the rubber tube, he'd been injecting his left arm, so that fit. Was he the one who gave Bill a punch? "Squatters have been camping under the bridge. I talked to one earlier about a panhandling situation," Holly commented.

Then he rotated the head and peered into the mouth. "Looks like he's been living outside, no frequent showers, shaves, or shampoos, but he's had some dental work in the distant past. Silver fillings, nothing fancy. A few teeth missing. Fights. Falls. Poor nutrition. Gum disease. To be expected." He took a temperature and nodded to himself. "Cool back here in the woods. I'd say he died sometime last night, if the rigor isn't lying. We're lucky the damn bears didn't get to him, nice chunk of steak like that."

"An overdose? With all of that gear, it seems obvious." She swept a hand over the scene.

"Sometimes the most evident answer is the real one. Don't look for no zebra in a herd of horses." He picked up the plastic bag. "Hardly anything left. His last fix. Poor sod went out with a bang...or a whimper. Dropped dead on the spot. Just enough time for an uh-oh. Give the immediate area a sweep in case he's tossed sharps into the bushes. Kids come here, I imagine. Ride their bikes up the creek trail."

"Yes, and now there are caches in the area." She explained the concept.

He was looking inside the pencil case. "Extra syringe. Cotton pads." He opened a tiny bottle and sniffed. "Bleach. Primitive sterilization but better than nothing."

"That pencil case looks ancient." When someone's possessions were boiled down to whatever they could carry, the items provided an often poignant flash of humanity. Had he been holding fast to this item from childhood? Bought it at a second-hand store? Innocence mixed with the most sordid of experience. "Any ID?"

"Getting to that, missy. Hold your horses. Don't act like you have something better to do here in Lotusland North." He slipped a thin leather wallet from a pocket and opened it, pooching out his large lower lip. "Driver's license. Ontario. How about that?"

He cocked his head. "Looks like our man is Joel Hall. Whoa. Here's a CT credit card in the name of Phillip Blunt. Twenty bucks. A lottery ticket for last week. Super Seven. Not enough numbers circled to win."

"Wouldn't that make a great story? Guy's found dead with a million-dollar ticket?"

Snorting, he fingered his way under an interior flap. "My oh my. A hundred dollar bill? And another?" He flicked one with his nail. "Brand new, too. If he was selling, it wouldn't be for this much at one crack. Maybe it came from Phil's wallet."

"I doubt he was a dealer. Usually they have a place to sleep, not to mention wheels."

"Unless the dealer turned doper. Shot up the profits." He held up a picture. "Who's this angel? Too young to be his mother. An old girlfriend? Or a wife?"

"Or a sister. Let me see." She held the small black-and-white photograph by its edges. High-school graduation package size. Judging from the hair style, it was definitely Seventies. She'd seen her mother's yearbook from university. Bouncy hair, fluffed up, "teased" had been Bonnie's word. Pouffy angora sweater. Ring on a chain. The woman was attractive, and her smile was full of youthful hope. Something was vaguely familiar about her. On the back was written in teenage script with a little heart over the i: *Love and kisses always, Judy.* "If only there were a last name on this. Judy's probably married now, too. And anyone can get a driver's license. It's out of date, too. With no picture like the new ones in this province."

"Another lost soul, I'd say. Doesn't look like he's had much of a life. Just an accident waiting to happen. But someone meant something to him once. Maybe she's still thinking about him. And that cash has me scratching my head." As Holly got up, he took her seat with a groan. "Knee's screaming blue murder. I oughta get a replacement, 'cept I'd have to wait six months."

"I'll check the backpack."

He put a warning hand on her arm. "Go slow. You don't know what might be in there."

She carefully looked through the pouches and zipped pockets: Soap, a ratty towel, a disposable razor, and a couple of t-shirts that had seen better days. Nothing was outstanding. Two pop tarts were crumbling in their packets. The flotsam and jetsam of the bottom rung of society. "Nothing to speak of. Not even a secret hiding place."

She gave the area a once-over. Needles were everywhere these days, even collection boxes in the ferry bathrooms, and the exchanges for addicts were attacked as "enabling" despite the fact that they minimized the HIV infection rate. Recently the fixed exchange location in downtown Victoria had drawn so much criticism that in its place, a mobile van cruised the streets. With the apparent inconvenience of finding the vehicle, many were reusing dirty needles. "Harm reduction" was a tough sell for activists battling more conservative citizens. Fortunately, in Canada health care was regarded as a right, not a privilege. Since its inception, no prime minister had dared prod the sacred cow.

To be as thorough as possible, she established a fifty-foot perimeter. The scraggly undergrowth defied combing. Sword ferns dueled with deer fern and bracken. Pick-up sticks of skinny alders blocked her progress, and the prickly weave of tiny ground blackberries threaded together the tapestry. Nothing more turned up except a beer can with fresh butts. Prints probably, DNA possibly. For good measure, she paper-bagged everything, peering at the water bottle, which seemed to have three good latents. In the distance, the wail of the ambulance could be heard. They'd probably been jammed by a fender-bender. Travel in the summer on the two-lane to Victoria was getting slower every year now that the housing developments in Sooke had ballooned the population. Hadn't anyone thought about infrastructure when that Sun River development of five hundred people had begun? And west of Fossil Bay, the Jordan River plan, involving hundreds of hectares of former clear-cuts, now stalled in the zoning, foresaw another nine thousand people. The traffic ramifications reminded her of sand dripping in an hourglass.

"Here are the ETs," Boone called, making final observations in a notebook. At least his purpled face had returned to a normal colour. This kind of exercise was taxing for the old man, but she liked working with him, trusted his wisdom.

They made their way back to the parking lot after the body had been removed. Boone drove off in his Jeep, the tailpipe dangling with baling wire. Surprisingly, the Jones family was still there. She walked over to thank them again. In the back seat, the kids were watching a video.

"Everyone's getting hungry, and we're due in Port Renfrew, where we've reserved a campsite," Chrissy said. "I don't think they got that close a look at the poor man. Frank saw him in time. Let's hope it's not quite real, only a bad memory. I told them that he had a heart attack. It seemed easiest."

Nothing wrong with a white lie now and then. "One last question. Did you find that cache?" Holly took off her cap to wipe her brow.

"Are you kidding? We got out as fast as we could."

For safety, Holly waved them back across traffic onto the busy road. Geocaching sounded like fun for kids. A real game in the real world...except that in this case a corpse had joined the party. As a first step, she'd run his name through CPIC. In all likelihood he had a record, perhaps even outstanding warrants. She respected the humanity, the mother who had borne him. But he had committed himself to a maverick lifestyle and removed himself from a world of cares.

Under the bridge, Bill's old lawn chair still stood, nearby a coffee pot and enamel cup beside a careful fire pit with a metal screen on top. She tested the ashes and found them cold. His meager belongings, consisting of a wheeled dolly with a shock-corded milk crate, sat beside his backpack. This way, hitchhikers could carry more, and the dolly could go into a trunk or truck bed. Odd that he'd left it so trustingly, but probably it held nothing of value. She'd lived light too, possessing no furniture that couldn't be left behind in the places she'd rented. But didn't everyone want a room of his own? Her mother would have expected her to reach out a hand, not be judgmental about those who lived on the street...or in the forest.

Chipper capped a bottle of spring water and wiped his mouth with a snow-white handkerchief. Other than her father in courtly mode, he was the only man she'd ever seen use one. "Everything go okay?" he asked.

Holly cocked her thumb. "That old guy I met the other day, Bill. Did you see him when you got here?" She explained in brief what Boone had found.

"No one was around but the family. Is that his stuff? We should be talking to him." Chipper looked disturbed, as if he had failed to secure the scene. "We *definitely* should be talking to him."

Holly checked her watch. With all his gear here, he wasn't going anywhere. Or had he been involved in the death in some way she wasn't discerning? Was this all that they might see of Bill Gorse? If they couldn't find him again, his estranged family might have some answers.

FOUR

The next morning, moans filled the house as dawn blushed over the hills and set the water shimmering in tiny wavelets. Shogun began howling, an eerie sound. Holly rubbed her eyes and glanced at the clock. Five a.m? "Coming," she called, grabbing a robe. How did mothers deal with children?

"Are you all right? Do you need anything?" she asked, pushing open the door to her father's room. Stupid question. Getting him to the bathroom at midnight had been a nightmare which challenged his dignity and her lumbar region.

"It's been nearly a whole day, and I can hardly move. I refuse to submit to being an invalid. Think about it. In...valid. That sums it up." He tried to sit up and yelled, his fist pounding the mattress. "Get me more of that ibuprofen...please. Make it a handful. My liver will have to fend for itself."

After giving him the medication and refreshing his water, Holly poured some orange juice to wake up. Then she brought his coffee. "Your usual oatmeal with extra bran?" Since they were in the Seventies, no need for that steel-cut stuff that took half an hour. If he could eat, she'd feel better. Why was she so worried? It was only a strain. The Mayo Clinic website said that ninety per cent of back pain disappeared within a month. It might seem like a year.

"The pain is making me nauseous, but I have to keep up my strength. Maybe a banana. A small one...diced...with cream... but in a few minutes."

As he sipped the brew and the pills kicked in, his face eased for a moment. He hadn't even been able to clean up yet, and she realized that people took their abilities to care for themselves for granted. Suddenly those TV ads for walk-in bathtubs were beginning to make sense. "Would you feel better with a shave? I can bring your electric razor. How about a hot towel?"

"That's the least of my worries. Your mother always told me I looked better with a beard. I had one for my first job interview. It added gravitas." He scratched his chin and tried for an ironic laugh but merely coughed.

She stood with her hands on her hips, aware that she needed to take a stand as a parent to a parent. Someone had to act in his interests. The world's most rational man, even in pain likely bearable to women, he was incapable of coherent thought. "I'm making a call. There's a good masseuse in town. We met the other day."

"Massage. Used to be a code word for something else. Now it's sissy spa stuff. Oils and stones and seaweed. No, no and no." He stuck out his jaw defiantly.

"Yes, yes and yes. Mother always said that you were stubborn." Bonnie would have trumped his self-pity ace with a withering word. She'd once let her appendix suppurate for hours down the Transcanada from Campbell River to the General so that she could drive a woman in need to a safe house. Norman roared at a hangnail.

He winced as he shifted. "Maddie did suggest a treatment. Can't hurt. Just once, mind you. It's not going to become a regular thing. Imagine the cost. Rich I am not."

"You told me that your university plan covered eighty-five per cent. Why are you quibbling about a few bucks? Sheesh, Father. In the words of your favourite show, *Get Smart*." Oops. Maxwell and crew had aired in the Sixties for the most part but ended in mid-1970. That Norman didn't catch her on that showed his distress.

Holly went back downstairs to find Marilyn's number in the phone book. Under "Massage", she saw several entries, all in Sooke except for Serenity Cottage in Fossil Bay. Marilyn offered a plain deep-tissue Swedish massage along with rebalancing, whatever that was. No exotic extras like heated rocks, ocean water droplets or detoxification via the feet. Norman would accept a therapeutic service without the pampering frills women enjoyed. He could think of it as a sports thing.

"Of course I can take your father, " Marilyn said. "I have two clients this afternoon, but I always leave room for emergencies. It's hard to turn away a soul in pain. Is an hour from now too soon?"

Holly sighed with relief. "It'll probably take us that long to get downstairs to the car, but we'll make it."

"Sounds like a muscle strain. They're severe, but they usually respond to heat and cold and go away in a few days. And watch yourself moving him. Even a young person can lift the wrong way."

"You're an angel. You can't imagine. My dad is beside himself."

"Oh my dear, but I can imagine. I see it every day. That's why I'm in this profession."

Holly returned upstairs. "Want me to help you dress?" She thought again of his bell bottoms and Nehru jackets. How far was he going to take this? She sympathized with her mother about the banalities of his career.

"Just my bathrobe will do over the pajamas. I'm not standing on ceremony in this crisis." She helped him into the paisley robe and left him sockless in his shearling slippers as requested.

Having forded the stairs on his hands and knees, Norman allowed himself to be loaded into his toy car, which was higher and more open to entry than the low-profile Prelude. The short kilometres in silence to Fossil Bay felt like eternity. Holly was beginning to experience the stress of living with someone unwell. She couldn't imagine what Marilyn had been through.

On the corner of Sea Breeze Avenue stood the quaint ivy-covered brick cottage that Holly had passed many times without note. Across the street, oceanside with an acre or two, it might have commanded a million, but its modest lot was shielded from the noisy road by a neatly trimmed cedar hedge. Holly pulled into the driveway beside the carved wooden sign reading "Serenity". She admired the giant red and yellow rhodos and inhaled the sweet perfume of matching white and purple lilacs. A perennial garden with ivied arches and pergola surrounded the house English style, delphs nodding acquaintance with daisies and wild pink foxgloves. As Holly turned off the motor, Marilyn came from the house, arms spread wide in welcome, a fat cream cat swirling at her feet like an angora fog. Its luminous golden eyes surveyed the inferior species. "Come, come, you poor man. Relief is on the way. You have my solemn word." Introductions were unnecessary. The place felt like home.

"Prince Chunk, clear the path." Marilyn swept the cat aside with a gentle foot movement, and the animal disappeared under a hydrangea bush, flashing its tail in haughty challenge.

The women guided Norman up a wheelchair-accessible ramp into the front room, which appeared to be the treatment area. Certificates lined the walls, and Holly gave them a quick scan. British, Canadian, even Californian. A bookcase held a collection of medical texts, including cranial facial neurology and spinal therapies. The typical depiction of a human muscle system stood beside a skeletal diagram of stress points. The air currents traced the healing scent of lavender from a fresh bouquet in a simple Japanese vase.

"Would you like music? It relaxes some people and helps with the drone of traffic," Marilyn said as Norman disrobed behind a lacquered ornamental screen. She and Holly exchanged womanly glances at his continued groans. "Do you have...anything from the Seventies?" Holly asked with an eye roll indicating that it wasn't her choice.

A CD collection in front of her, Marilyn turned slowly. "Wouldn't he prefer classical music? A bit of Mozart?"

Holly shook her head. "It's a long story which involves his job. I'll explain later if he doesn't."

Marilyn folded back the flannel sheets on the treatment table and adjusted the headrest. "My repertoire is somewhat limited. Sounds of the sea all right? Gentle lapping waves?"

"Uhhhhhh" was his non-committal response.

Marilyn set the music, chose a few oils like a chemist and turned to Holly with a confident smile. "We'll be finished in an hour."

"All yours." She felt as if she'd dropped off a whiny child at a very reliable daycare. Men were such sissies. Nature knew best where strength was needed. Back at the detachment minutes later, before she could get into her office, Ann pointed to the phone. "For you. It's Boone. Test results no doubt. That unfortunate homeless man. Word's already out in the community."

"What do you mean?"

"I had coffee at Nan's and heard the craziest rumours about drugs and gangs. People were comparing it with Vancouver. Next we'll get suggestions about pulling up the drawbridge or signing up vigilantes."

Holly huffed out a breath. "Our crime stats are still minimal. It's not like we have a serial killer on our hands. Or a mass murderer."

When she answered, Boone got quickly to the point. "I called in a few markers to get the tests run fast. It's an overdose, like we thought. On city streets, common enough. Guess it's more unusual out here."

"So what's the product? High-grade heroin? Too much of a good thing?" Addicts were always chasing a greater rush. That was the insidious part of the drug scene. Holly had enjoyed the odd clandestine beer as a teenager and drunk wine, even her father's wretched homemade efforts, but she had never tried marijuana. Now that she was a law officer, even that popular herb was no longer an option. On the other hand, if any place in North America was going to legalize pot, B.C. was in the forefront.

"It's a mixture we see now and then, but rather puzzling. Seems that the heroin was mixed with Fentanyl, a synthetic morphine used to treat extreme pain. It's eight hundred times stronger."

"Wow. Hard to imagine. The wonders of modern medicine." Holly rubbed the back of her neck. "That cocktail must cost. I thought dealers used sugar, flour, quinine, starch, other cheap fillers."

"True. But a kilo of heroin is cut a bunch of times as it makes its way to the streets. Not enough to dilute it too much, though, or bye-bye sales. Junkies are very discriminating. Word gets around."

"So choose something more expensive for street people? That makes no sense." Her brow furrowed in question.

"Could be a marketing strategy."

"What? Are you serious?" She didn't think of the common drug trade as Madison Avenue thinkers, but if competition was tough...

"Basic economics. Law of supply and demand. When too much junk hits the streets, and prices drop, the competition gets hot, and dealers wise up. A batch of super-strong stuff might tip the balance. Problem is, having people die from your product isn't very good advertising."

She couldn't stifle an ironic laugh. "Damn straight. Should we be worried?"

"I called an ME buddy in New York City for the big picture and the trends. A few years ago, across the States, addicts were dropping like proverbial flies. Hot spots were Camden, Harrisburg, Philly. Officers even tried giving out leaflets in Chicago to warn addicts."

"How did that work out?" Would they have to do the same? Conservative Canada lagged behind the cutting edge of bad things.

"More people than ever turned out to try the big bang. If it doesn't kill you, you get a monster high."

She slapped at her forehead. "That's crazy. And in the province?"

He paused for a moment. "Big, bad Vancouver had a few deaths last year. Nothing on a large scale."

"It's possible this guy brought it with him. He looked like a drifter. Maybe it was a free sample, because if the lab is right, no one takes this twice and lives."

"I'll look into it. If there's a run of this stuff on the island, we need to know about it...if only for the sake of the emergency rooms when overdoses arrive." One of the first things ER staff did with injured patients was ask about drugs, in case anesthesia might be compromised.

When Boone had called, she had been on a search for Joel Hall on the CPIC site. His name hadn't come up anywhere. No outstanding warrants, no record. An invisible man. "Did you run the prints from that beer can? He may have aliases."

"It's going to take another day or two. Big backlog in the summer with short staff. Since this recession, the cutbacks have been brutal."

Holly added, "Ann traced that Canadian Tire card. A wallet was stolen from a tourist in Victoria. Inner Harbour area. Crowds are trolling spots for pickpockets. He didn't know it was gone until he got back to the hotel. Meanwhile, a sixty-dollar Visa cash advance was charged at a nearby ATM. The card's probably trashed by now. That activity tracks quicker than bank card use."

"What about the hundreds? Did they come from the same guy?"

"Says not." Bank machines usually gave out twenties. Many businesses wary of counterfeit money refused the unprepossessing brown hundred-dollar bills.

Later, Holly contacted the drug units at the West Shore RCMP, largest in the area, and at the City Police Department in Victoria. The capital city was one of the twelve places in B.C. with its own police force. It was a great draw for officers who wanted to avoid the family hassles of constant relocation and the high risk of big-city crime. Fentanyl had turned up in an overdose case about a year ago. "It was a fluke," Corporal Danalyk told her. "Nothing before and nothing since. Only an idiot uses a highly-controlled drug to cut heroin."

"So he brought it with him." But they should keep current. Hanging up, Holly told Chipper, who loved surfing the net, to begin monitoring the databases to see if Fentanyl was popping up anywhere else.

"I've got a super link," he said with a proud smile. "Marketplace. ca. Covers all the Canwest Canadian newspapers."

Holly's Timex beeped, reminding her that it was time to collect Norman and get him home to bed. Surely life would soon return to normal. She found herself counting on Marilyn's promise. "Sorry, Ann," she said. "Hold the fort. I won't be far, and I won't be long."

"I saw you come in with that baby car. Something wrong with the Red Rocket, or are you voting for the Green Party? Do I see a wind turbine in your future up there on Otter Point Place?"

"Might be an idea for the next power outage." Norman refused to get a generator, and for once, she agreed. Too expensive for him, too noisy for her. Holly explained about her father's injury, knowing that Ann would sympathize.

Ann flashed her a thumbs-up sign. "Good choice. I don't believe in energy fields, white magic or woo woo, but Marilyn *is* a miracle worker. Her hands connect with your body, and she can feel the slightest difference as the paths open up. She was able to diagnose a slight case of scoliosis before the damn CAT scan turned it up. That could be why my back gave out years before it should have. If we had more comprehensive health coverage, I'd go every week."

When Holly explained how they'd met, Ann nodded. "I was sorry to hear about Shannon. She was a sweetheart. As I was leaving the cottage once, she was returning from pulling a double shift in the ER after a pileup on the Malahat. Every doctor asked for her, especially the neurosurgeons. Then a year later, she had deteriorated so far that I barely recognized her. Marilyn had a wheelchair ramp installed and retrofitted one bathroom. I don't know how she nursed her as well as running Serenity. Then the lottery. Go figure."

"The lottery?" Gaming was big business in Canada.

"They won nearly a million on the Super Seven. At island real-estate prices, not that much." Everyone knew that B.C. stood for "bring cash".

"My mother used to call it a tax on stupidity. She was even against bingo."

Ann gave a sad frown and sipped her coffee. "Funny how it happened. Someone handed her the ticket as a tip. Marilyn is no frivolous person. She and Shannon had plans for a wellness centre in the hills about an hour west of here. Now she'll have to do it alone if she decides to follow through."

"That's a long way to drive unless you're spending the weekend. It's not like Tofino, where there's a whole town for entertainment."

"She had her eye on a property in East Sooke. Glenairley Centre of Earth and Spirit. An order of aging nuns owned it. But the asking price was several million, so she searched farther from town. The House of Alma, she's going to call it. Weird name. I don't think it's religious. She told me it came from some Latin word for soul."

"That's ironic, isn't it? Money can't buy health. She'd probably trade it all to get her partner back." Suppose Holly had all the cash in the world? Could Boone Mason, with his private-investigator skills, find her mother?

Back at Serenity, crossing her mental fingers, Holly knocked and let herself in as she heard light laughter. Her father was tipped nearly upside-down in a zero-gravity chair, his face relaxed, a twinkle back in his eyes. "I'm almost normal," he said, relief apparent in his vocal tones. "My muscles were putty in her hands. It seems like I was fighting myself for the first half hour. Then I fell asleep."

"Wonderful," Holly said, trading glances with Marilyn, who was washing her hands, a beatific smile on her pleasant face. She wore light yoga pants and a scrub top. Now that things were more relaxed, Holly couldn't help noticing a portrait of Shannon and Marilyn in pride of place over the carved mantel. They seemed her age, in their prime. The photographer had caught them looking at each other with amused confidence, the sea splashing behind them, twin halves of a single committed

66

soul. She thought of that last touch of their fingers, that gold ring. How long had they been together?

Marilyn turned her way and gave a bittersweet smile. "Tofino. The Wickaninnish Inn. We went stormwatching there one weekend."

"I visited Tofino about fifteen years ago. It was still at the back of beyond, full of hippies and recluses, not the tourist trap it's becoming," Holly said.

"Is that hot tub revved up?" Norman asked Holly with a wink. "I have a prescription for half an hour. Never thought I'd use the silly thing." He had bought it for her mother, another romantic touch to save the union, but somehow evenings soaking under the stars never materialized. Bonnie was on call 24-7, rarely home on weekends when he was free. Why did some people feel that what mattered or didn't matter to them worked the same for others?

"That aromatherapy helped, too. Marilyn says there's an organic lavender farm in Metchosin. I'll get some this week." Norman flipped back up and as Marilyn steadied the machine, he began to slip out of the ankle cuffs. "My angel of mercy."

A year ago, Holly wouldn't have believed this. He'd been such a hermit since her mother had been gone. Yet Norman was an attractive man with the capacity for a relationship. She arched her eyebrow in wonderment and said, "Thanks, Marilyn, or should I say doctor? Any other orders?"

"Oh, please. I do have a doctorate in naturopathy, but titles are so stuffy. We worked on his breathing first. The Hindus say it's the key to the system. Without oxygen, cells can't work properly. Fundamental, like drinking enough water. His skin tells me much, too. More hydration." She gave him a mock warning finger. "Practice your breathing every night and drink two extra large glasses of water. Green tea would be even better for its antioxidants. Add fresh lemon or lime juice. Vitamin C maintains a strong immune system. I recommend goji berry juice, too." She opened up a file cabinet, riffled through folders and passed him some xeroxed sheets. Holly wondered if Norman's menus were headed for a vegan or macrobiotic turn. Popular Culture was tough enough, but expecting him to change at his age was unrealistic.

Norman reached for his wallet and pulled out two fifties, stopping short of bowing. "Here, my good woman. Please accept the rest as a tip."

Marilyn put a hand to her cheek. "Far too much. I can't—"

"Give it to charity, then. Or use it for your centre. You'll think of something. I insist." He folded his arms, signifying that he would not take no for an answer.

Holly nearly had to grab her jaw to keep it from hitting the floor. Norman ripped paper towels into quarters, rationed toilet paper and coddled his mutual funds like spoiled puppies. He'd stopped subscribing to the paper as soon as he found the *Times Colonist* website. He'd brake for beer cans to get a five-cent return. To spring not only for a massage but to offer a tip of probably forty per cent, guessing at the going rate, that was a revelation. What next? Yet if his pain had been eased, she understood the gesture.

As they were leaving, an ancient Maltese hobbled into the room. "Brittany, do you want out? Good girl for telling Mom," Marilyn said as the animal came over for a head rub. Despite its age, the grooming was impeccable, and it wore a cute Harley Davidson bandana.

Norman stood slowly but with minimal effort. "Pardon me if I don't stoop over. She looks like a venerable old dear. My border collie runs me ragged. Guess my daughter will have to pitch in until I'm fit for service." He ignored Holly's sharp glance.

Marilyn scratched the dog's ears and brushed hair from its

bleary eyes. "Cataracts are coming on. She's eighteen. Old even for the breed. Very bad arthritis, especially in the rainy season. Until lately she responded to glucosomine and chondroitin. I give her massage, too. Dogs love it."

"You could do well in Victoria," Norman said, retying his bathrobe and smoothing his hair in a rare vain gesture. Every time they watched *Gone with the Wind*, he looked more like an aging Leslie Howard. "A dog lover's paradise, and plenty of money. You can tell by the number of specialty stores for pets. Raw food. Clothing. Doggy day care, for lord's sake."

"Cities are too fast-paced. I prefer the quiet life. Out here people are often on limited incomes and can't spend that kind of money on their pets." Marilyn clasped her hands together. "And I have plans for a wellness centre. Now that Shannon is...gone, I intend to work harder than ever."

"My coworker Ann is one of your clients. She said something about your...House of Alma, as I recall."

Marilyn beamed, as if she remembered all her charges' histories and took personal gratification at their improvement. "How's Ann doing? I haven't seen her in awhile." Laughter creased her face. "That's probably a good sign."

Holly thought it best not to reveal personal details about her staff. "She's...much better than when I met her. It's been a long struggle for such an independent woman." She gave her father a warning look. "I hope she doesn't overdo it, though. But tell me more about your place."

"I've bought an old church camp north of Jordan River in the San Juan Hills. Far enough to give the illusion of wilderness. Close enough to make Victoria in a hour and a half. There's one good drilled well with plenty of water. A beautiful creek runs nearby with a Zen garden of rocks in the summer. All the buildings are sound, and it overlooks the ocean from a hillside. There are already rustic hiking trails through the rainforest."

"So you won't have to build from scratch, then. It's always hard to find workers on the island."

"Just renovations, really. The bunkhouses can easily be converted to single and double rooms, and the other outbuildings can be used for offices, a cookhouse and treatment modules. Shannon had made a comprehensive business plan. She had such a mind for details and priorities. That's an ER nurse for you, not a masseuse. I'm much more scatterbrained. When we get things going, we'll have a staff of seven. Our dream is to help people find balance through yoga, meditation, tai chi, herbal treatments, every healthy alternative. Once we establish the clientele, they'll be back, and they'll tell their friends. The expense of big-time advertising would be beyond us."

It was poignant that she still spoke of *we*. With the irony of her partner's death, Holly could sense Marilyn's purpose and focus. Could she claim as much? Policing was merely the act of allowing human activity to take place in an atmosphere of safety. They were both part of the larger goal.

With hardly a complaint, Holly had her father back home and relaxing in his blue velvet recliner in the solarium. She opened the patio door and slid the screen into place, letting in the ocean breeze. With all of the massive glass windows facing south, the room heated up in summer. Still, it was better than the long gloomy rains of fall and winter when Norman wouldn't allow the propane wall stove to be used until January.

"I'll make you an egg salad sandwich on whole wheat for lunch. I'm sure they ate those in the Seventies. I'll leave it in the fridge. There's buttermilk, too." She handed him the *Times Colonist* someone had left at the detachment.

"Sorry to be such a baby. Here you are, taking care of me." He skipped to the business pages and checked the TSE. "You will use Miracle Whip, won't you?"

Grrrrrr. She checked her watch surreptitiously. Time to get back to work. Thank god he was on the mend. "I will. But think of it as payback. Except for when you pinned me to that diaper."

Later, he sipped the green tea she brought. "Your mother made sure I did my share. But usually I did it so poorly that she had to take over, especially the bathrooms. I scattered Comet around and never wiped it up properly."

"You still don't. That's why you're the cook, and I clean house." Bonnie had taken Holly to work before her daughter was old enough for school. She had a crib with toys set up at the small law firm in Sooke where Bonnie worked before she tired of wills and real estate transfers and set out on her own. Her talents led her to become a fundraiser for women's causes, especially Coastal Salish women. She travelled the island arranging for shelters, transition houses and training. With a few exceptions, she encountered disgruntled men whose girlfriends, wives and children were pawns to their bloated egos and quick fists. On one hand, she could count those who took anger management courses, stopped drinking and mended their families. There was a dangerous side to helping people. Sometimes Holly wondered if...

"I see a hot tub in your future," she said now, "preferably before bed. Don't start without me. It's tough to get in and out of the unit. That stool is wobbly." Often she discussed her cases with him, but this was not the time. One detail did interest her. "And next time you're on the computer, date a piece of memorabilia for me, please? It's James Bond on a pencil case. Sean Connery, the original." Norman had been late to twenty-first century computing, but he used eBay to seek out knickknacks for his collections.

"Film merchandise is all over the map. Seat-of-the-pants reckoning, I'd go with around fifty bucks, depending on condition. Now with Shirley Temple, you're talking big money."

"Or that first *Mad* magazine Mom threw out."

His expression spoke of financial pain. "Two thousand dollars down the drain. And Holly..."

"Yes?"

"Have a nice day," he called.

FIVE

W asn't that a laugh? She thought about a smart answer, then remembered that he was back in character. "Catch you later." A blown kiss, and she was out the door.

On her way to the detachment, Holly took a call on the radio. On the back burner for far too long, the radio communications systems had improved in the last year from the stutter-starts on the bony ribs of the island, but an officer could be totally out of touch inland. Ann said, "There's been another break-in on West Bay Road. That's the third in two weeks. I suppose it's the usual teens out of school and into trouble." She gave Holly the contact information.

"At least Sooke has the soccer field, the pool and the skateboard park. I feel sorry for kids stuck out in Fossil Bay."

"Oh, come on. Someone has to live out here."

"The younger ones get into mischief, even vandalism. This sounds like kids over sixteen with access to a vehicle. They're not going to be found humping a plasma TV on their bikes or skateboards. Remember when we broke the last ring, two fourteen-year-olds and their brother driving Dad's truck."

"I wouldn't live farther out if you paid me double. My condo in Sooke's much safer, and I can see the harbour from my balcony. Sure, it's by a school, but my working hours cover that. And I can walk to everything I need, lattes included."

Holly thought about replying that anyone could make his

own coffee but decided that perhaps Ann enjoyed the company as much as the brew. Social isolation had never bothered her, but she knew Ann had hated her former post in far-flung Wawa. It would be tough raising children in the boonies. Either you'd be driving them on a twenty-four-seven basis, or worse yet, they'd want their own vehicle.

At Bailey Bridge, Holly saw Bill standing to the side with a pole and line in the water, where a deep gravel hole held small trout. So he was still around. What did he know about the overdose and the identity of the victim? She hadn't questioned whether he was a user himself, though he hadn't appeared to be lying about his stance. Would legalization of drugs result in more deaths or merely fill the public coffers and eliminate one significant level of crime? Reformers in North America were still evaluating Europe's programs, especially in the Netherlands. It was a hard call. Enablement or risk reduction? Methadone had caused such controversy yet hardly earned a ripple now.

She pulled in with the Smart Car and climbed out as Bill came down from the bridge into the parking area, pole over his shoulder, a wiggling steelhead in his hand. "Pardon me for a second. I want to clean dinner." He gave its head a quick knock against the cement bridge. Then he gutted it with a Swiss Army knife, put the garbage in a bag, and placed the fish in a Tupperware container, which he secreted in the cool shallows under a rock. Call her squeamish, but she preferred her fish and local crab delivered on ice.

"Speaking as a taxpayer of sorts, I approve of your frugal car. B.C. always leads the nation," he said. "Anyway, I have some news about Derek Dunn. We spoke about him in connection with that camcorder."

They ducked under the bridge. A round of Douglas fir served

as a seat for her, and he took his lawn chair. "Word in town was he'd been a bad boy. Broke the window at the liquor store. I found him in jail in Sooke sleeping it off, as they say. Visitors aren't encouraged," he said, swatting at a rare mosquito. "I left him some candy bars. Can't kick a guy when he's down."

"It's just a holding area en route to West Shore then the correctional facilities. I came to talk to you about Joel Hall."

"Joel? I haven't seen him. Sometimes he goes up the creek to sleep. The guys trust me to look after their gear." He took a wad of pink gum from under the chair arm and popped it into his mouth. "But he never does. Has he been up to something? I didn't like the cut of him."

She realized that nobody had been at the bridge by the time he had returned. It wasn't like he was going to see it on the news or read it in the *Times Colonist*.

"We found his...body back up by the creek. Or a family of tourists did."

"Holy crow. I had no idea. Are you saying that kids..." He removed a large, battered straw hat, and his grizzled face fell into creases of concern. "What the hell happened to him? Some pretty steep places up that hill."

"An accident's our best guess. Unless someone *wants* an overdose. His arm tracks indicate that he had some savvy in that regard." She watched Bill's demeanour carefully. Tone spoke more than words, and body language spoke loudest.

His light brown eyes were sad as a bloodhound's. She hadn't noticed how clear and white the sclera were. Not a user, then, nor a drinker. "Can't say I'm surprised. I warned him to stay off the junk. Crack, meth, coke, they're killers. If an infection doesn't get you, the poison will."

"It wasn't merely the drugs. His stash had been adulterated

with something quite toxic." She explained the circumstances.

He sat back in the creaking chair, staring at the ground. "God almighty. I've heard about that. Thought he'd be smarter about his sources. He lived a long time, considering his habits, I suppose. But you spin the roulette wheel enough..."

Holly took a deep breath, looking up at the bridge as a motorcycle roared overhead and a trickle of dust filtered down. "Two problems. We need to know where he got it in case this is happening elsewhere on the island. Users need to be warned. You can help us there. Tell me about his contacts." Her heart went out to this well-educated but still homeless man. He had no addictions, nor was he mentally ill, unless he was a clever sociopath. Why live such an uncomfortable life away from society? Had he exiled himself? Maybe she should run his name as a precaution.

He shrugged. "That's none of my business. I didn't ask him where he bought, only that he keep it out of camp. Look in Sooke, maybe Victoria." He swept his gaze around the area. "This is hardly a hotbed of drugs."

"I trust you, Bill. You seem like a straight guy, but I'm only doing my job, so please don't get offended. Second, his name isn't Joel Hall, unless he's squeaky clean, which is highly unlikely. There's no trace of him in the system. We'd like to find his family. They may want to take him home for burial, wherever that is. He may have been gone for years. On the other hand, it may be a case of good riddance. What do you know about his history?" She couldn't help thinking that Bill's situation paralleled Joel's. What she was saying might be stinging. To her, the saddest thing in the world was an unclaimed body. Everyone was somebody's child.

"Hell, he hardly opened his trap. I tried to be friendly at the start, offered him my reading glasses when he had a paper. Wasn't my kind of man, even though he talked some with Derek when they shared a bottle." Gulls screed down on the creek side where a chip bag pirouetted in the breeze. A wise bird picked up his prize and whisked it away, chased by jealous juniors flapping their anger. "But he seemed to know his way around this part of the island. Didn't ask the usual questions of a newcomer."

"That is strange. Didn't he just arrive?" She was thinking about the wallet theft in Victoria. It was possible that he'd gone back and forth more than once. The buses were regular, even if they took all day.

"*I* sure as hell never saw him before, and I've been here off and on in the summer for the last twenty years. There's not much to Fossil Bay, never was. Sooke is another story. He knew all about the free lunches and coffee. Good corners to hitch a ride. Location of the best dumpsters. When the food stores put out their old produce. Sometimes it's possible to make a few quick bucks doing odd jobs. Folks are pretty trusting around here, and there's lots of seniors. Once he stole a dozen eggs from a roadside stand."

"All the lavender and flowers he could want, too." She thought about all the survival skills that the homeless needed. "What else did he say?"

They watched a dragonfly hover over the creek, snagging midges. Its dazzling blue isinglass wings and sectioned, tubed body gave it a science-fiction appearance. Bill tapped his temple as if to prod his memory. "Let me think now. He mentioned Whiffen Spit and said he liked to fish there. Offered to let him use my tackle, but he laughed. Said he had easier ways of making money. Also asked about Algie's Fish and Chips by the high school. That place has been closed a long time."

"How long?" Knowing that might tell them when the victim had been here last.

"Ten years at least. I used to wash dishes there once a week before my pension kicked in. For awhile I thought Algie's widow and I might..." He kissed his fingertips. "That's another story. I wasn't about to get a ball and chain along with a daily plate of fish and chips, even though I'm a sucker for halibut."

Holly gave Bill her card. "I know you probably can't call, but it's a short walk to the detachment. If anyone turns up here who gives you trouble, give me a shout."

"Hey, I'm no squealer. I mind my own business." He folded his arms.

She met his wise old eyes with a sincerity he couldn't ignore. "I can put you or anyone in need in touch with social service agencies. This happened on my watch, and I feel responsible. We don't want anyone dying from neglect. Sometimes a bit of care can prevent more serious health problems. Diabetes is particularly deadly if undiagnosed."

"I hear you. Buddy of mine lost his leg to an infection. He begs from a wheelchair down at Bastion Square."

She thought of the roving nurses in Victoria who ministered to the street people. Monitored their meds, clipped their toenails, bandaged their wounds. Unsung Mother Teresas all.

He nodded and ticked the corner of her card with his thumb before tucking it into a pocket. "Will do. And thanks, Cap."

Cap, Guv, where would it lead? But nicknames meant someone liked you. She sympathized with Chipper. He'd grown up in a less than multicultural neighbourhood and had endured considerable ribbing until he'd changed his name at ten. His father had understood, but his mother was very traditional and insisted on calling him Chirakumar.

Several hundred yards later, she turned right down West Bay Road, a transitional enclave which in typical island fashion mixed a variety of real estate. Deep and dark forested lots where the lights burned all day sheltered mossy-roofed doublewides, hunting or fishing cabins from the Fifties, A-frame kits with ramshackle add-ons of rough, greying lumber, then a spurt of neater box-house bungalows on quarter-acre lots, and finally the newly rich with their mansions. Snapping up cottage properties like great white sharks after chum, they dozed the structures, landing with large footprints and at least five bathrooms. Their long, winding lanes began with mammoth wrought-iron gates and stone posts bearing electric lanterns. Many gigantic cedar signs bore picturesque names: Hurricane Ridge, The Buck Stops Here, Tickety Boo, and the more literary Kenilworth.

Now that school was newly out, she wasn't surprised to be sent on a petty theft report. With their jurisdiction extending all the way to Port Renfrew, the police often answered calls to summer cottages. The absentee owner in Seattle or Houston arriving in June might discover a broken window and general ransack. A bush bike had been stolen from a shed. Chainsaws and generators, portable property, were very popular. Leaving liquor in a cottage was stupid, because it encouraged thieves to stop and party, an enticement to trash the rooms and leave a pile on the carpet in a primitive gesture. Houses on West Bay Road were year-round, complete with nosy neighbours, and thus less vulnerable. She pulled up to a modernized two-storey log cabin with a bright red steel roof. A B&B sign featured a classy soaring bird with a white head. Eagle's Nest.

A knock at the door brought a woman in her forties. She wore cutoffs and a scooped neck blouse. Behind her the screams of young kids playing in the yard made her shield her ears. "Sorry, it's summer. Please wake me when it's over."

Holly introduced herself and was led around the side to a

quiet corner under massive spruces with branches trailing like ball gowns. A guest cottage with a spectacular ocean view had a window which had been jimmied, perhaps with a screwdriver or knife. "We were so embarrassed," Jean McNair said in a slight Scottish accent. "Our guests were from Ottawa. They had the place for the week and spent two more nights away at Bamfield. Since we weren't booked, we let them leave some belongings. When they got back, they found the theft. They left early this morning to get the ferry to Anacortes. Of course we'll reimburse them from our insurance once the police report is made. I can't even tell you on which of the two nights it happened."

Holly followed her into the small cabin. Like most upscale boutique places, it had a cozy bedroom with pillows, bolsters and nautical-themed drapes and covers. On the glowing honey pine floors, dressers, bar fridge and sofa along with a small table and two chairs completed the furniture along with a plasma tv and microwave. "There's a four-piece bathroom with jacuzzi. Sleeps four with the pull-out sofa. Parents take the bedroom. Kids stay here." She reached over to a vase of larkspur and bluebells backed by salal leaves and nipped off a faded blossom. A bowl of potpourri scented the air with jasmine.

The small villages along the coast, under pressure from businesses like Jean's, had discouraged the usual accommodation chains through draconian zoning and were able to charge from one hundred to two hundred dollars a night with bookings made through the internet. They boasted super breakfasts, including fresh baking and even eggs Benedict. In contrast, the nearest motel, a refurbished but ancient model, was far down the road in Sooke. "What was taken?"

Jean passed Holly a paper. "They left their video camera in the room those two nights. It was giving them trouble with the electronic settings. The man dropped it when they were taking pictures of the gardens at the Sooke Harbour House."

"Wish I could afford to eat there," Holly said by way of conversation. *Condé Nast* had called it the best small inn in Canada. There was a knock-three-times special price for locals.

"We try to serve as an information agency for our guests. See that they enjoy all the highlights of the area according to their interests. Some like to hit the beaches west or whale watch. Some come for the Art Show in August or the Fall Fair in September." She pointed to a table set up with brochures of local attractions, including the Tugwell Creek Honey Farm and Meadery.

"And a Rolex watch, too?" Holly said, scanning the information in the paper for her report. "That's traceable." The police had solved an international murder case in England by matching numbers. Who would have thought that a body cast into the Atlantic would have surfaced tangled in a net? Karma.

Jean put her hand on her chest. "I feel so responsible. Things were kind of hectic. They had a teenaged girl who complained all the time, and you know what they're like to motivate on a trip. The Rolex number's on the paper. And the serial number for the camera. He said that the watch had cost him over ten thousand dollars, and he'd taken it off when he went into the hot tub."

Holly checked her bargain Timex to date her entry. "Your notes will be a great help. I wish everyone kept such good records."

"Better than Bo. He was absolutely useless." She pointed out the window at a snoozing form which might have been a very fat dog or a small calf. "He's an English lab. They're much stockier." Holly's assessment put the dog twenty pounds overweight.

"Can you give me an approximate timeline? Anything at all."

"We're not even sure when it happened. They came in from their trip at midnight Saturday and just went to bed without noticing that the window had been opened. Nothing in the room indicated anyone had been there."

Holly did a brief survey of the perimeters, looking past Jean. "You're pretty closed in. Could the neighbours have seen anything?"

"I asked. No luck. The dirty rat, pardon my French, could have snuck through the shrubbery. There's a vacant lot on the other side. Kids take the path to the ocean at Scorpion Beach, a little cove. It's odd. We moved here for the quiet. Never had a break-in before when we were in Langford."

"It's becoming a crowded little island, at least along the edges, and with that comes trouble. You'd be wise to get one of the alarm services. Most people on private lots do."

"It all seems so expensive, though I suppose it's a tax write-off."

"Very true. The cost is nothing next to the peace of mind. Or you can set up motion detector lights. That should scare someone off if you're out." Or get a German shepherd, she thought. Her dad had a fake protection shield sign stuck in the cribbing at the gate. Some generic name like Guard-All which wouldn't fool a savvy thief.

As Holly closed her notebook and tucked it away, a curious frown crossed the woman's bright face. She fooled with the end of one strand of hair. "Aren't you going to...what do you call it... dust for prints?"

Holly suppressed a smile. Thanks to television and films, everyone was a detective these days. And results, even of DNA, were expected wrapped in a silver package between commercials. "How many nights are you booked each month?"

"Mmmmm. In a good season, fifteen, even twenty. It's been slow this year with gas prices so high."

Holly's palms went up in surrender. "That's my point. Over two dozen people could have come through, and your place is cleaned daily, I'm sure. It's nearly impossible to solve crimes like this in a hotel or motel setting, even if we had the resources and the prints were on file from a known felon. Your best hope is that the camera or watch turns up in a hock shop in Victoria. We'll get a bulletin out this afternoon to the dealers." She recalled what Bill had said about Derek "winning" the device. Camcorders were ubiquitous, but perhaps because of the proximity there was a connection.

Jean blew out a long, disappointed breath. "Oh dear."

Feeling as if she should try to do more, Holly gave the list of particulars another quick scan. "I see it's a Sony. We might have good news for you."

Back at the detachment, Holly grabbed a coffee and went to her desk. Then a call from Pirjo Raits at the weekly *Sooke News Mirror* came in. Fatal accidents in their community were rare, but they did happen. Two teenaged boys had recently perished in a crash. The utility pole still bore traces of their descanso, which was filled with seasonal flowers. Meeting Pirjo once at the Village Market and recognizing her picture, Holly had learned to pronounce the woman's melodic name. Like vireo.

"I'm planning an article on the homeless, including what happened to that poor man at Bailey Bridge. Won't make me any friends, but we have to deal with realities. Too many 'we should's' and not enough 'we will's,'" Pirjo said. "We're into a development boom, and more housing should be geared toward lower incomes. Instead, it's going the other way." Across the island, hundreds had become homeless when their trailer parks had closed and their units were too old and impossible to relocate. Laws protecting these elderly people lagged behind *faits accomplis.*

"I agree. Hold their feet to the fire."

"Most people don't realize that many hardworking families are a paycheque away from losing the roof over their heads." Recently the sub-prime mortgage crisis in the U.S. had been bringing this reality home. Thanks to stricter lending laws and only five major banks, Canada had a buffer.

Holly thought about the average house price of over $525,000 in Victoria, including ramshackle bungalows and barely-converted garages. Out here everything was twenty per cent less, but still higher than any place in Canada other than Calgary or Vancouver. Holly noticed that Ann was coming over with requisitions to be signed, which she left on the desk.

"Anyway, I don't want to keep you," Pirjo said. "What can you tell me about this individual? Sounds like a human interest story. Had he been ill? How old was he? Most important, who was he? I can get down there for a shot of the scene. Pictures always punch home the point better than words."

"Hold on. Slow down." Holly related the slim facts about the case. "We don't have the identity yet. Pursuing the IDs in his wallet hasn't turned up anything solid. The credit cards were stolen from a tourist."

Holly pulled Boone's report from the file to give Pirjo a more accurate description of the deceased. "It's possible that he might have lived around here many years ago. If nothing breaks, we might be able to get a picture from the morgue. That's usually standard procedure." Gruesome though it was, sometimes family or friends recognized the face of a lost one. Programs were more sophisticated these days, especially with the eyes no longer suspiciously closed. Fortunately this was not a case of serious disfigurement.

"I'll run this next Wednesday. Suppose he has some contacts

in town, maybe even a relative? Five-ten, one hundred and sixty pounds, brown hair shading to grey, dressed in a sweatshirt and jeans. Could be fifty to sixty. Carried a picture of a young woman signed 'Judy' with a Dolly Parton hairdo. Have I got it right?"

Holly was familiar with the styles of the decades from Norman's old *Life* magazines. "Sounds like you got everything. There weren't really any other personal belongings." She saw no reason to mention the 007 pencil case. *Sad evidence of a soul.*

She heard Pirjo pause and the paper rustle. "Judy was a more common name once. I must know six or seven from my older sister's friends. Anyway, cause of death was an overdose? That's not going to get him much sympathy."

"Heroin adulterated with a very strong pain medication. Like a loaded gun."

Pirjo gave a shivering sound. "I hate what's happening to our community. This kind of thing used to be confined to Vancouver. Is this called progress?"

"I hear you. Look at the crystal meth epidemic. Still, it would be worse if a younger person were involved. This individual had a long history of addiction. It was probably a matter of time."

"We can't hide the truth. Maybe this brings home to young people that the drug scene isn't glamourous, but deadly." Pirjo paused. "That could be a good approach for another story."

An award-winning journalist, Pirjo knew all the angles. She was a one-woman crusade and didn't mind rattling cages.

*　*　*

When Holly got home just after six, her father was already in the kitchen, a good sign that things were stuttering toward normal. Tony Orlando and Dawn were tying a yellow ribbon. In the yard corner, a small oak tree bore that trademark. Vietnam, the Gulf, Afghanistan, now Gaza again, did anything ever change in the outside world? The smell of baking bread met her nose and reminded her that she'd had only a chocolate milk for lunch.

"I checked that pencil case. More like seventy-five dollars. Circa 1972. If you're thinking of my birthday, I'd rather have a Victorian chocolate box from the Boer War. 1900. My collection from the Oughts needs work."

"Thanks for the research." She noted that he moved slowly but more easily. Marilyn's miracle was worth a hundred dollars. "I'm glad to see you up and around."

"Package arrived for you, sweetie. It came UPS. I left it on the cube seat in the foyer."

"Funny. I didn't order anything." At one time, getting presents from her mother had been a regular occurrence—when Bonnie was visiting remote communities, some accessed only by boat. That shawl with a turtle pattern. She'd been cramming for a math final, and her gratitude was lukewarm at seventeen. Only years later did she admire the subtleties of the colours and appreciate how it warmed her shoulders on cold nights outside in the fall looking at the sky, trying to find Jupiter to the south. Her mother had traced Orion's belt as she pointed out one of the brightest constellations. Coming up behind them in a rare moment of family warmth, her father put his hands on their shoulders as he quoted Bette Davis in *Now Voyager*. "Don't ask for the moon. We have the stars." One was Hollywood, the other her heritage. If she could return to being a teenager, she'd show her mother how much she loved and respected her, but that wisdom came with age or with a tragically premature loss.

After changing into sweat-suit civvies, Holly came down the stairs and hefted the large, light parcel, taking it into the kitchen, accepting with a managed smile a brimming glass of her father's homemade fuchsia merlot, and sitting at the table. Glimmering in silver on the strait was a small cruise ship, and she picked up a set of binoculars, amused that passengers might be staring at her like zoo visitors. What did this house look like? What thoughts entertained them as they relaxed on deck chairs, sipping margaritas and hoping to catch a glimpse of a whale?

Her father, wearing his George Jefferson apron, put his hands on his hips and stretched backwards. "I'm nearly eighty-five, no, eighty-seven per cent normal. I was embarrassed at first, but Marilyn explained that deep tissue massage applies greater pressure than conventional relaxation techniques. It can be used to release trapped nerves and address damaged muscle tissue. Do you know I'm unbalanced?"

"Let's hope it doesn't run in the family."

"Run in the..." He broke out in a forty-carat grin. "You kidder, you. Marilyn is a rebalancer. The Osho system was developed over twenty years ago in India to put the body in tune with the emotional, energetic and spiritual aspects. And she uses oil of bergamot and lavender to provide helpful sensory stimuli. Speaking of stimuli, how's the wine? I gave it an extra fortnight. Should be choice." He took a large draught and wiped his mouth with a serviette.

Better not discourage him in this upswing. "Even better than the chardonnay." Not a lie. Both wines were sour enough to curdle all the way down the pipe, but at four dollars a bottle, the spirits flowed. "Anyway, I wonder what this package is."

"Don't look at me. You're not the birthday girl." Holly was an even-tempered Libra, the scale signifying her profession. Her mother was a Gemini and her father an Aries. An ugly combination. Even in the Chinese system, they were rooster and monkey, notorious bickerers. The stars had conjoined against them in more than one culture. Her father pulled a crusty loaf out of the oven and placed it on the tile counter, tapping its toasty perfection for the hollow sound.

With a mixture of curiosity and suspicion, she examined the postmark on the brown-paper package with shaky block lettering: YOUBOU, BC. She looked up with surprise and guilt, a flush of shame spreading from her breastbone. "It's Great Auntie Stella Rice." The kindly Coastal Salish princess, now in her eighties, had raised Holly's mother when her own sister had died far too young from resurgent tuberculosis in the former logging community. A year before that, Bonnie's father had suffocated when a bulldozer had rolled on him during the stump removal and re-seeding of a clear cut on the north side of the Cowichan Valley. In their tightly-knit community, someone always came forward to raise a child. And if anyone under fifty needed a rap on the head from Stella's cane, she accommodated.

Holly's father tightened his narrow lips, and a muscle twitched in his lean jaw. Quiet but resolute, the native side of the family had cut all ties with him when her mother had disappeared. They hadn't approved of her marrying outside of her people, much less a professor with his head in the clouds. His rapture with popular culture they found debased and trivial, as had Bonnie when the first blush of love had paled. "You sent her a Christmas card telling her you were living here now, didn't you? It's important... to keep in touch with family. Bonnie would have...they're good people..even if they don't..." His voice sputtered out of energy, and like a dog making distracting gestures, he started to mix sauces for the beef fondue, a jar of mayo at his side along with chopped garlic and a blender of hollandaise redolent of lemon.

Holly grabbed a knife to open the box. Removing its contents from a tissue-paper wrapping, she gasped in delight. On her little farm, Stella raised goats and spun her own yarn for traditional Cowichan weaving and knitting. She was never without sets of needles in her purse and had turned out socks, hats, and scarves for Holly in sizes baby to adult. Holly's visits to the reserve had tapered when Bonnie's activism had started taking her all over the island and stopped altogether when Holly had left for university. And here was Stella reaching out to her. It was only a few hours to Youbou. Why hadn't she made time for a visit? She didn't deserve this present.

She unwrapped a thick cowled sweater in undyed wool with a charming pattern of a deer amid cloven-hoof prints. "This is lovely," Holly said, feeling the woman's arms embrace her as she tried it on. "This white contrast to the browns and tans—I've never seen it before." She touched the soft fabric to her cheek.

Norman gave an approving nod, his sleek eyebrows rising as his voice softened, taking his absent wife's role. "The deer is your totem. Remember what your mother said about its powers when she took you camping at Nitinat Lake on that spirit quest. You were so unhappy when she told you that you didn't get to choose. It chose you."

"I wanted a bear or a cougar and pouted for a week. Guess I wasn't the easiest kid, and lucky a chipmunk didn't find me." Then she read the enclosed card, the writing spidery but exact. "She says she'll be in Sooke the 20th. Hey, that's this weekend. She's coming down by bus to talk to a local weaver about selling her wares at Duncan during the International Indigenous Games in August."

"Paper said that they're expecting over twenty thousand people. The city will be jammed and pretty damn hot at that time of year." Norman cleared his throat and began portioning out the sauces in custard cups. "About this weekend, she's welcome to stay here if she—"

"That's generous, Dad, but it wouldn't be a good idea. Stella's made it clear that she wants to meet me at the T'souke reserve down at the harbour. She'll be staying with an old friend." Holly turned to the window and forced the last swallow of wine, a weight of unfulfilled responsibilities over her head. This fall it would be another year that Bonnie Martin had been gone. Yet there was no grave, no scattered ashes, nothing but a lack of even questions.

Coming back in touch with her mother's side of the family brought the deep ache back to the surface, where it asked for attention. All the time Holly had been learning her trade at her first postings, she'd thought about applying her new talents and resources to finding out what had happened that terrible week. Since returning last year, she'd made slim progress. There had been contact with an old social worker boyfriend of Bonnie's, the stunning news, confirmed in a letter, that she had been ready to leave Norman once Holly was in university. A silver amulet of Raven which had turned up at a nearby thrift shop might have been her mother's, yet it had surfaced long after her disappearance. Holly had been given a chance to read the case records in Sooke a few months ago, but when she tried to talk to an inspector in West Shore, he'd told her that the case was very cold. All the leads had been traced years ago, and he disputed the ownership of the amulet. "You're too personally involved, a bad mix. Doctors shouldn't operate on their own families," he had said to her, rudely checking his watch and picking up another file. "Give it a rest. People often wait years to come out of the woodwork." Was that supposed to be a consolation?

She had stuck out her jaw and announced that any personal time she had would be dedicated to solving the mystery. "If you think I'm waiting for a deathbed confession, think again," she had said, turning on her heel. "What if it had involved *your* mother?"

Lately the *Times Colonist* had been running a cold case series. She'd called the journalist in charge, but the series was full for the time being. "Call me in six months," he'd said. "We're getting a lot of good press."

After dinner, Holly cleaned up. Norman came from the video room, rubbing his hands. "How about a game of Pong? I can set it up on the computer. Then the next *Godfather*? Or did you bring home work for tonight?"

"Crime themes are too close to home." When she saw his surprised look, she added, "Close to my job, that is. Let's do *The Odd Couple*. I need a laugh." Though Bonnie was never far from their thoughts, discussing her on a regular basis would have been too painful. She would have wanted life to go on. But how could it without any resolution?

Just before she turned in at eleven, Holly went to her deck off the master suite to find Venus rising across the strait. No streetlights clouded the view, no fortifications obscured the sky. The glow flickering over the eastern hills was the lights of Sooke, but ahead the firmament was black as her mother's eyes. From her childhood Holly recalled the storms those eyes held when her mother's work brought frustration, when Norman persisted in his chatter about his latest period toy or recipe, or when Holly had put her life in peril and nearly drowned at Mystic Beach trying out a surfboard. How she missed the warmth they held when Bonnie had embraced her daughter and planted butterfly kisses on her cheek. When had she grown too old for that, eleven?

"Your love of the natural world of plants and animals came from my side, your academic pursuits came from your father. I suppose you're going to teach in a university like he does or do research." She chucked her teenaged daughter under the chin.

"Come on, Mom. That's so boring. I want to be a ranger and work in a park. Maybe on the mainland. Anyway, you went into law," Holly would say, setting aside her insect collection for Grade Ten biology. She'd just mounted a stunning sheep moth and had been admiring the black Hebraic markings on its delicate pink and ochre wings. "You could have been defending the innocent. Making the big bucks, too. Like on television."

A brief smile flickered across her mother's face, revealing her wry sense of humour. "You're very dramatic, my dear. Like me. It's the devil's profession, but I found a good use for it. Fight evil with its own methods and cut it no slack. Turning the other cheek only encourages bullies. Now I have a mission, not only for women but for my own people. And for yours, little freckle pelt."

Holly took a quail feather and marked a page in the *Trees and Plants of Coastal British Columbia* that her mother had given her for her birthday. "Are you saying that you want *me* to be an activist? An environmentalist?" Her parents had never pressured her. Their trust in her to make the right decisions was precious.

"Use your gifts. I expect you to set and achieve your goals on your own, wherever they lead. But what an impetuous girl. Not patient, but a watcher like the deer. A creature of instinct and grace, not a predator." Bonnie shook her head in mock frustration, retying her shining ebony hair in a ponytail.

Now Holly looked to the wall at the deer mask her "Uncle" Silas Seaweed, Bonnie's childhood friend, had sent her when she was ten. "No deer were harmed..." he had told her when she worried about the animal's fate. "The buck left us his antlers one spring so that he could grow newer, stronger ones." The mask had a human face, black painted hair with cedar bark strips falling down on each side. Shiny golden brows stood over an eye mask of red, streaks falling like tears of flame and a broad red mouth. In a curious feature, it looked behind her as if "watching her back".

"Where are you, Mom? Why didn't your totem protect you? The cougar is strong," she whispered again as she had many nights. But even bears and cougars were powerless over some evils. Her mother would never have abandoned her. A tear sneaked down her hot cheek. "I'm not crying. I...am...not." She blinked away the traitorous moisture and flicked off the light as she heard her father's door close.

SIX

You have grown tall, girl. You are a woman now," said the venerable Stella Rice, her black-olive eyes creasing in joy as she enveloped Holly in a powerful hug that scooped her up. She packed power into her five feet. "You have been such a stranger. Children must not stay away so long. Were you good, or should I get my applewood switch?" Stella had threatened, but she'd never applied the rod. One hot glance of her eyes stung more than a thousand words or a hundred blows.

"Sorry, Auntie Stella. I was in university, and then posted across the country. But I'm back now." With the cool morning and a fog rising, Holly had worn the sweater. "Thank you for this gift. What beautiful patterns. This wool is so soft. Is it a different breed of goat?" Sometimes the weavers worked in feathers, bark, or other natural sources for colour and interest. A hundred and fifty years before, the arrival of the Hudson Bay blankets had eclipsed the weaving industry, and drab grey machine product had replaced the works of art. Now artisans were reviving their craft.

Stella let a wisp of a smile crack her broad mahogany face. Large, square red glasses magnified her eyes. Her totem, the owl, had been well chosen. "You have heard of the Salish wool dog? They are very small, like coyote."

"My mother told me. But I thought they were extinct by World War II." Holly felt the warmth of family love. How quickly they returned to the familiar comfort. It was as if they had never parted, and yet Stella moved a bit slower than last time.

"A new secret for you. My cousin's cousin on Tzartus Island had a pack his family had kept separate for generations to protect the line. I took the ferry from Port Alberni for a clan gathering there this year. Because of my knitting, I was allowed to take a pup. So that she doesn't mate with our local dogs, she will soon be spayed. I call her Puq, which means white." Stella formed the words with the trademark glottal sounds that Holly couldn't reproduce.

"Maybe when I'm in the Cowichan Valley, I can see her."

"*Maybe* is not a strong promise word. I expect you very soon." Stella tapped her temple. "This I know."

They sat in rocking chairs on the porch of Mary Wren's small cedar-shake cabin on the T'souke reserve. In mid June's cool mornings, a cedar fire in the wood stove kept off the chill. A grassy expanse merged with the pebble beach, now at low tide, the flats dark grey and murky with the sea tang. Across the Sooke basin were the majestic, smoky hills of East Sooke, where the Martins had once lived deep in the great dark woods. Holly sipped aromatic camomile tea and nibbled on bannock heaped with purple salal jam. As usual, Stella's strong and talented hands worked her knitting. "I tried to visit you my first summer in university, but you were in Northern Alberta staying with your grandson. Wasn't he working on the tar sands project?"

"His first job, and his first baby. The young need the wisdom of the old. Thus it has been and shall be." Stella's eyes crinkled, every wrinkle earned in a hard-working time on earth. She must be closing in on seventy-five, nearly as round as she was tall. Her thick silver hair was gathered in two great braids down her back, tied in red ribbons, her signature colour. The cotton dress was plain as a nun's habit but had complex embroidery depicting a thunderbird. On a side table lay the conical reed hat of the Salish.

Mary quietly sat at her loom inside, glancing up now and then with a friendly smile. A small yellow bird trilled from a gilded cage on the table. The cage was open, yet it never emerged.

"You used to come sit on the sheepskin with me by the fire, and I told you the old stories, like I told your mother." Stella took Holly's head in her hands and pursed her lips with the cool assessment that had made her a leading elder. "You look some like your father. That blond man. Your hair is lighter than your mother's. But the nose and mouth are hers. As for what lies inside you, I wonder if your heart remembers the first and most important legend." The test had arrived.

Holly grinned and pointed to the ceiling, letting her fingers flutter down. "We are the people who fell from the sky." Their culture was oral. Though little remained for long in the wet climate, continuous settlement dated from at least five thousand years earlier, and middens from two millennia demonstrated a fondness for shellfish, especially littleneck and butter clams. Weirs were established on the major rivers, and deer traps woven from cedar bark. Of all the places in North America, the coast was one of the richest for foodstuffs due to the mild climate and marine location. No roaming Anasazi these, ravaged by droughts, but a people whose meat came easily to the table. When the government had banned the potlatch in 1870, a feasting tradition involving much gift-giving, Salish culture had gone underground for more than two generations. Now legalized since World War Two, it was returning with renewed pride.

The rocker creaked as Stella continued her questions. "Do you remember the twelve names?" Long before the Great Flood, a dozen separate human beings had fallen from the heavens, bringing different gifts.

Holly took a deep breath. Stella always asked her that. The

96

names were difficult, but she retained their phonetic memory if not the spelling in the Hul'q'umi'num language, with its disconcerting apostrophes, a dictionary created in the last century. The Warmlands, or Quw'utsun, was the alternate spelling for Cowichan. The land bore the history inscribed upon it. The huge boulder left on top of Mt. Prevost, aka Swugus, had saved people in the Great Flood. A giant boulder near modern Mt. Roberts had been flung by a chosen warrior to kill a monster octopus.

The Salish occupied a territory that stretched from Washington State to Alaska. It contained seven peoples, including the Tlingit, Haida, Tsimshian, Northern and Southern Kwakiutl, Bella Coola, Nootka, and the farthest south, the Coast Salish. Bonnie Martin, nee Rice, had belonged to the Cowichan band around the big lake. She had won scholarships to university, where she'd met Norman in Toronto as she was finishing a law degree at Osgoode Hall. An odd couple, they had connected in the first blush of their twenties before their personalities were firm and while they still bathed in romantic ideals.

"I thought you would become our medicine woman," Stella said with a mock pout, her tangled steely eyebrows warring. "You were so interested in our plants, learning all the time from those books your mother gave you. Every time you came, I took you into the woods to gather the sacred herbs, roots and flowers. Teas and tonics for stomach, eyes and arthritis. How to tell the death camus from the nourishing blue camus." Patches particular to families were as close as these people came to owning property. They hadn't understood why the white man wanted to cut down the riches of the land to plant his demanding crops in their stead, when hunting and gathering filled the belly.

Holly put an arm around her. "And you taught me how to make a horizontal cut and pull the red bark from the Tree of

Life to make baskets and mats. Or reap the yellow cedar with its waterproof pitch for robes and hats."

"The cedar is our mother. It gives us everything. Wood for warmth and building. Bark for cloth and baskets. Women used to chew the green cones as a contraceptive."

"Maybe it worked. I don't imagine cedar breath is attractive."

Stella paused and settled her hands in her lap. How knobbed from arthritis her knuckles had become, but they would never rest until her last heartbeat. She pointed at the flames licking at a driftwood fire some boys had made on the beach. "Cedar warms us, too, even now when our hydro goes down in storms. And when the white man came and saw our huge, fine houses, he could not believe that we had hewn wooden planks with only stone tools. Cedar is soft but durable. It can be split easily, a willing wood."

Then Stella grew silent and seemed to be thinking. Her creased lids fluttered shut, and she began humming a melody as old as her people. The "Slug Song" was Holly's favourite. "*Imush q'uyatl'un*," it began. "Walk, slug." Then "What is wrong, slug? Smile, slug. Speak, slug." By that time Holly would have fallen asleep, slow as the invertebrate.

The venerable old woman gave a deep groan and let her knitting drop onto her lap. "Your mother. It is not good. She doesn't rest."

There it was. The reproach Holly had known was coming. Did she mean this literally? That without a body, the soul wandered? "You believe she's dead? You said that about Mimi, too." Her mother's rowdy older sister had left the island at eighteen, stealing her auntie's purse and going east with a drifter. To their increasing shame, word of her felonies and scams had reached the family, but no one had mentioned her for years.

"Mimi became a ghost to us when she harmed others, but your mother lives in our hearts."

Holly bowed her head. Passion denied it, but her mind had accepted it long ago.

"I know it, child. I feel it here." She tapped her great bosom. Sadness pulled at her face like gravity as she gave the sigh of ages.

"But what can I do, Auntie Stella? Ten years have passed. I've tried through official channels, and there's no..." She didn't know how she could communicate the frustrations of a bureaucracy to a woman who thought with her feelings and never respected a door closed against justice.

Stella smiled and pulled at one long brown earlobe. "Did you ever wonder why you didn't follow the medicine? There was another purpose for you. Find her. And when you do, you will understand why she left us." She ran a finger along a string of yarn. "Seek the thread and follow it to its origins. You must be as patient as a spider and as powerful as the ladybug that drank up all the floodwater." She stabbed the ball of yarn with the needles, as violent a gesture as she would ever make. "Your mother and I have waited long enough."

Holly nodded as she stood and looked out at a giant hulk listing on a sandbar in the harbour. Once a proud tugboat, then abandoned, it had caused a ruckus in the small town. Jurisdiction was murky. There was something about appealing to the Minister of Wrecks, but only after two years. Meanwhile, it lurched in large reproach. "Take care of me," it seemed to say, a metaphor for Holly's burdens.

When Holly got home, Norman was on the phone, an irritated look on his face. He beckoned to her as he closed a hand over the mouthpiece. "Can you take Shogun to the vet for his shots? This call just came in, and I have to deal with it." He was talking to the dean about a problem student whom he had failed. "Says he's going to sue the university. Big shot athlete. But he plagiarized his paper on Lincoln Logs. I caught it with Google. This old man is not behind the technology door."

Holly gave him an okay sign and grabbed the leash. Minutes later at the vet's in Sooke, she saw Marilyn hurrying from her Audi, the little old Maltese cradled in her arms in a blanket, only its black nose and grizzled muzzle in sight. "Something wrong?" she asked, opening the clinic door and keeping Shogun close as he struggled to smell the other dog.

"Brittany's in too much pain. She can't even walk now. Or won't. It's cruel to make her go on. Dogs know when they want to leave. She overstayed her time because of us." She wiped away tears as her voice trailed off in despair.

Holly swallowed back a lump in her throat. *What a second blow for the woman, and yet how often life worked like that.* "So are you..." She inclined her head toward a door to the back area. From the sympathetic look on the approaching tech's face, she suspected that animals in distress were rushed with discretion and dignity to that room, a place of merciful release into the afterlife.

"Dr. Joe is very gentle. In a few minutes she'll be running free at Rainbow Bridge." In the waiting room, an older man sat with a King Charles spaniel pup cupped in his hands. The old generation giving birth to the new.

Perhaps that bridge was a childish concept, but it had helped Holly over the death of her two shepherds. Her mother had told her the story about old and sick pets becoming young and strong and helped her write a poem as a memorial message. Their graves in the backyard had gradually surrendered to moss.

With quiet efficiency, the vet tech led Marilyn into an inner office. Minutes passed with no sounds. Even the waiting room was dead still. Then Marilyn emerged. Her eyes were red, but she looked at peace, as if she'd made the decision a long time ago and had been in denial. Behind her, the vet tech carried a small plain cardboard box. "Can you put...her in the back seat, please?" Marilyn said. "I have a lovely place already picked out at home. Overlooking the strait and the sunset. Brittany always loved to sit with us at the end of the day."

Holly held the door for the tech. Shogun was being unusually well-mannered, as if sensing the solemnity. Then again, a vet's office wasn't an animal's favourite venue. With a bittersweet smile, Marilyn stroked him. "Lovely coat. So this is Shogun, the big barker?"

"That he is. I'm glad my dad adopted him as a rescue." A thought occurred to her. "Say, maybe you might want—"

Marilyn's eyes filmed with moisture. She shook her head as she heard the car door shut outside. "It's too soon. Much too soon."

Holly flushed and ran a hand over Shogun's silky head to calm herself. "I'm sorry. I shouldn't have..."

Marilyn gave her a hug, still redolent of lavender. "You mean well, and that's what counts."

*　　*　　*

Back at the office late that afternoon, Ann reported that nothing had turned up on Joel Hall. "But we know why now. The prints belong to a man called Rick Fagin, aka Jim Hickok and Jeff Custer."

"That's a comedy in itself. Couldn't he choose more normal aliases? What's his rap sheet like?" Holly poured herself a coffee and took one of the oak chairs across from Ann's desk. "Are there any threads to follow which will give us his real name?"

Ann leafed through it. "It goes way back. First he turns up in Winnipeg in juvie court at sixteen, or so he claimed he was. Shoplifting. Couldn't find his family through the names he gave. Maybe he was just stubborn, or maybe he didn't want anyone to know how he turned out. They put him in a foster home on probation, and according to them, a minister and his wife, he was an ugly customer. They weren't sorry to see him leave a year later when he tried to seduce their daughter."

"Nice. What else?" She looked at the mug shots. He'd been a good-looking guy in his youth. She recalled his face in death. The bone structure was there, despite the hard life. Bill had said that he could still attract women on his own level. Clearly family meant nothing to him. Perhaps he'd even been abused. Bonnie had often said that some people were too broken ever to be mended. She had been a pragmatist. She left romantic notions to Norman.

"Let's see." Ann turned a page, then another, then another. "What *didn't* he do on the way up the ladder as a career criminal? Break and enter. Selling stolen goods. A couple of assaults. In and out of jail like a revolving door. Isn't that pathetic? Over fifty, and he spent most of his life behind bars. With the three-strike rule in the U.S., he'd still be in a cell. Some people never learn. I just hope he never married some unsuspecting woman. That would be a mess. Not to mention passing on these genes."

"What's the last sign of him?" Holly asked. If someone was going to put out this much effort, they should have a fortune to show for it.

"Outstanding warrants in Toronto, but you know what happens when these guys cross provincial lines. Once they're out of a jurisdiction, it's too expensive to get them back. Unless they're wanted for murder."

"Con Air has only so much cash." A recent hotly-contested

campaign had begun in Vancouver where businesses made contributions to fly the ne'er-do-wells back to where they came from to face warrants. Running them out of town wild-west style. Legal processes had threatened to derail the plan.

Ann flipped to the past page. "Then he got into drugs as an independent. Made himself a chunk of change until he started bothering the competition in Windsor and dealing across the river. The big boys in Detroit gave him a royal beating. He was in the hospital with a concussion, a broken arm and jaw. Left the hospital and never showed up for his trial. Since then, two years ago, he hasn't turned up in the system."

"Lying low, or too old to run with the young dogs. Wonder what brought him here?" She told Ann about Bill's idea that the dead man had a general familiarity with the area.

Ann looked out at the fog rolling across the strait. "The perfect climate?" They both shared a laugh. "Anyway, about that theft at the McNair B&B. I called all of the pawn shops in the Capital Region. Nothing recent. But what about trading posts or junk shops like Diesel Debbie's. If he didn't have a car..." Her voice trailed off in the obvious question.

Holly shot her a finger pistol. "Good thinking."

"And that guy you told me about who 'won' the camcorder. Coincidences like this bother me." Ann turned back to her keyboarding. "Can you find him, Holly?"

"He's a guest of the province.Remember that broken window at BC Liquors?" Ann's was a well-known face at that venue. Neither of them pretended that she was on the wagon. What she did on her own time was her business. It was healthier not to tiptoe around her taste for a drink. It was the painkillers that Holly worried about. Since she'd started the exercises, she seemed to be improving.

Diesel Debbie's was a ramshackle converted barn on Oak Ridge Avenue on the west edge of Otter Point. The property had a proud history as one of the first local farms. Over the years, the land had been sold off in parcels. Now the old barn with spavined roof was all that was left of a dairy flourishing in 1890 and passed down for three generations. Up and down the quiet street, ominous yards signs announced the March of Zoning Progress: condos were sprouting like mushrooms now that sewers had arrived, allowing lots to split.

Holly parked and went into the building, passing a row of pressed-back chairs, a dented washboard and a balloon-tired bicycle. Inside was a packrat's delight as dust motes rode the warm air and a trapped sparrow flapped for release.

"Hold that door open, will you? A bird in the house is bad luck." Debbie was sitting in a battered leather recliner, too heavy to move except for fire or the prospect of a buck. Rumour had it that she'd gained her name from having been a long-haul truck driver on the ice road over Great Slave Lake. Too many hot turkey sandwiches with fries had robbed her of her minimal mobility, and now she had a disability pension. "Hello, my favourite officer. Haven't seen you since your dad was in here looking for Depression glass."

"He's into the Seventies now." Holly watched as the bird sailed free into the air.

Debbie brightened. "Seventies. You're in luck. Hey, I got a lava lamp." She hoisted herself up, a woman of only forty. At hand were a litre of Coke and an empty box of Joe Louis. "Ooo." She clumped to a table, picked up the lamp and handed it to Holly. Then she collapsed in the chair.

"You need an assistant, Debbie. A little monkey to run around for you."

"Considering all I make is peanuts, that's a great idea."

Holly rotated the strange apparatus. A red lump sat at the bottom of a clear, viscous liquid. "Might make a good present. He's hard to buy for. How much?"

A twenty pleased them both. "And it better work, or I'm bringing it right back." Holly's voice grew more serious. "Listen, I know you deal in...electronics." From where she stood, she could see several televisions and more delicate instruments in a glass case.

"Sure do. Need a camera? A nearly new Nikon D80 came in yesterday. I can do you a wingding of a deal. Discount for the trade."

"It's a stolen camcorder I'm looking for." She watched the woman for a reaction, but Debbie's plucked eyebrow barely rose.

"Stolen?" Her tone even, Debbie flicked a speck of dust from her cardigan. "I don't mess with that. Do I look crazy?"

"Of course not. But accidents happen." Holly levelled her eyes at the woman then softened her glance and waved a hand. "Summer is busy. Paperwork's such a bummer."

Humping over to a huge bound record book on a nearby roll-top desk, Debbie confirmed that two days before, a man called Steve Riordan had sold her a nearly new Sony camcorder for fifty dollars. Except for the name, the description sounded like the man Bill had described, down to the truncated finger.

"That was a good deal for you, Debbie," said Holly. "Weren't you a tad suspicious? Be honest, now."

Debbie cleared her throat before walking to a cabinet, removing the camcorder and handing it to Holly. "Depends what I get for it...would have gotten. Second hand is second hand."

"What about a Rolex?" Holly checked the serial number of the camcorder against the one in her notebook and showed the result to Debbie.

"Hell, no. This isn't a jewellery store." Debbie's broad brow furrowed into lines. "What now? Are you taking me in?"

"Consider yourself on unofficial probation." It might have sold in a few days. This was a spot of luck. "I'm not surprised that he didn't give his real name. Did you ask for any ID?"

Debbie gave an embarrassed grin. "I had one super headache that day. Maybe I wasn't as sharp as usual."

"Under another name, I believe that 'Steve' was taken into custody for drunkenness and vandalism. If I can confirm his identity, I can tie him in with a robbery in Fossil Bay."

"Anything I can do, ask. I always cooperate with the law. For sure."

Holly took the camcorder as evidence and gave Diesel Debbie a receipt. "I'll bring back a picture of this man. As soon as we get an ID from you, we're on our way."

"Whatever you say. The law and I are good friends." Debbie added an icing of sincerity to this cupcake.

"Oh, Debbie. One thing," Holly called over her shoulder.

"What's that?"

"Stop being so soft-hearted."

Shortly after making a quick call, Holly was heading down Sooke Road for Langford, where West Shore was located. It was a huge detachment policing five communities, with a staff of officers, civilians and volunteers. Heading up the unit was a Detachment Commander. With units for Major Crime, Street Crime, Firearms and Fraud, it was a hive of activity. Holly had no desire to work in a large detachment, despite the possibilities for promotion, but it was the only way she could get involved with the canine unit, an idea she had recently. Drug searches, lost children, exciting field work.

The complex was perched at a busy corner at Goldstream

and Veterans Memorial Parkway, so she parked around back and returned to the front, going in the large doors and up the steps. At the reception desk, she asked for her friend Sergeant Cliff Lloyd. "I'll buzz you in, Corporal," the secretary said, hitting a button for interior access. "He's downstairs, first door on the left."

"Hello, Cliff," she said a few minutes later. "When are you going to send us some of those spiffy new Impalas?"

"Out there in the boonies you probably could handle crime with a five-speed bicycle."

"Built for two. Point taken. Anyway, what about Derek Dunn?" She explained the original complaint and the tracking of the camcorder.

Cliff motioned her to a chair and sat back at his desk, biting on an apple. Given his seniority, he had an undemanding PR job of supervising community policing projects, leaving him on cruise control to sixty-five. "I checked the files. Derek has been a very bad boy. Picked up in Sooke for drunk and disorderly. Seems he threw a trash can through the window of the BC Liquor Store at midnight. Grabbed a forty-ouncer of Canadian Club and guzzled half of it before our patrolman got there. He was taken to their cells to sleep it off, then brought here. Tomorrow he'll have a bail hearing. With his warrants in Vancouver, he'll be waiting for trial at the Vancouver Island Correctional Centre."

"We won't miss him out in the beach-belt, but I need to talk to him about a camcorder theft," Holly said, feeling somewhat claustrophobic in the windowless office. This job was even more boring than hers.

"I'll run off his picture for your ID purposes, but it sounds like he's your man." He turned to the computer and punched in some data. The photos on his desk of a Malinois dog in action drew her attention. Almost as good as a shepherd.

"That would help. I also need to know if he had a Rolex on him. One was also stolen from that B&B."

Cliff smirked as he pulled out a black and white picture from the printer, put it into a manilla folder and gave it to her. "Now *that* baby I remember. It's in a box downstairs inventoried with his empty wallet. Nothing else on him."

"Lead on."

Shortly after, they were let into a locked storage room and, after consulting a register, Lloyd took a coded box from a shelf on the wall. He pulled out the Rolex and dangled it. "Wish I could afford something like this."

"It might be a knock-off." She checked the number in her notebook. 1690011835. "Perfect match. And they call this work?"

"Let's have a chat with him. We put him in the drunk tank just in case he hadn't sweated it all off in Sooke. But he's not in the most hygienic state."

"Doesn't say much for your concierge services." She wrinkled her nose. "Promise me I'll still feel like lunch."

On the upper level flush with the busy five-corner intersection outside, the cells had attractive glass-block windows for maximum light. Each room was empty and pristine, the floor whistle-clean. The drunk tank was more austere than the other cells, with smooth surfaces, a drain for easy cleaning and no sharp corners. Derek was snoring on the long stainless steel bench, scruffy head pillowed by his hands. Traffic purred by between flashes of sunlight, hardly audible thanks to the thick walls.

"Derek, wakee wakee," said Cliff, playing the bars with a clipboard. "Room service is here."

Derek sat up. He was dressed in an orange jumpsuit over his small frame. He was in his early twenties and still had a boyish look. Brushing sleep from his face, he tossed back a hank of hair covering small plum-coloured eyes. A wispy moustache made him look more like a baby Fu Manchu.

He blinked at Holly. "What's going on? I already told them I didn't do nothing with that window. Other guy did it, not me. Bastard ran off, but I was too wasted to get away." He swallowed in discomfort, then took a sip from a plastic bottle. "Could use some hair of the dog."

"Breaking a window's bad enough, but you're in deeper waters, Derek." She explained about the camcorder and the watch.

"Big deal," he said, raising his right hand to nibble at a nail. "So I found it like the camcorder. People should take better care of their stuff."

"If you find valuable property, turn it in. Don't hock it at Diesel Debbie's, especially under a false name. We frown on that."

One case closed. The evidence would keep him off the streets for awhile. Then another thought struck her. "I also wanted to question you about Joel Ha—"

"Oh shit, yeah. I got the buzz about him. Tough break. He was an okay guy. Offered me some of his stash, but I don't do drugs. Gotta draw the line somewheres. Look where it got him." He gave a shiver and tried a crooked smile, which might have worked ten years ago.

"We're still trying to find his real name. He has several aliases."

"All's I know is Joel Hall is what he called himself. He's dead, right? Who gives a fuck now?" He seemed more puzzled than rude.

With a disapproving grunt, Cliff stepped forward, reached through the bars and took Derek's collar in a meatloaf hand. "Watch your mouth, son."

Holly waited until Cliff had backed off. "Someone might

have cared for him. A mother? Wife? What can you tell us? Did he ever mention a family? Why was he here? Bill seems to think that he once lived on the coast long ago."

"Billo has tough rules, but he was fair. He and Joel traded a couple of punches last week." His eyes grew narrow and calculating, and his thumb flicked at his nails in an almost feminine gesture. "I might know something. What's in it for me?"

Holly sighed and traded glances with Cliff, leaning against the wall with his beefy arms crossed. The usual back-scratching game. But wasn't it played on the highest floors of Bay Street as well as the alleys of Skid Row? "That's up to the Crown Prosecutor. We'll tell her you cooperated." Holly put her hands on her hips. "This isn't a state secret. Jailhouse snitch on a murder rap. We just want to know who the man is." She couldn't keep her voice from rising in exasperation. Interrogation skills, Grade C minus.

Cliff stepped forward. "You'd be doing yourself a favour. This will be taken into consideration in your plea. Be smart for once."

Derek rolled his head from side to side as if banishing a headache. No doubt he had one. "Okay. But I only talked to him once or twice. He wasn't real conversational. Said he lived in Sooke as a kid. Dropped out of high school and hit the road a long time ago."

Holly's heart pumped up a beat or two. "That's interesting. You're doing well so far. How long is a long time?"

"Jesus, I'm doing my best. How the hell old was he? Figure it out for yourself."

Holly tried to remember. If he'd been a teen when he left and was upwards of fifty now...he'd left in the Seventies. That jibed with the picture of Judy. Sometimes her dad's studies came in handy. "What else?"

"And he hadn't been back. Not ever. Who'd blame the guy. Knocked up some chick."

"He had an old picture in his pocket. Judy. Mean anything?"

A raucous laugh escaped his mouth. "Judy. She's the one. He showed it to me. Popped hers, he said."

"What else did he say about her?"

"Ask her if you want. She works in Sooke at the A&W."

SEVEN

Holly smacked her fist into her hand. "I thought she looked familiar. People change in..." Thirty-five years? What would *she* look like? Her mother, a woman frozen in time? "Did he talk to her? I mean recently?"

He shrugged. "Guess so, but it's not like they were getting back together or nothing. He learned about his kid. All growed up now and working in Alberta. He was kinda proud, though he didn't show it. Tough guy, know what I mean? Maybe his heart was broken."

Holly let that observation pass. It was important to get as much out of Derek as she could, even if some memories were an alcoholic blur. Otherwise he'd move on into the system and might do time far from the area. "Anything else? Even little details can help."

Derek tipped back his head and closed his eyes. Cliff sent her a "forget it" look, but she waved it off. Then Derek snapped his fingers and started to laugh, an ugly sound. "When he was high, he used to sing a crazy song about Spain and France. What a wingnut. Then something about a queen, and the Rennie Saints. In a funny accent." He puzzled at the idea. "I've been to Port Renfrew. They don't have no team, not even a junior high."

"And you said he went to school in Sooke. But an accent?" *Stranger and stranger.* "Wasn't it English?"

"Yeah, it was English. What kind of idiot do you take me for?

112

The melody was 'God Save the Queen.'"

Satisfied that he had no more to give, Holly nodded to Cliff and turned to leave. "Do us all a favour, Derek. Find someplace else to spend your summers."

"Damn straight I will. It's too friggin' cold here!" He wrapped his thin arms around his shoulders and pretended to shiver. "Can you get me a blanket? And when's lunch?"

He wasn't the only hungry one. Holly took advantage of her location to grab a plate at the nearby Smokin' Bones Cookshack. Barbequed brisket sandwich with slaw on the side. Despite the token offerings of mustard greens and sweet potato pie, this was no place for vegetarians. Meat eaters pigged out on the luscious selections like pulled pork and ribs.

Might as well use the trip back through Sooke to check on Judy. Probably she would have the key to this sad man's identity. Twenty minutes later, Holly stopped at the A&W. Did the woman still go by that name? She parked in the lot next to a couple of gleaming Harleys ridden by retirees with frizzy beards, their wives on the one-up seats. Behind her on the grassy knoll, a few homeless people played cards, their mutts lolling beside them. As for what the brown quart-sized bag contained, she'd rather not know. This wasn't her turf, and she wasn't sorry. Down the street, young vandals had smashed cars at the Used Auto Lot, forcing the owner to erect a chainlink fence and take one step forward to resembling shell-shocked Los Angeles. Everyone knew who was responsible, but no one could prove it.

Inside the restaurant, she watched the brown-shirted staff greet customers. Nostalgia posters lined the walls, featuring a '57 Chevy and a roller-skating waitress. "Rock around the Clock" was playing at a discreet level, and a woman with ivory hair was doing a crossword in ink and singing along, pausing to sip from a frosty root beer. Holly walked over to a teenaged boy with apple cheeks and a cowlick who was filling the bussing dish with glasses and cups. "Yes, ma'am?" he asked.

She smiled back to put him at his ease. "Does a woman called Judy work here? Perhaps one of the senior staff."

He brightened. "Judy's one of our managers. Judy Springer."

"Is she here now?" Three other workers were in sight, but all too young.

He shook his head. "She does her shifts Wednesday to Saturday. Opens up the place."

"Do you know where she lives?" At his puzzled expression, she added, "We need some information from her. An identification. Someone she might have known."

"Karen, come here for a minute, please," he asked a bean-pole lady placing a bag of Chubby Chicken on a tray.

Following the directions, Holly drove to Grant Road, a busy, transitional area, main bus thoroughfare, and a popular shortcut. "Pulling a Grant" meant that an individual ignored the stop sign at West Coast Road and streaked at an inviting angle west towards Fossil Bay. The long road consisted of small hobby farms of a few acres, tract houses, about the only apartment building in Sooke, recent affordable townhouses on postage stamp lots, and a few monster homes West Coast style. Nine-thousand-square-foot lots were marching forward. It was a matter of time before sleepy Fossil Bay woke beside its giant neighbour.

Judy had a cozy little doublewide with an extra shingled roof for protection and a white plastic miniature picket fence. Tomatoes grew in clay pots along with herbs. A birdbath sat in one corner of the sunny space. Planted as a buffer between hers and the lot beside her was a cedar hedge, neatly sculpted. In the distance, Holly could hear the sound of a trimmer. Clearly, Judy maintained the small property with a sense of pride. The siding was pristine and no moss turfed the roof. To mar the picture, a smear of acrid smoke rolled down from the hill where someone was burning brush. It made Holly's eyes water. She rubbed them with the back of her hand, blinking back tears.

She walked up the neat slate path and knocked at the screen door. From inside came the sound of a late afternoon talk show. Single voices were interspersed with the hilarity of audience participation. Nothing happened, so she knocked again, harder.

"All right, already. Hold your horses. Is that you again, Al? Hope you brought your own beer this time," a low drawl said from another room before its owner materialized in front of the screen. The older woman, her hair in a bouffant that had gone out when Annette had left the Mouseketeers, was dressed in yoga pants and an oversized men's white shirt. A bottle of hard cider was in her hand, and a cigarette hung from her full lips. Seeing Holly's uniform, she widened her dark brown eyes and stood straighter. "Officer, is something wrong at the restaurant? I hope..." Her gravelly voice trickled off as happy sounds came from a commercial.

Introducing herself and confirming Judy's name, Holly saw a neighbour crane her neck toward the door and asked, "Could we go inside and talk? All I need is some information about someone you may know."

"Not one of my kids at work? Pam's been having trouble with her—"

"Not at all."

"Hate to drink alone." Judy flipped off the television, then provided a glass of iced tea, which Holly took partly to diffuse the tension. It was sickeningly sweet, but she sipped it and nodded in appreciation. Then she took out her notebook. "I'll get right to the point, because I don't want to alarm you. A few days ago a homeless man died of an overdose—"

"I saw the story in the *News Mirror*. Put two and two together. The description fit." Judy's voice sounded more resigned than sad. Then her gaze dropped, and shiny glints appeared at the corner of her eyes. She shook herself and found a steel backbone after the years of betrayal. "Never thought he'd come to anything but a bad end. Just dumb luck it took so long." Close-up and with no makeup, she had the hormonal challenges of errant chin hairs of those past fifty, but good bones, and the pretty girl she had been wasn't far below the surface.

"I'm hoping you know his real name." She opened the large brown envelope she'd brought and took out a picture of Joel's most recent mugshot, passing it to Judy.

The woman took the picture, her hand shaking. She gave a brief nod then swallowed the last of the beer and put down the bottle. "I need something stronger. These kind of days don't happen very often." She got up and went to the cupboard.

Judy returned with a glass and a fresh bottle of Captain Morgan Dark Rum. Twisting off the cap with adept fingers, she poured herself two inches, blinking as she swallowed it all in one gulp. "God, what would Mother say?" she said with a laugh. "Roll over in her grave if she had one. She's out there on the roses instead. Six feet tall like she always wanted to be."

Another siren sounded, going the other way. Holly let the woman monitor herself. It didn't help to hurry anyone. This was their show. Her job was to keep them on track and get the facts, in either order. "His name?" she prompted.

"Joel, Joel Clavir." The tones were hushed, almost wistful. At one time they might have been a prayer, not a curse.

Holly's pen stopped as she snapped to attention. "Pardon me?" Cylinders of a lock were falling into place. The name Clavir was very unusual, and this was a small community. Marilyn and Joel were in a similar age group. A former husband? A bitter divorce and a lifestyle change? Or a brother. In any combination, another piece of bad news for the woman. She was a magnet for tragedy.

Given time for thought, Judy barely restrained a hiss. "Yes, Joel. He turned up like a bad penny after all these years. But let's be honest. We never would have made it." She gave Holly a quizzical look. "How in god's name did you know to come looking for me?"

"He was carrying your picture. From a high-school year—"

"That sentimental old fool. Who would have thought?" She gave a reluctant sniff. Her small chin started to wobble. Then she poured a solid triple and downed it like milk. Holly thought about saying *Hey, take it easy.* She didn't want the woman blitzed out of her head and unable to think straight. But Judy put the bottle back in the cupboard, a good sign, and sat down again. "I'm not totally stupid. That's enough for me. It's gonna give me reflux, and I'm out of Zantac." She tapped at her breastbone and gave a small burp. "'Scuse me."

Holly considered saying that she was sorry about the loss, but somehow it seemed like history. "So you and Joel..."

"Joel and I were a pair in high school. Mr. Personality. Smile like the sun. Had us laughing day and night. And could he dance. We were going to get married when we graduated, at least that's what I thought. You should have heard his line. Men. It's bred in the bone, I guess. Then he left me high and dry. Never trusted one after that. Well, maybe this one. 'Cause I raised him to respect women." Her gaze went to a framed picture on the table. A big strong man in his thirties, arms folded in confidence, standing by a late model car. Hills and mountain in the background. She touched it lightly with her finger.

"Are you saying...I mean were you—"

"Pregnant. Sure, they had birth control then, but Sooke is a small town. One doctor for all of us. The condom broke. Hey, it happens." Judy gave a bitter chuckle and threw her arms up. "Nature, what a joker. When you're ripest for sex, it's all out of control."

Holly nodded womanly support. "You wouldn't be the only one." She looked at the picture. "Nice dog. Malamute."

"My son, Shiloh. Against all odds. But I did get a job as soon as I delivered. God, I must have juggled plates and washed dishes in every restaurant from here to Victoria, any one on the bus line. It was tough. My parents had no money. Dad hurt his back on a hali boat. We ate a lot of macaroni. Mom bought peanut butter by the gallon. Made our school lunches, and we damn well better eat them."

So Holly had her identification. She could get this case off the books if... She held her breath. "Clavir is an unusual name. Did Joel have a sister?"

Judy smiled and waved her hand. "Sure, that's Marilyn. I see her around town at the stores every now and then, not that she comes into the restaurant. Junk food isn't her thing. She's okay, not snooty. I kind of like her. No fault of hers that her brother was an asshole. She went into massage therapy and has a nice little place. Sort of woo, woo, but hey, if it works..."

Holly sat up a few degrees to signal to herself that she needed to leave. There was bad news to deliver. "I'm glad that you've provided identification for Joel, but I have to wonder why he came back after all these years. Was it to see you? And why now, of all times? Had he kept in touch?"

"He could have been on the moon for all I know. That bastard never sent me a friggin' buck. He had no idea I worked here until I saw him ripping into the dumpster when I went out with the trash. Gave him a piece of my mind, all the things I'd wanted to say. Know what?" She eased back and took a deep breath. "It didn't make me feel any better. He was just a pitiful character. Like an old whore. His looks and body were gone. Only a mother could love him, as the saying goes."

"So why—"

"Why did he come? For nothing but his own benefit, I can tell you that. Maybe he wanted to score off his sister's lottery win. It was in the papers. People turn into jackals." She shivered to add to the effect. "Catch me winning, I'd move to Maui in a heartbeat."

Holly remembered that ironic piece of fortune. "Good point. We know he's been in and out of jail most of his life. Theft, drugs, assault. Who knows what he got away with?"

"Assault maybe, but nothing worse. He wouldn't have the guts. Joel was sneaky, but he was a coward. I should have seen that, but you know what it's like when you're a teenager. Love is deaf, dumb and blind."

They went back outside, and Judy coughed at the smoke, banging theatrically at her bird-like chest. "Damn. Can you do something about that? I have to keep my windows closed some hot days. Isn't it illegal this time of year? I saw the sign at the Fire Hall reading Danger: High."

"Everyone's still burning off the trash from the storm last winter. I don't like it either. But it's not my jurisdiction, I'm afraid. Call the Fire Department. They're the enforcers." The area, still largely rural outside the core, was in conflict about burning laws. Closer to Victoria, the rules were strict. Out here, people felt like they had a right to burn even garbage. And then there were the enormous piles dozed up and left in clear-cuts. In the dry season, there was a moratorium for the companies. Even a spark from a dozer could start an inferno.

Back in Fossil Bay, Holly stopped by Marilyn's, but the car wasn't in the drive. She tried her cellphone. "Marilyn, please call me. It's Holly," she said, leaving no message because of the sensitive subject. With the work beginning at the wellness centre, perhaps she was out there supervising. A third body blow after Shannon and Brittany. She hoped that Marilyn had close friends. She hadn't mentioned any parents. At her age, perhaps they were no longer alive. As Holly headed back to set up a speeding check at Jordan River, a call came over the radio at the giant lighthouse. "Another weird one," Ann said. "We have a complaint about a dognapping at the RV park. Go figure."

It was a new one, all right. Boomer the beagle belonged to a former Vietnam vet who lived on Fossil River Road near an RV camping park. His dog made the rounds every afternoon in search of an occasional hot dog. This time, Boomer had been grabbed by a tourist family.

"I'll check it out. By the way, we have an ID on our victim." She told Ann about her talk with Judy.

Ann whistled. "Marilyn's brother? She never mentioned him, not that she got that personal with me. She'd always tell me to relax and breathe deeply, not gab during a massage."

Shortly after, Holly reached the RV park on the river flats. The people camped next to the dognappers, a couple from Calgary, told her what they had witnessed. The man put up his hands defensively. "I didn't learn about Boomer being a local until later. This guy, his wife, and kid from Switzerland, said that they had found the dog and were going to take him camping for a month up island."

"Take him camping? Then what?" Holly asked.

He shrugged. "Leave him off at a pound or something. Say they *just* found him."

"Do you have any idea where they went?" She had learned the license of the rental Cruise Canada Class A. She could hardly initiate an Amber Alert or an All-Points Bulletin.

He scratched his head and looked at his wife. "Port Renfrew, then Lake Cowichan? That sound right, hon?"

His wife agreed. "They had a map which showed the rec sites. Basic and cheap. Must be five or six around the lake. Can't say which one they picked."

Back in the car, Holly glanced at the time. Five p.m. Friday. The Cowichan detachment wouldn't appreciate chasing after dogs, and the rec sites had no phone access, often only a camper host who collected the money and was paid with a free site. Tomorrow, other overdue personal plans could piggyback upon the trip. She could still hear Auntie Stella's voice: "Your mother and I have waited long enough."

EIGHT

Port Renfrew, a tiny fishing town of a few hundred, hadn't changed much since Holly's last visit in high school. Then it was all bush roads requiring four-wheel drive. Now bridges had been refurbished by the forest companies, and roads had been surfaced to urge tourists to take the Great Circle Route. Marilyn was still not answering her phone, and when Holly passed on her way out of town, the Audi was missing from the drive. Business on the mainland again? As Holly had suspected, a check on Joel Clavir had yielded nothing. Off the island, he'd never gone by his real name, having left his life behind in more ways than one.

Botanical Beach had often called Holly to its unusual shores. At low tide, the marine life on the protected rock-shelf beaches drew international attention from scuba divers or rubber-booted strollers. But she passed Rennie with Pandora Peak in the distance, turned north, crossed two bridges at the San Juan River, and headed east on Harris Creek ML (Mainline) toward Fairy Lake. The miniature bonsai island close to the highway, a popular picture, brought cars screeching to a halt.

As she travelled in and out of clear-cuts across the high hills, the sights reminded her that over ninety per cent of the island had been logged once, twice, if not three times. In her heart she almost welcomed the recession and the lowered demand for wood. Maybe the government would wake up and stop exporting raw logs, a self-defeating concept.

She left the San Juan watershed and headed up in a cloud of dust toward Harris Creek and the legendary spruce. The giant Sitka stood a few hundred feet in, as old as the first of the Tudors. The new fence gave little protection against harm by some fool with an axe. Noble giant companions sat nearby in the cathedral grove. In this accessible area, the largest trees survived on a combination of water sources, or the whims of a beneficent timber company officer. "Hello, old friend," she said, pouring a libation of club soda over the fence.

An hour later, having crossed Robertson Creek, turning at Mesachie Lake, and passing Honeymoon Bay, she found the Swiss family on majestic Lake Cowichan at a rustic site with no more than a water tap and outhouse.

She hoped that the sparkling blue lake was as clean as it appeared, yet with the many creeks flowing in from cut areas, appearances were unreliable. For over a century, companies had bought or leased the land for peanuts, supposed stewards of the renewable resource. Every now and then, as in the Clayoquot Sound initiative, the world paid attention and saved a few trees. Some land was being returned to the First Nations, but they were attracted to jobs too, and some had been tempted to welcome mining ventures on the vulnerable territories.

Fifteen dollars a night attracted frugal families. Four or five cars were parked in the camping areas with one tent trailer and several tents. Kids were splashing in the shallow waters, their happy cries bouncing off the natural sink.

The Cruise Canada RV with a red-and-white flag stood out. A clothesline was strung for towels and bathing suits, and under the awning shaded by the huge trees sat a couple in their late thirties. Their young boy, possibly ten, was playing with a beagle with a ragged ear. Boomer. Holly had put on her uniform for emphasis but not the stifling vest. Already she was taking chances Ben wouldn't approve of.

"Officer? Or are you a...ranger?" The man's tone was respectful. The dog got up, trotted over, and jumped onto her pants, leaving dust marks.

"*Otto, komm hier.*" He waved it over, and the dog came, tail wagging. A shiny blue collar was around its neck. At his request, the pale boy clipped on a leash and took it back to a picnic table, where he gave it a piece of cheese.

Holly was surprised that the dog had mastered German so quickly but supposed that the universal hand gestures did the trick. She introduced herself. "I'm afraid that back in Fossil Bay, you may have taken someone else's dog...by mistake."

With broad shoulders and a Teutonic lantern jaw, the man looked like he was accustomed to getting his way by mere posture. "That cannot be so. We found Otto a couple of days ago. He had no collar and was to us a...stray as you call it?"

"He's not a stray, and he must have slipped his collar." Her language was neutral and her smile polite but not overly friendly.

"Miss, officer." He bent forward, lowering his voice. "My boy has many health problems. Life for him has few pleasures. He loves the dog."

Holly softened for a moment. "I can see that, but Boomer's people love him, too."

His wife muttered a few words to him, and he bit his sculpted lips, swallowing a retort. Did he imagine he'd be sent to jail? "We don't want any trouble."

Sensing tension, the boy started to cry. "*Bernd. Nein.*" The mother put her arm around him as tears streaked down his face.

Holly let the boy give Boomer a final hug, then loaded the

mutt into the rear seat and drove off. This was a no-win situation for everyone.

Heading back east around the north side of the lake, and seeing the mile marker for Youbou, she felt nervous about seeing Auntie Stella again. The old woman might imagine that Holly's resources would allow her to begin the long trail to Bonnie. That simply wasn't the case. Not only had years gone by, but investigatory processes weren't for her personal use.

In an hour, she was driving past the town in all of its summer finery, flower baskets and bunting. The small former logging community had a healthy population of Natives and a thriving reserve. Like other parts of the island, it was becoming gentrified, huge summer homes going up for the wealthy as they took over cottage properties along Lake Cowichan. The first wave of three-storey condos had surfaced as if a Monopoly board game had come alive. With mall shopping in Duncan and Victoria only an hour away, the Warmlands community would get its share of retirees.

Travelling up Rice Road, named for a family that had been here before recorded time, she stopped at a familiar century cabin within a grove of apple trees. Memories of delicious fruits came flooding back. She'd bitten into many pallid imitators since. Stella had explained that the harvest had three seasons: early, mid-season and winter. Duchess and Melba varieties were best straight off the tree. From the Cox's Orange Pippin and King, she made her famous hard cider and sold it in a roadside stand. And the winter Belle de Boskoop and Calville needed ripening in storage to enhance their flavour. Any tyro who imagined that all apples were Red Delicious was in for a pleasant shock.

Stella had five acres cleared for hay cutting and backing into the hills. A small barn and corrals helped manage her goat herd.

A runty but perky white dog with snowy fur trotted out barking. It seemed to have fraternity with everything from Pomeranian to chow, spitz, husky and even poodle. Friendly but wary, it drew back from Holly's outstretched hand. In the back seat, Boomer gave a bark and pawed the window, sticking his head out. "That's enough, you. My car is sacred," Holly said, opening the sun roof for ventilation and leaving the windows down. The day was mild, and a stiff breeze rustled the leaves, sending a rooster weather vane creaking slowly.

Out of the front door came Auntie Stella, brandishing a broom. "It's you, sweetie. What is that dog you have with you? I hope not a male. We can't have any lovemaking with Puq. She won't be spayed until the end of the month. I'm bartering two wool sweaters with our vet."

Holly nodded. "No worries. He's in custody."

Stella shook flour from her apron. She wore a generous gingham dress and a pair of soft moccasins. "So how do you like my new baby doll?"

The small dog had overcome its initial shyness and was rubbing its head on Holly's leg. The blue pants didn't take kindly to dog hair. Looking into the sharp brown-marble eyes was like reading a history book. "Who would have thought? Bringing the breed back from extinction. It's better than *Jurassic Park*."

Following Stella inside, Puq snuggled down on a comforter in a willow-wicker basket, head between her paws but her eyes tracking her mistress. The house had a wood cookstove in the kitchen and living space with a bathroom and two bedrooms in back. Stella laid a plate of seed muffins and a tub of fresh churned butter onto the large cedar-slab table with five hundred years of growth rings She took one for herself and slathered it. No one ever went hungry in Stella's house, nor did she stint herself. Her first words jolted Holly back to reality and confirmed her own inadequacies. "What is the news about your mother?"

Holly swallowed a mouthful of her auntie's aromatic cider. "I...well...I'm not making excuses, but..." From outside, an errant goat gave a protracted baaaaaaaaah.

Her auntie flicked a glance at the window then narrowed her round eyes at Holly. Though blearing lately with cataracts, they seemed to penetrate to her soul. Nobody put anything by Auntie Stella. If you didn't have her good opinion in the community, you might as well leave town. "No? Listen to your own words. I'm not proud of you."

Holly flushed, her appetite gone in seconds. She reached for the glass and saw that her hands were shaking, then clasped them in her lap. "But Auntie Stella, with a full-time job...it's not like on television, where information comes at the push of a button."

Before Holly could crawl like a guilty worm, Stella's voice softened with the emollient of mercy. "That's good that you're working hard, making the island safe. But nothing is more important than your duty as a daughter. She would have moved heaven and earth for you. That was her job. This is yours."

"I know." Holly's heart lost a beat, then picked up the pace. Was she mistaken, or did the cider have a kick?

"And much time has passed."

"I did learn—"

Stella raised a hand that could part an ocean. "This morning I saw a deer track across the crimson sun. In the Warmlands is your mother's ancestral home. Your journey starts here."

A modern day shaman, her auntie had a gift. Though she was untutored in academic knowledge, her intuition and common sense helped her find lost children, rescue marriages and solve problems beyond the abilities of so-called geniuses. As a judge of people, she was peerless, never suffering fools gladly. For the last twenty years, she had headed the tribal council and pushed through countless incentives to nourish and succor her people. Holly gulped back a lump of anticipation.

Stella began slowly rocking, as if it helped her think. She picked up her needles and yarn and paused to consider her pattern. "This is the hub of the wheel. Your mother came here often in the course of her efforts to help her sisters. You were with her, sometimes, until you went away to school. That was part of a plan. On that you have not faltered."

Memories were returning. Happy, painful, necessary. With her interest in the natural world, Holly had paid little attention to her parents' jobs. Her father's campus she had visited to use the library or go to concerts. Bonnie had taken her to work until she began school. Stella was right about the hub idea. Her mother must have used the area as a mid-island base. From that point, it was possible to drive north as far as Port Hardy or west to Alberni, Tofino or Gold River in less than a day, weather permitting. Many isolated communities remained on the island, most without doctor's care and few with schools or libraries. Bonnie took the resources where they were needed.

"Is there anyone I should talk to?"

Stella pointed at her eyes. "You need to look first before moving. Even a deer knows that." She was off on her allegories again.

"But I don't know—"

"Your mother used my spare room as an office."

Holly stood up, her body pointed toward the bedrooms. Why hadn't she thought of this? Her mother may have acted like a one-woman travelling band, but she had paperwork, even with the confidentiality of her job. "Her records are here? Why didn't you tell me?" She recalled her mother's faithful Bronco, filled with boxes of files and supplies, everything she needed at hand. Holly could count the Christmas holidays they'd spent together on the fingers of one hand. What holidays meant to Bonnie was more alcohol to fuel domestic disputes, the saddest time of year.

Stella shook her head and tucked her knitting into a woven bag. "*Uw-wu*, no, don't go so fast. Your mother left no more than a small box that she kept in a closet. I found it the other day. At my age, bending down is not a position I enjoy."

"What was in it? Did you learn anything that would help locate her?" If only the SUV had turned up. But the vehicle had been old and of little use if recognized. It might have had its number filed, been sold on a casual basis, or perished in a junkyard crusher.

Stella waved her porky hand, knobbed with arthritis. "Seventy years of milking goats. Puddling in papers isn't my strength. I like numbers no more than letters. And besides, do I look like such a meddler? I gave it a little shake for my own curiosity. Perhaps the box is empty...but it doesn't feel so."

"But surely—" Stella was handing the torch to Holly after so many years. How well she remembered the fatal week when her mother had failed to arrive at her destination. "Go back to school," her father had protested a few days later, his voice hoarse with strain. "You can't do anything more than the police. That's what she would tell you herself."

Holly had changed majors after the semester. The natural sciences held little interest for her when real life had interceded. Nor did she ask divine guidance. No fan of conventional religion, she found her cathedrals in the woods.

Stella rose and took Holly to a work room in back. Inside were a handsome carved whorl for spinning, two looms, a carding machine, knitting needles lined up in gallon pickle jars, and built-in racks of patterns. The wall held a dozen elaborate fetish masks, worth thousands of dollars in the native shops. Holly looked at the proud eagle, his craggy beak and determined stare. Now *that* could have been her totem. Anything but a helpless deer.

Stella knelt stiffly, opened a small closet and took a box from the fir-plank floor. "Give me a hand up, girl. Go to my room and sit on the bed. It may take awhile, or it may not. Either way, I have things to do." The stuttering roar of a helicopter made them both turn toward the window. The trademark yellow of a rescue flight flew low, heading west. Possibly someone was in trouble along the West Coast Trail. Three or four times a summer, hikers often tumbled into crevices, or sprained an ankle and needed to be lifted out. Holly needed to finish up and return to her territory.

In Stella's room, monastic except for a single bed and dresser along with a scent of rosemary from sprigs in a clay bowl, Holly sat on the wool blanket and opened the file box marked "Bonnie". As she had finding out about her mother's raven pendant, she felt something warm resonate inside her, a connection across the years and miles. How she wished that she could have convinced Bonnie's lover to give it to her. She hesitated for a moment, afraid to continue. A diary? At least an itinerary for that fateful weekend?

Holly had been returning to UBC for her final year, and Bonnie had taken her to the ferry. "Be careful, Mother," she had said, wearing the lovely beaded deerskin jacket she'd been given. "Sometimes I wish you drove a Hummer." Travelling was risky on the north island. It was only September, but in the higher elevations, snow was possible. That the jacket had been stolen on the trip made her feel worse. She should never have left it "saving" her seat when she went for a coffee.

"My Bronco, my pony, will take me anywhere," Bonnie had

said, laughing at Holly's concern. Her shiny black hair was pulled back with a leather clasp.

"I know you love your job. It's just…"

"Better that you look after your father," Bonnie said. "Life isn't quite real to him. He's always miles away in his little world. If he is as happy there as I am in mine, why should we complain?"

Gold River had been her destination, yet she had never arrived. A call from a motel in Campbell River before she headed west had been her last message to them. Praying with all her heart that something useful lay within, Holly opened the box. Instead of files, all she saw was a battered map of the island, a pack of index cards, a small piece of paper and a blank notepad. A sob left her lips. Why had Stella raised her hopes? Why hadn't she opened it and saved Holly the first-hand despair? The answer was easy. Her great-niece was no longer a child.

The paper was a receipt from Otter Aviation, a small company which ran tourists around the interior of the island. Operating out of Chemainus, they flew float planes and a few fixed-wing machines. The receipt read "Bonnie Martin. One way flight to Williams Lake. September 13th, 20—. Two thousand dollars." Holly whistled. Stiff fees, but what did anyone expect for private flights, perhaps at the last minute? Why Williams Lake in central B.C.? That made no sense. Her mother had been safe at home that night, a week before she had disappeared. The timeline had been so important to Holly years ago. She and her father had chewed over it, beaten it to death so many evenings with no results. So she hadn't taken the flight. But why pay for it? Was that where some of the ten thousand dollars she'd taken from a joint account had gone? Not enough to establish a new life. Yet Bonnie had left several hundred thousand dollars of their mutual funds intact. Because two signatures were needed for such a transaction? Holly hadn't thought about that before. Another of her mentor Ben Rogers' corollaries about perfect crimes affirmed that there were only imperfect investigations.

Disappointed and confused, she picked up the notepad, half an inch thick, several pages torn off. *What could you tell me?* she thought, flipping through it like one of those cartoon pads where a character moves in stuttery fashion. Then as she turned to the light, she noticed indentations, as if someone had pushed down hard with a ballpoint on the previous sheet. Sometimes Victorian forensics trumped rocket science.

She took it to the kitchen, where Stella was peeling potatoes and humming to herself. "Do you have a pencil?"

Stella laughed, her eyes crinkling like shook foil. "The policewoman doesn't even have a pencil?"

"We use ink in our notes and reports. I need a pencil to shade this. Something's been written here." Holly showed her auntie the notebook.

"So there *was* something useful. Let me get my glasses on." Stella popped them onto her face, then rummaged in a drawer for a stub. "Here's a tiny one. It even has an eraser."

With Stella standing by and peering through her thick lenses, Holly sat and slowly shaded in the paper, her smile widening as she put the letters together.

"*Flight confirmed. She leaves on the 13th at 10 p.m. Get the rest of the money in twenties. Send taxi to McD an hour early. LS will be there.*"

It was her mother's angular script, nothing like her father's careful cursive. She'd thought faster than she wrote. Often Holly would have to ask her for a translation. These were notes to herself. Perhaps some of the last notes Bonnie had even written. She heard Stella grunt behind her then move to the table.

132

"Is Otter Aviation still in business?" *And who or what is LS.* McD could be a street or the golden arches.

"The Hamilton place? The older brother Bernie was killed in a crash over Denman Island. I think Phillip sold the business. What have you found? I couldn't read that writing. Your mother never got better than a C in penmanship." Stella put potatoes into a pan of cold water then dried her hands on her apron.

Holly shrugged and ticked off points. "We have an expensive flight she didn't take. Talk of more money in small, transferable bills, like a getaway stash. I don't know if I told you that Mom closed out a joint account with my father before she disappeared. He didn't even tell me at the time. It wasn't important to him."

Her auntie stared at her then snapped off a sentence like the crack of a whip. "She did not *steal* it."

Holly spoke with caution as she saw the hurt on Stella's face. "Of course not. I wasn't saying that." Despite the cider, her mouth felt dry. "It's possible she was helping someone leave the island. A woman, of course. But who?"

"It wouldn't be the first time."

"So you agree with me." She had never been privy to the inner workings of her mother's trade. It was as if Bonnie were Superwoman and that to intrude upon the prosaic details of her business would have spoiled the magic. More than that, Holly had been a typical teenager, not a biographer. By little more than osmosis, she knew her parents' parents, where they had been born, where Bonnie and Norman had studied and lived as adults. Self-absorbed as she was, nothing more concerned her.

"She helped many women get away from abusive relationships. Sometimes when mediation or intervention failed, that was the only choice." Stella's crossed arms indicated that she'd brook no criticism about Bonnie for taking that risk.

So her job had been more than arranging for support. Halfway houses, access to training and education. "What does 'get away' mean exactly?" Had Holly's father known the risks Bonnie was taking? Or wouldn't he dare to ask? The answer for someone in that ivory tower was obvious. It was a miracle that their marriage had lasted as long as it had.

"Get away and stay away. Start new lives with different identities. It was harder with young children."

"Different identities? Easier ten years ago, but it costs money, no matter how often it occurs in the movies."

These details were sketching a new and fearful picture of her mother. Money changing hands. Secret plane trips. Angry men looking for her. "Sounds like she should have carried a gun," Holly said, regretting as a law-abiding Canadian the very idea.

Stella's even white teeth showed in an amused smile. "What makes you think she didn't?"

"Did she mention any names?"

"Never. Bonnie was very disciplined. It was better that I not know. She would tell me that she'd had a call from this one and that, that they thanked her. Nothing written, either. That's why she had so few files. She liked keeping things in her head. Bonnie had a photographic memory." Stella tapped her temple with one stubby finger.

Holly remembered how her mother could read a page and recall it days later. She envied that gift. Norman used to joke about Bonnie never needing to pull an all-nighter. "But it's a burden, too," Bonnie would say. "Just try to forget what torments you. That's impossible."

Holly's head was whirling. She needed to get organized, to take one small step at a time. Start with the cold facts. "Is this Otter Aviation place still on Poirier Road like the receipt says?"

Stella's brow furrowed. "I'm not familiar with the new owners. They fly a lot of rich people around the island and to the mainland. Fishing, hunting, even honeymoons. Your second cousin Terry Hart used to work there as a mechanic."

"Used to? What happened to Terry?"

"Now he's in Sidney at Eagle Air. He does well for his wife and children. The training he got paid off."

Stella sent Holly off with a half dozen muffins, a bag of dried Winston apple rings, and a jar of blackberry preserves. "Don't be a stranger. You are home now. Come to the games this summer."

"I'll try. In another few years I could be transferred." It could be anywhere across the country. She was here now, and she had to make the best use of her time.

Stella placed her hand over her heart. "A job is important, but without family we are rolling stones. Do not waste a minute. Something sent you back."

"Are you talking about fate? Karma?" Holly searched her auntie's face for the pride she had seen there as a child. But pride was earned.

"The exact words do not signify. In all beliefs, the meaning is the same. Justice."

A bark sounded from outside. Stella waved her off. "You're on a trail now. You won't disappoint me."

The old woman showed such trust and confidence. Holly gulped back a lump in her throat and thought about her next move. The later afternoon was heating up, warmer than she was used to with the strait winds. She brushed a bead of sweat from her lip.

*   *   *

Otter Aviation occupied several acres out of town down Route 1, outside the tourist mecca of Chemainus with its famous murals and summer theatre. A windsock flapped in the breeze. A small floatplane was taking off as Holly arrived, its tiny wheels spinning under the grey metal pontoons. Two hangars and a cinder-block building anchored the small complex. After parking amid the vortices of dust in the lot, she opened the door. A desk and file cabinets and two folding chairs filled the room, along with a wall calendar, bulletin board and coffee service.

"Hello, there. May I help you?" said a pleasant, gap-toothed lady in her forties with sleek dark-brown hair.

Holly showed the woman the receipt. "I need some information, but I understand that the Hamilton family no longer owns this business."

The woman shook her head. "It was a tragedy for the family. Bernie went down in a swamp in an accident. His brother Phillip couldn't make himself carry on. I can't tell you where he is now. Went back east somewhere." Odd how people spoke. It was never back west. The frontier went in one direction.

"Records must have been kept. I'm interested in files from ten years ago. Flight plans. It involves my mother. She went missing about that time. This business and a trip to Williams Lake were mentioned in a note. But it wasn't...specific."

The woman put her palms up in a gesture of futility. "We retained the files back thirty years, but they were lost in a fire shortly after we took over. Some electrical problem. You'll notice this building is new. Everything was burned to the ground, not that there was much of it. One of our planes was damaged, but the rest were safe."

"That was fortunate. Thanks for your time." Holly accepted the woman's card as a courtesy. "Do you have a phone book I can use?"

Unless a miracle happened and she located Phillip Hamilton, Terry Hart was the only one left with possible information. The last time she'd seen him, they'd been around fourteen. He'd taken her halibut fishing in his small boat off Chemainus. The more moderate Strait of Georgia was benign, nothing like the wild waves on the Juan de Fuca. Thanks to his advice and strong arms, she'd caught a twenty-five-pound chinook beauty. Auntie Stella had cooked it on a cedar plank, nudging Bonnie, who was serving. "Only one I know who can bugger up fish and a flame," she had said. Bonnie had stuck out her tongue.

Holly dredged up an old plastic jug from the trunk and gave Boomer a drink from the tap at Otter Aviation. "You're going home, pal. But I have one more stop. Cross your fingers."

She used her cell to get the number for Eagle Air. "Terry?" the manager said. "You're out of luck for now. He and his family went up to Yukon for a month-long trip. Fishing for him, hiking and camping for the wife and kid."

Holly thanked her and hung up with a mild curse. Stopped in her tracks. Would Stella understand this frustration? In her slow and methodical mind-set, where five centuries nestled in oral traditions, she would have the patience.

As Holly headed down the perilous Malahat, through death-defying high-wire scenery looking across the Georgia Strait to Vancouver and majestic Mount Baker, alarming news came on Northwest Public Radio, a powerful American station which always gave the Canadian weather. Summer was erupting with a vengeance. In Washington State east of the Pelouse, blazes were raging. The area had experienced an uncharacteristically light winter, and like the island, was parched for rain. The preponderance of thunderstorms with lightning was making the situation worse. Arson was suspected in a number of

137

central Vancouver Island burns, and over 200,000 hectares in the province had been affected. At one point, with nearly eight hundred fires raging, the province had more aircraft aloft than the entire Canadian Air Force. Holly thought of the local fire protection, one lone station at Otter Point Road for all points west. Flames would be fanned into hell on earth from those ocean gusts. Burning ordinances at parks would be easier to enforce with a $345 fine for illegal campfires, but an errant cigarette from a car might torch the bush.

An hour later, as she sheared off Highway 1 heading towards Sooke, Holly snapped back to reality. It might be the weekend, but she still had to find Marilyn and tell her that her brother was dead.

NINE

The next day, having seen the Audi in the drive, Holly stopped at Marilyn's. Behind the Audi was a flashy Mini Cooper. A flat of purple petunias sat ready to plant in a border bed. Trust Marilyn to take time for flowers to feed her soul. Under a shady plane tree, an unusual sight on the island, was a small mound planted with marigolds. Brittany had a super view of the strait.

The rounded-top cottage door opened, and a very thin lady in an Indian print dress and sandals strolled out, waving behind her. Glancing with surprise at the police presence, she got into the car and slowly backed out of the driveway as if she were taking a learner's lesson. Marilyn stood at the door, a quizzical look on her face. "Oh dear, I hope this visit isn't bad news about Norman." She craned her head as if to see if he were along.

"No, he's fine. Never better in fact. I think your massage has made a new man of him. It's...something else."

"Come in, please, I was just about to relax for an hour between appointments. Sometimes the masseuse needs a massage. Rather like the shoemaker's children going barefoot." Her voice was musical.

"It must keep you in shape," Holly said. Marilyn's upper body looked strong and toned. In long shorts, her legs were well-muscled, if untanned like most of the islanders'. She wore comfy pink clogs.

"We'll have some tea. And I have some wonderful flax coffee

cake from a client. They're generous with their baking and jams. I simply don't have the time."

"Thanks." Holly entered the house and was taken through the front work area to a rear sitting room, where a wood fireplace with an ornately carved mantel provided a cozy atmosphere. On the walls were collages and still-life paintings of pears and other fruits. A Grandma Moses-style picture had a small farm with cows, a bull, sheep, goats, ducks and pigs.

Marilyn saw Holly admiring it. "Lovely, isn't it? In the nineteenth century, wealthy farmers would commission an artist to commemorate their property. There's something so simple and gratifying about the rural life. That's why I like it out here. I'd prefer to have lived in those golden days, but I doubt my massage business would have thrived. Frontier women were not so self-indulgent."

She poured fragrant mint tea into Holly's cup. A bright floral service of Royal Winton had two cups and saucers, a creamer and sugar holder, and a small pot made for two. "Debbie has wonderful things if you know how to look. Antiques from an age in which people cared, instead of the Styrofoam generation. This pattern is called Summertime. They're reproduced now, but these are originals from my Aunt Dee."

Holly found a surge of hope. "Do you have relatives nearby?" This felt as phony as the "are you sitting down?" routine.

"Aunt Dee's here. She raised me. My mother died in an... accident, and my father had left her a widow when she was thirty." Marilyn mentioned the bare facts with no self-pity, as if it had proofed her in a cauldron of challenges.

Holly thought of Joel. No father figure for him. And yet some young men grew up to live productive lives. Why make excuses for a felon? No wonder the aptitude tests placed Holly low on the scale for social work. "How old is your aunt?"

Marilyn answered with pride. "Eighty this year. She was in a small downstairs suite in town. When Eyre Manor opened, she moved right in. Shannon and I offered her the spare bedroom, but she was firm about living where she could socialize. Sharp as hell. I hope I take after her." The new facility had recently opened with great fanfare in Sooke. Its proximity to the legion was helpful for those residents who liked a social beer, card games and bingo.

"There's a picture I took of her with my old Polaroid. It's a shame how the colours fade." Marilyn pointed to a framed photo of a small woman with a strong face, her hair in curlers. She wore a flowery house dress complete with full apron and was brandishing a rolling pin in a comical candid shot, a mischievous expression common to those who would never grow old. "God, could she bake. She must miss that the most. Sometimes I have her over for a meal and let her go wild in the kitchen."

With a warm, enveloping smile that made friends of a stranger, Marilyn looked relaxed and revitalized. Perhaps she was finally seeing her life come back to normal, and now... Holly girded herself. Although Joel seemed to be a good-for-nothing, who knew how his sister had felt about him? Without siblings of her own, Holly couldn't imagine. Her parents had probably stopped at one by choice, or perhaps Bonnie, an idealist, wanted no more "complications" in the disappointing marriage.

She put down her tea and lowered her gaze, searching for words. Her hands she placed in her lap, lacing the fingers and squeezing them so that the knuckles hurt, though the tension was invisible. Delivering this information was far more painful when you knew the person. "I have some bad news for you. Forgive me for the delay. It's the worst part of my job."

Marilyn cocked her head. The corners of her mouth drooped.

"I thought you said your father was...you don't mean Aunt Dee. I was just talking to... And how could you have known that she—"

Holly shifted and barely managed the last swallow of tea. Maybe she wasn't cut out for more than traffic complexities. "I'm afraid it's about your... brother. I'm sorry that...I—"

"My brother? Joel?" Marilyn's cup shook in the saucer, and she put it down. Where her body had been a supple thing and her posture natural, now she seemed tense. With a bitter laugh, she hurried on. "He's in jail again? You're not surprising me with that news. They say blood is thicker than water, but in this case..."

Holly's news was pre-empted by Marilyn's surprisingly harsh attitude. "Did you know he was back here?"

Marilyn passed a hand over her forehead. Small points of red began to appear on her cheeks. "Yes, I...saw him last week. After all that time. I thought he was out of my life, dead even, and frankly, I didn't mind. I've spent so long trying to..." She looked to the photograph of Shannon as if seeking strength.

Holly decided to let the woman talk. She'd already made a mess of the announcement, and it was too late for Joel.

"He showed up at dinner time. Wouldn't that be the case? I gave him supper. He ate like there was no tomorrow. I did feel bad about that. I've never gone hungry in my life."

"Did he say why he'd come?"

She waved her hand. "Money, what else? I gave him what I had. A few hundred. Not that I keep a lot around, but some clients pay in cash. I told him he could stay the one night, and I was firm about that. He looked terrible, but what would you expect? The man was a con artist, and a poor one at that."

"From our records, he spent much of his life in jail, off and on. So he didn't have a more positive reason for coming? Starting over, for example."

"He was hardly wearing a suit and wingtips. It wasn't as if he was going to find a job, although I did suggest it. Normal work was always beneath him. He would rather have been the president of nothing than make an honest day's wage. Don't think he always looked like a bum. He was a handsome kid at eighteen when I last saw him. I suppose he was into drugs. That's why he wanted the money. Do you call what I gave him enablement? What could I..." Marilyn's voice trailed off, and she raised one hand as if to say "enough".

Now that she knew that Marilyn couldn't stand the man, the rest should be easier. Holly took a deep breath. "Joel was found—"

Marilyn stood up, a pulse beating in her temple. She felt blindly for the mantel, steadying herself. The room grew very silent, as if the air pressure had changed. Outside a tiny tree frog whirred and cracked its hopeful song. "Was *found*...are you saying? An accident? He had no car unless he stole one. Don't tell me he was hit walking the highway?"

"I've done this all wrong," Holly said. "Let me start again." She reshuffled her mental cards. "He overdosed, the medical examiner said. It seemed to be an accident, not...suicide."

As Holly continued, Marilyn rubbed at the bridge of her nose, where parallel lines bisected. "But why didn't you..." She braked to a discreet halt, her voice unsure with confusion. "Sorry, I'm not criticizing you. I've been away supervising the work at Alma. Probably you didn't want to leave a phone message...under the circumstances. I'd hate to be the bearer of bad news, too."

"With the life he'd been leading, few possessions, fewer friends, he wasn't easy to identify. We didn't know his...Joel's name until yesterday. His wallet contained..." She hesitated against adding the theft charges, but clearly the woman knew her brother. "False identities, stolen credit cards."

Marilyn gave a knowing laugh. "Same old Joel. Aliases, you mean. I watch occasional crime shows, and I read to relax. Everything seems to come out so right in fiction. Justice always prevails...unlike in the real world." She squared her shoulders, took a long breath and exhaled slowly as if she were counting to ten. "I wouldn't wish anyone dead. But I'm not going to pretend that I'm grieving. No one can turn back the clock. I mourn the boy he once was, but even by age ten, he'd made very bad choices."

"Was there trouble when he was growing up?" Abnormal psychology had been one of Holly's favourite subjects. Nature, nurture, or both? Here was Marilyn given the same genetic assets and liabilities, yet with a productive life helping others.

Marilyn crossed her legs and folded her long fingers on one knee. "You see, when our mother died, Aunt Dee stepped in without a word of complaint. Never married, she had built a profitable house-cleaning business, but was very serious about education. With Joel, it didn't take. There was a bit of the sociopath in him; he made his own rules. Despite his charming side, his only consideration was what was in it for him."

"That must have been hard for you. I'm an only child myself. And I...grew up with both parents." Now was not the time to recite her own history.

Marilyn met her glance with a smile. "You know, it feels good to talk about this. Bring it all out from under a rock. In later years, if people asked, I'd say I was an only child. Shannon knew because we'd grown up together."

Psychologists estimated that perhaps ten per cent of the population had sociopathic tendencies. They weren't all serial killers. Some found great success in heading up companies and leading in professions but let no one stand in their way. "What happened to your father?" This family had too many strikes against them. Holly wasn't going to speed things up by hastening the interview, especially since she'd taken her own sweet, pathetically incompetent time getting to the point.

Marilyn sat back and half closed her eyes, but her face was growing peaceful. "Dad's family had a history of heart disease in the days when, without apparent symptoms, that condition went largely untreated. God love him, but I suspect he had terribly high natural cholesterol, even though he was skinny as a rake. He was an avid jogger and loved to charge the hills. Like that runner who died young. Jim Fox, or Fixx, was it? We never suspected. Dad came in second in his age group in the Victoria 10K once. He was my hero. He didn't make it past forty, and I never saw him eat an egg, much less bacon or junk food."

Holly needed to get back to the detachment, but she wasn't going to interrupt this therapy. Marilyn could take as long as she needed. And now that Aunt Dee was in the picture, she'd have some much-needed support.

Marilyn went to a large secretary desk and pulled a pack of pictures from the bottom drawer. "We weren't much for albums. This is all I have, isn't that pitiful? Mother never liked having hers taken. Kind of vain about her Roman nose. Here are the four of us at the PNE." Holly looked at the snapshot taken in what she presumed was the Seventies. Marilyn and her brother were very similar in build, wiry and lithe. The father had the characteristic long hair of the period and stood by the mother, who wore slacks and a light sweater. Characters in a Diane Arbus picture, static but full of tension. Marilyn was looking proudly at her father, and he was smiling. But the other two? What was that saying? That all happy families are alike and all unhappy families... It sounded dour.

Marilyn gave a bitter laugh. "It's so odd about Joel. He took no care of himself, lived on the streets, yet he outlived Father by

145

nearly twenty years. Must have taken after Mother. She had the heart of an ox." Her steady voice showed that grieving would not be an option. Then a thought seemed to occur to her. "Aren't you supposed to show me a picture?"

Only now did Holly realize that she was holding that large envelope. This was no time to compound her actions by making a mistake about identity, no matter how far-fetched. "Uh, yes. I brought a recent one from his records."

Marilyn took the picture and grimaced. "He'd grown coarse as he aged. But it's Joel."

Holly felt a reminding pulse in her forehead. "There is something else. Maybe there's no point in mentioning it."

Marilyn steeled herself for another blow. "He didn't harm anyone, did he? Essentially I always saw him as a coward."

"He had a few assault convictions, nothing more than the usual brawls. Hard to escape that in the drug culture."

"I don't know much about street drugs, other than marijuana. Shannon had it prescribed for her pain, and it was a godsend. Do you mean heroin or cocaine? Or is it that meth they talk about? My business uses nature's healing herbs and potions." She gave an almost imperceptible shiver as she rubbed her shoulders.

Would Marilyn want to assume the responsibilities of a funeral? It seemed unlikely, not to mention unnecessary. Yet she was the closest relative. Why communicate these sordid details if not for the wish to tie loose ends? "It was unusual. In his stash...his bag of narcotics, mixed with the heroin, was a dose of a powerful synthetic opiate."

"That's not so strange, is it? Who knows what's on the street? Call me a crazy liberal, but I'm getting close to wanting all drugs legalized. Let's level the playing field."

"He kept his drugs in a 007 pencil case." Holly shook her

head in disbelief and felt a bit silly. "That sticks with me for some reason. Innocence and experience."

Marilyn gave a little start, and her strength began to melt away. "I gave him that...on his...tenth birthday. And we took the bus downtown. One of those huge movie theatres they've closed." Her voice grew soft and almost nostalgic. "All these years. How many people with a life like that keep things from childhood? He probably crossed the country more than once."

"Our records show that most of his time was spent in Toronto."

"Where the action is. When mother was going to move us there, he was so happy." Marilyn's eyes opened as if she had awakened from a bad dream. "But the drugs. Was he selling as well as using? Even to children?"

"Who knows? The idea that all drug dealers drive around in shiny black Escalades is a myth."

"I imagine you're concerned because it's so deadly. If even Joel could make that mistake—"

"There wasn't much left, just enough to do the job. We're trying to track down the source. That overdose potential could be very dangerous, even for other addicts." Chipper was supposed to be working on it, as time allowed. He'd been out the last few days with the summer flu. Though he offered to come in and work in "quarantine", the small post couldn't risk anyone else contracting it.

Marilyn nodded. "I don't know what more I can tell you. Obviously we didn't discuss his drug habits. He said, did say, that he'd just arrived on the island. So maybe Vancouver—"

"Yes, he came over on the noon ferry from Tsawwassen. We found the stub in his wallet."

"Anything goes across the strait. Look at Hastings Street. One of my clients went into a ladies bathroom to change her son's diaper, and a man was shooting up. There was a tie looped around the baby-changing table as if it had belonged there. As long as they're away from schools, I'd rather see safe injection sites."

Holly understood the public's frustration, but it wasn't professional to get into the debate. "It's hard to draw the line between harm reduction and enabling." She paused as Marilyn checked her watch. Probably another client. "We should talk about the...process for his remains. As far as we know, you are the next of kin, and—"

"I don't see Joel as having a wife, though who knows? I'm sure you'll think I sound cold, but I can't see how I'd want to plan any services. Funerals depress me, and it seems hypocritical at this point."

"There is the former girlfriend." Holly explained about the picture in the wallet and how they had tracked her down.

"Judy?" Marilyn gave a bark of amusement. "She's hardly likely. She was very wounded about his leaving her pregnant. Then as the years passed, she got smart and wrote him off as a bad debt. If he'd wanted to send child support, he could have contacted her family. They still lived here, and she lived with them. He had absolutely no sense of responsibility. I tried to warn her in high school, even if he was my brother."

"That fits with what Judy told me. It's your decision, of course." She gave Marilyn the contact numbers. "We'd like a formal identification, too. It won't take long. The...morgue's in Victoria at Royal Jubilee Hospital. I'll call, and if you like I can—"

"I can manage that, but if I don't want any more to do with him..."

Holly thought for a moment, then answered without judgment. "The province would probably step in. That's the process when we can't locate any next of kin."

"Kin," Marilyn said. "An overrated word. Some people don't deserve love, sad as it is. But I suppose a simple cremation would be the least I could do. His keeping that pencil case touched me for some stupid reason. And once he smacked a boy who was pulling my hair while we waited for the school bus."

Holly nodded. "You'll probably feel better in the long run."

"Carrying grudges is like adding to a sack of potatoes. All you get are sore shoulders as it grows heavier. That's done, then. Thanks for tweaking my conscience. There were a few good memories." A beat of quiet passed as she clasped her hands in purposefulness. "He had a tree fort at the big old house on Booster Ave before we moved to a duplex Aunt Dee found. Last time I passed the whole block was getting dozed for another development. Maybe they'll save that Douglas fir with the big arms we used to sit in, and I'll spread the ashes there. I'd rather remember him that way instead of thinking of his spirit lurking around my home." She gave a shrug. "Not that I'm superstitious."

"His possessions weren't much. A backpack with old clothes."

Marilyn's face was softening, perhaps overcome by better motives and a filial bond. "I'd like to have that pencil case as a memento."

"I'll make a note about that. All the storage is in Victoria." As she stood to leave, Holly hoped to turn the conversation to something positive. "How's your project coming?"

Marilyn went to a desk and picked up a file folder, removing glossy photos and blueprints, clearly pleased at the change of subject. "Renovations at Alma have started on the main buildings. I have a terrific carpenter, Mike. He's recently retired. He hired a mentally challenged boy who just graduated from high school and was trained in a special program through Rona. Mike says

149

he's a fast learner. With a bit of luck and a couple of volunteers I've rounded up, we'll have the place open in the fall. Thanksgiving for sure." She showed the plans and preliminary sketches. Rustic it was, but the design suited the rolling hills. Clearly Marilyn was a woman with vision. The island abounded in spas, but this was close to Victoria and yet quite rural. The 180° view of the strait, capped by a pillowy fogbank, added to the drama.

"Impressive. I love the stained glass window for the main building."

"Local artist. She's a genius. Wins every year at the Sooke Art Show." Marilyn grinned, energized by talking about her project. "Call me in the late summer, and I'll give you a tour. We can even have lunch. I'm lining up a cook who specializes in food grown on the island. All organic, of course. A couple of farms in the Otter Point area are signing on."

"Sounds good. Maybe I can get my father interested in one of your weekends." He might become more flexible about his popular-culture diets.

"Tai chi. Hot and cold yoga. He's a tense man. Tries not to show it. Often cool cucumbers hide their feelings under a protective shell. Does he get colds and flu more than normal?"

Marilyn had seen through his façade to the passion within. He was not an old fossil, an enigma of a faithless professor. He was her father, a human being with harmless foibles. "He takes pretty good care of himself. And I'll remember your offer. It would make a good birthday present."

*   *   *

The next day, on a routine tour around Fossil Bay, Holly saw something on the pavement in front of Marilyn's. "Fuck you, Bitch" was spray-painted in white letters five feet tall, an arrow pointing to the cottage. Holly got out and knelt down to inspect the fresh work of a coward. Marilyn's car was gone and the shades drawn.

Next door was a modest bungalow. Farther down, the street ended in a cul de sac and a greenbelt with trails to the clear-cuts beyond. She knocked at the door of the bungalow. From the living room window, a strange, whiskered face looked at her, ears twitching. Out of reflex, she stepped back. A weasel?

A trim woman in shorts and white athletic socks answered. Curly hair framed her face like a Madonna. For some reason, she was partially blocking the opening with her body, shifting her legs. No one liked the police at the door unless invited.

"Yes, officer? What is it?"

"I just—"

Before Holly could look down, a sleek brown shape scuttled out and raced for the bush. "Teasel!" the woman called, slamming the door behind her. "Dear god. He's loose again. Help me, will you?"

"What do you want me to do?"

The woman motioned her to come along, and they both headed to the end of the road, where Teasel had disappeared into a thicket of berry bushes. The flowers on the salmonberries had just appeared, bringing out the trill of the Swainson's thrush in nature's orderly enfolding, and the blackberries were close behind. Heavy salal crowded the underbrush.

The woman, whose name was Kate, she told Holly breathlessly, was panting, hand at her chest. She seemed close to tears as they stopped at the cement barrier blocking cars and trucks from the trails. "It's too thick. I'll never find him."

Holly moved a few branches aside, then looked at her, helpless at the distress. "Does this happen often?"

"Never. I'm very careful. There are cats in the neighbourhood, and the ferrets are so tame that their lives can be in danger. Luckily Rosey didn't get out. She's albino, a perfect target for predators." Her eyes were wild with love and fear. "Albinos are rare for good reason. She's called a sprite. That's an unspayed female."

Holly put her hands on her hips to buy herself a minute's thought. Another one of those cat-up-a-tree situations that tied up police and fire resources. Still, public relations were important, and she hated to leave someone in panic. Perhaps the ferret would scuttle home on its own. No one ever found a cat skeleton in a tree. "I'm not sure that we—"

"Can you sing 'Morning has Broken'?" Kate's pink cherub face wore one last hope. "Or just hum along. The louder the better. It drives Teasel crazy."

"Won't that make him run even farther?"

"Oddly enough, no. He'll try to get me to stop."

More than self-conscious, Holly cleared her throat. At a pitch note and the count of three, she and Kate began their duet, Kate singing an alto to Holly's soprano.

At last there was a rustling in the bush, and a brown face with a sharp nose poked out. Intelligence gleamed in its beady black eyes. It bore a clear resemblance to a meerkat, and Holly half expected it to stand and peer around. "Teasel! You come here, and you come here now, mister!" Kate bent down to scoop up the ferret and wrap him in her bush jacket.

"They must be high energy," Holly said, wiping her bloody hand where a bramble had scraped it.

"Not so. Ferrets are very calm and laid back. They sleep much of the time. Sometimes you can see their little bodies expand and contract as they breathe. It's very restful."

They were both laughing as they came back down the

street, mission accomplished. "I noticed this spray paint. It wasn't here yesterday," Holly said, scanning the area in case the can was still around. "That's destruction of public property. Do you know who did it?" She took it for granted that young people had been involved.

Kate shook her head. "Like the rest of us, Marilyn can't stand these kids on their noisy quads coming through to access the clear-cuts."

"They're not supposed to run on roads, even to cross," Holly replied. The other day, some young man in Sooke had received a ticket of over six hundred dollars for driving down Otter Point Road.

"Marilyn's had some harsh words with them. Her partner was so sick, and often the noise kept her awake. Said she was going to phone your detachment. The riders don't even have licenses, much less insurance." Kate bent closer. "Sometimes only a man can get through to them. I thought of calling my cousin."

"Have you seen the ATV? Colour? Make?" Holly took notes.

Kate described the machine. It had a death's head on the tank. Expensive custom painting. "On weekends, that's when they usually arrive. This boy's thirteen or fourteen. Sometimes friends on bush bikes come with them. Sometimes during school hours, too. How many PD days do those lucky teachers get?"

"Not enough to make me sign on. Anyway, school closed last week, so it will only get worse. That death's head shouldn't be hard to trace. I'll ask at the gas station. I doubt they fill up with a jerry can. Too much bother."

Bush bikes and other off-road vehicles had grown in popularity, despite the rise in fuel costs. They operated on a sneaky basis, in and out for gas after dark, accessing roads and alleys to get to the clear-cuts. Once there, they found their way around the locked gates. What business did a kid have with a ten-thousand-dollar machine?

Holly called Marilyn that night and explained about the graffiti. She answered the phone as if she'd been waiting for a call.

"I thought it was the Jubilee calling. They're keeping...Joel there until I can make arrangements. They've really been quite kind. And a staff sergeant from West Shore helped me locate the pencil case. And the money I gave him, too."

"I'm sorry you had to get involved with this petty vandalism after what you've been through."

Marilyn gave a self-deprecating laugh. "I didn't know writing on the pavement was against the law, but the language is offensive, and it is paint, not chalk. I suppose I angered that little...young man when I complained about his machine. Don't they have mufflers? I make noise, therefore I am. Maybe I was sarcastic. I haven't been sleeping well lately."

"Let me take care of it. I'll find out who the bike belongs to."

"Thanks so much. Who would have thought living out here could have such problems. What purpose do those gas-guzzling monsters serve?"

"Hunting or just raising hell. I suppose they have their uses on farms or in remote places. Like snowmobiles." She thought of her own small red Bravo, sold when she left The Pas. She'd enjoyed the freedom of the winter, heading over swamps and through country only a moose or rabbit could navigate. Now she'd have to go up to Mt. Washington if she grew nostalgic about the white stuff.

At the Petro Canada station in Fossil Bay, Holly spoke to Mac, the genial giant with a billiard-ball head who ran the place. When she described the bike, he snapped his horny fingers. "I know that one. Scott Bouchard's a spoiled brat. His family lives on Sproat Road. The father, Paul, is away on business most of the time. Leaves the kid to his wife, who thinks the sun shines out of his ass. Remember those broken tombstones at the old pioneer cemetery? Just got to wreck something, but try to catch them at it. My granddad is buried there. Next thing you know it'll be chain-linked. Just plain disgusts me." He gave her a brief description, and they checked the address in the directory.

The Sproat Road home was dark. Nobody home. She left her card with a "please call us" stuck in the door crack. As she headed down Otter Point Place, she noticed a strange bird standing in a driveway to the Dodo Farm. A turkey vulture. No obvious wounds, no broken wing, just calmly turning from scavenger to roadkill, prey for the next car rushing by. She debated catching it for the Wild Arc rehabilitation people. But without a net... It would have to take its chances. Like Joel, some creatures were too damaged for a normal life span.

Driving slowly by as the bird hopped a few feet, she checked her mental calendar. Tomorrow morning she was due for a taser upgrading seminar in Nanaimo. She wanted that paint off the pavement. Chipper could talk to the boy. His interview skills were progressing nicely.

TEN

Chipper gave himself a final once-over in the washroom mirror at the detachment, surrendering a slight frown and brushing lint from his dark blue jacket. From a kit bag he retrieved a small comb and tweaked his short, curly brown beard. Some Sikhs saved their hair and nails, but he wasn't that orthodox. After adjusting his turban, he rinsed the sink as his mother had taught him.

He thought about the office. Ann was only fourteen years older than he was, but with her grown son, she was more like a younger aunt. He got along well with her and had been prepared to accept her as his new boss. Then came the accident, and Ann's career had taken a left turn into a desk. Had she handled the situation by the book, or had she taken one chance too many?

In another few years, like her and like Holly, he'd be a corporal. By thirty-five, a staff sergeant with a command of a dozen. To be posted to a major city in B.C., he'd have to leave the RCMP. And wearing the red serge, even if only on formal occasions, was a matter of great pride. Like many other officers, he was disturbed by the negative publicity the force had been getting thanks to a few bad apples. The taser deaths and other scandals had hit them hard. They weren't adapting to the twenty-first century as quickly as needed but were preserving elitist mindsets, some thought. One political party had recently suggested a return to the provincial police system. BC. without the mounties?

Unthinkable. Every time he saw a light in the eyes of a boy or girl when he went to the local grade school, it made a difference.

Holly had briefed him on the pavement painting. Though not classified as a hate crime, this graffiti was nasty and mean, a personal attack, not a mere ego tag. He agreed with Holly that he was a better choice to connect with this boy. She wasn't a micro-managing control freak. Building on their individual strengths was part of her leadership challenge.

He decided not to phone the Bouchards. Their failure to call the detachment as Holly's card suggested spoke volumes. An unannounced visit would give the boy no opportunity to prepare a story. It was the first week of summer vacation, so Scott Bouchard would have more time to ride. Not that he blamed the kid. Truth to tell, he liked these quads, and during the last big storm, had enjoyed one cool weekend on a big monster, helping with emergencies when roads were blocked. His thumb had tingled at the sheer power and noise. Holly didn't understand guy things.

Meanwhile, a CD of the Arrogant Worms played a song he missed since coming to the island, "Last Saskatchewan Pirate." He thumped the wheel to the lyrics. "Cause it's a heave-ho, heave-ho, comin' down the plains/ Stealin' wheat and barley and all the other grains." He'd loved the wide open nature of his last posting, not to mention the hot summers. The island made him feel claustrophobic, like a bug in a shoebox.

He parked in front of the house, noting the expensive quad with the skull decal inside the open garage. Though he knew that some of these death signs and Goth bravado meant nothing, they could frighten a woman living alone. He stood straighter and adjusted his vest, prepared to ride forth as Ms Clavir's knight.

From a window came the sound of loud television, the inane

audience roars of a game show. He knocked, then knocked again as hard as he could. The door was answered by a young teen, who wore a t-shirt with cut-off sleeves. His arms were pasty white and skinny. A nasty rash of acne covered his cheeks. His platinum blond hair was shoulder length.

Chipper introduced himself, pleased to be looking down from his height. "Are you Scott Bouchard?"

"That's me," Scott said from behind a fringe of double eyelashes, dark in contrast to the hair. He seemed wary at the sight of the uniform. "Are you looking for my dad?"

Chipper tipped back his hat and gave the boy an assessing look without the nuance of a smile. "Yes, I am, Scott."

The boy made a dismissive sign with one hand and folded his arms in a stubborn posture. "What's this all about? What do you want, anyways?"

Chipper noted that no "sir" followed any of Scott's answers. This was one tough little nut. He hoped it wouldn't boil down to a he said/she said argument. "Is your dad home, then? Or your mom?"

"She's up in Parksville. He's watching TV." As Scott gestured to the other room, his jaw tightened, though his brow remained blank. "There's no school now, or haven't you heard?"

"I'm not here about school, Scott. I'd like to talk to your dad." Chipper spoke as loudly as he could, not having been invited to enter. Stepping forward, he placed a boot inside the door. His father would have flattened him if he'd talked like that. Not with his fists. With his mild and hurt expression.

"What the hell are you doing out there? I thought you were bringing me a goddamn beer. It's going to be warm by the time you get back. Hustle!" a rough voice called. Then a man in a Ducks Unlimited sweatshirt and jeans came to the door. His cheeks wore a "wife's not home today" stubble. "Hey, what's the problem?" He looked from Chipper to his son.

Chipper introduced himself to Paul Bouchard, then looked pointedly up and down the street. "I think it would be better if we spoke inside. Perhaps at the kitchen table? I may need to take notes." The television roared again, and Chipper allowed himself a slight flare of his nostrils.

Paul reached around his son and pulled the door open, leading with his shoulders. They went down a hall into the kitchen. Chipper was surprised to see everything clean and polished, dishes and cutlery put away. All except a table where a box of fruit-coloured cereal sat beside a bowl, spoon and a quart of two per cent milk. Paul Bouchard disappeared into another room, perhaps a den. After another few minutes the TV went quiet, and as he returned, in slow deliberateness he grabbed a pop from the fridge, opened it and took a long drink.

Chipper waited until they were all seated. Bouchard lit a cigarette and pulled over a saucer, and his son slumped in a chair, his knobby elbows on the table and a sullen look on his face.

Bouchard said, "Yeah, so. What's this about?"

"Your son has been spraypainting the sidewalk on Sea Breeze Avenue. Writing nasty notes in front of a home owned by an older woman." For security's sake, he didn't add "living alone".

"Huh, that's bull," Scott said, but a muscle twitched at the edge of his mouth. He picked up a can of soda and took a drink.

"Says he didn't do it. There must be a mistake here," Bouchard said.

"We have witnesses." Including a ferret, Holly had said.

The father narrowed his eyes into slits. He might have been handsome at one time, before the onset of early middle age had layered fat onto his body like a snowball rolling downhill. He gave his son a light cuff to the head. "Are you lyin' to me?"

"Honest no, Dad." Scott pulled in his head like a turtle.

Chipper put up a warning hand. "Enough of that, sir."

"Who's causing all the trouble, then?" the father asked. "Some have a problem with riders?" His son sat quietly. To Chipper he didn't look like he was beaten on a regular basis, but he certainly was no stranger to a swat.

Officers were advised never to reveal more names than necessary at this stage. Vendettas had a bad habit of multiplying. "They're adults. Trustworthy sources. Your quad was described to the last detail. How many others around here have those distinctive markings?"

The boy shrugged, his chin jutting out. In a decade he'd be a clone of his roughneck father. "Did you lend it to anyone?" Paul asked.

Scott be confused about the merits of each option. He stammered without making sense, never looking his father in the eye.

Paul's fists gathered like a boxer's ready to brawl. "You'd better not be...that motherfucking bike cost me—"

"No, Dad. I swear!" Scott shrank in his chair, and his voice cracked into a higher register. Perhaps he and his father communicated at opposite ends of a belt after all. "What's the big deal over some paint on a road? Why doesn't that old bit..." He swallowed, and his lips whitened, "get a life and leave us kids alone?"

The father tossed the can into the sink then smacked the table with his meaty hand. "Watch that trashy language, you little shit. Your mom will hear about this. You'll be lucky to get back on that bike by next summer. I bought it to go deer hunting anyways."

Chipper took a deep breath. Easier than he had thought. Three men could sort it out. Some resolution was needed at this critical point. What did they say on those U.S. shows? Time to man up? End on a positive note. "Are you sorry you did it, Scott?"

An insincere nod. "Sure. What's going to happen now?"

"If you make restitution, we'll consider it a lesson learned."

"What's restit—"

"The pavement can't be cleaned. Not enamel spray. So you'll have to get some black driveway sealer and paint over it."

Bouchard waved off the suggestion as he scratched his armpit. "We have some in the garage. Scott will get right to it, won't you, you little bugger? I'll drive him over and make sure it's done by this afternoon. And stay out of trouble now that school's out. There's a cord of wood back of the house needs chopping. Make some kindling, too."

For Chipper, the appeal of parenthood was fast fading. Then he remembered his father. The product of a Scottish orphanage in India, Gupta Knox had added the traditional Sikh name Singh when he'd emigrated to Canada with his wife. Decades of hard work had taken their toll. "It's past eleven o'clock," his mother would say in a musical voice. "Your poor father must have dozed off. Go down and shut up the shop, then bring him upstairs. I have a hot bath and tea ready. And hurry, hurry." She clapped her pudgy hands, clinking her silver bangles. "You need your sleep, too." And there his father would be, sitting on a stool with his head on the counter at their convenience store.

"An apology to the lady would be the best way to finish. I suggest you go over in person. And remember, those quads aren't street legal. If you want to drive them in the clear-cuts or on private property, you have to transport them. In cases where hunting out of season is concerned or disruption of a salmon stream—"

A worm of a pulse began beating on the father's temple. "No sweat there. My buddies and I get our deer up north."

161

"The vehicle can be impounded. Confiscated. You know better than to drive on roads now, don't you, Scott?" Chipper flashed a dazzling smile.

Bouchard blew out a long stream of smoke through his wide nostrils. "He'd damn well better."

Scott stayed silent except for a slight nod. Then a gleam appeared in his soulless eyes as if he had remembered something useful. "Know what? I heard her in a big fight a couple of weeks ago. Some guy was yelling, and things were getting smashed."

A knot tightened beneath Chipper's shoulder blades. Things had been going so well. Now the blame game was starting. He refused to get sidetracked as he stood and closed his notebook with a decisive slap. "Arguing isn't against the law. Defacing public property is." Still, it didn't jibe with what Holly had told him about the woman, a masseuse who tended to her clients and minded her own middle-class business.

Back at the detachment over doughnuts late that afternoon, Chipper filled Holly in on his semi-success with Scott. "Good job. I knew he'd respond better to you," she said, resisting the urge for a second chocolate dip. "We don't want a major incident, but the kids need to know that not only is graffiti not acceptable, that threats can get them into worse trouble. So he agreed to apologize?"

"He'll probably scrawl a misspelled note and put it in her mailbox. But it should put an end to the nonsense. And I don't think he'll be driving the quad on the roads after seeing his father's reaction. I wouldn't be surprised if he gave the kid a whack. I felt like it myself."

"You said your father never raised a hand to you."

"But my mother wielded a wicked wooden spoon." Chipper paused for a minute. "Something weird, though, about Ms Clavir.

162

When you were writing up your notes this morning, you told me Joel visited his sister, didn't you? Sounds like there was some family trouble there." He told her what the Scott had said about a fight.

Holly took a serviette to wipe icing from her mouth. "She admitted that he came by, that she gave him money. We didn't go into much detail because it didn't seem relevant at the time. It seemed sad to me, because I was an only child, and I might have liked a big brother."

"I'm an only kid, too. Big brothers can stand up for you, but look at it this way: you had to learn to stand up for yourself. Good training for the job." He looked out the window to where an eagle soared in the distances, its peeping cry belying its noble reputation.

"But what about Scott? Do you think the kid made up the fight to shift attention from himself?"

"He might have heard something. You know how they embellish. But it was the perfect way to shift attention, if you think about it."

"I'd check with Marilyn again, but what's the point in opening old wounds by asking her if they had a brawl? It's kind of embarrassing." She shuffled a few papers. "Did anything ever surface on that Fentanyl check?" Making sure that the deadly drug was not circulating in their territory was still a concern.

"I made a couple of calls. Nothing yet."

"No news is good news where drugs are concerned."

That night, Holly stood on her bedroom deck as a large brown moth battered around the light. Across the black strait, pinpricks of bright red fires on the Washington side lit the night. Surely they wouldn't be burning off the clear-cuts in this dangerous drought. And was that smoke she smelled on the breeze? A forest fire had closed Route 20 in the North Cascades National Park, the news had reported. Suppose her area was threatened. Everyone was on wells, so there were no hydrants. Behind the parallel streets of development lay tinder-dry brush. The strait, from seven to eleven miles wide, was a buffer zone, and prevailing winds blew from the south, not north. As usual, the single coastal lifeline from Victoria to Port Renfrew made her uneasy. Where people went, fires followed.

* * *

The next morning, Holly passed Bailey Bridge on her way to work and saw Pete's rusty van with the Helping Hands logo. He was about to close the rear hatch when he looked up and waved a large bag of bagels. Stomach rumbling, she pulled in and rolled down the window.

"Have breakfast on me, officer. They're day-old but top drawer. Cobs Bakery donates their leftover goods. I even brought cream cheese." He held up a tub and rattled a bag of plastic knives.

Clichés like the cop taking a free doughnut flashed through her mind. But yesterday's bagel? "Very generous. If you have a spare, that would be great." Why hurt the sweet man's feelings? Though the "pastor" name was merely honorary, Pete spent his spare time making sure the homeless and poor had enough to eat. His food-bank drives cleaned out shelves in every house, and he made sure the supermarkets donated turkeys for a real spread at Christmas. Last year, Holly had helped serve and pass out toys to the kids. A crowd favourite, Shogun had attracted hugs and performed for treats.

"Is Bill around?" she asked, spreading the cream cheese and tucking in. Cobs was King of Victoria when it came to baked goods. Their artisan bread and cinnamon rolls were legendary, though pricy.

"Bill took his breakfast up in the hills to pick salmonberries. He's the last one left here…since…" He fingered the simple cross hanging around his broad neck. The man had the build of a Brahma bull and a bigger heart. His unstinted dedication to his community and reverence for humanity gave him deserved respect. In yet another initiative last winter, he had assembled kits for the homeless, a waterproof poncho, tent, clothes and boots, and distributed them at the Evergreen Mall.

"Since Joel Clavir was found." Holly completed his thought. "Did you know him? He also went by Joel Hall." The drifter hadn't been here very long, but Pete made regular rounds.

"Met him once, a very uncommunicative man. Not unfriendly, but taciturn. I saw right off that he would be a challenge. The readiness is everything. If the pitcher isn't open for the water of life…" His voice trailed off, leaving the homily unfinished.

"I couldn't handle your job, Pastor. You must run into resistance, especially with substance abusers." She finished the bagel, then reached into the car for her portable coffee cup.

"That's the odd part. I came by one morning with sweet rolls and juice. He asked me to keep something for him. For a week or so."

"Money? Valuables?" What about that three hundred dollars? Carrying that much cash was risky. How much had Marilyn given him? It wasn't Holly's business. But her radar went up with this new twist.

Pete shook his head and shifted his stance. A short and bowlegged man, he'd had a childhood operation on a clubfoot which had left him with a slight limp. "I see where you're going, and I wondered, too. It was a plain white envelope, business size, not that I did more than look at it in his hands. Couldn't have held more than a few sheets of paper. Smudged. Dusty. It's hard to keep everything clean when you live like this." He spread his arm toward the bridge's underbelly, where whorls of dirt spun in the erratic air currents. A squirrel scolded from the cedars, annoyed at the humans preventing it from foraging for crumbs.

"Did he say what it was?" She appreciated the problems of the homeless, who guarded their belongings in shopping carts and refused to abandon them to enter shelters. New initiatives for the ongoing problem included lockers. "That's stolen property," opponents of a move to allow the carts inside would say. "You're enabling thieves."

"No, it seemed intrusive to ask." Pete scratched a shaggy ear. Regular haircuts were not of concern to him. "Maybe it was a keepsake, or even his will."

"Why would someone like that even *make* a will?" But she remembered that he had learned recently that he had a son. *Someone like that.* She sounded like a snob. "An insurance policy?" Police work involved being in tune with details. How many scientific breakthroughs came when someone said, "That's funny" instead of the cliched "Eureka"? Might this explain Joel's shadowy past?

"I'm no expert on insurance, but don't you have to keep making payments? That would have been hard without a regular income. Anyway, it's a moot point. I didn't feel comfortable holding something valuable. People are in and out of our building at all times of the day, coming for a coffee, getting out of the rain. We don't have locks even for the cupboards. I hated to turn him down, but..." He shrugged. "I told him to take it to a lawyer or rent a safety-deposit box."

Holly gave him a skeptical look as she mused. It didn't sound like Joel had planned to stay, nor was he reconciling with his sister. Was he ill, returning like a sick animal to die in a familiar place? The autopsy had demonstrated neglect more than signs of serious health problems. Where had the envelope gone? They'd checked his belongings. Had Bill taken it? Derek, the video-camera thief? She'd put nothing past that opportunist.

A call later from work to the arresting officer, Corporal Barb Cottingham at the Sooke detachment, confirmed that Derek had had no envelope with him when he was apprehended in front of BC Liquors. For all of his travelling light, Joel seemed to be a man of many secrets. What about that suggestion from Derek that he had a ready source of money? Not Judy, though. She had total contempt for him. His sister's lottery win? He must have been drinking serious Kool-Aid if he thought she'd deflate her dream for him. Maybe that explained what Scott had said they were arguing about. Holly looked at her latest boring traffic reports and petty-crime statistics. Mourned by no one, Joel had died of an overdose, at the end of a self-destructive life. But the envelope intrigued her.

She saw Marilyn at the post office that afternoon mailing a letter. Dressed in casual jeans and a sweater, she turned with a smile, brushing back a curly lock of hair that had strayed over her eyes. "I wanted to thank you, or rather Constable Singh, for taking care of that paint on the road. It was embarrassing to have clients pass by it. You don't expect that kind of vandalism in Fossil Bay, though it only takes one teenager."

"Glad to do it. Graffiti, even if it's not as ugly and personal as yours was, can make an area look lawless and unsafe. Once it's there, like litter, more appears. The downside of human nature." Holly stepped back to let a bow-backed woman with a Yorkie get to her box. "Did the boy call you? I wouldn't have put it past him to send an e-mail or text message." Because of her business, Marilyn's e-mail would be easy to obtain.

"He came over and painted the road with some kind of smelly

driveway sealer, then left a short note in my mailbox. 'Sorry. Won't do it again.' Probably cost him a lot to write it. Video games would be his forte." She shook her head. "Listen to me sounding like the older generation. Most kids around here are decent. One does my lawn."

"Constable Singh told me that he put the scare of impoundment into Scott's father. A ten-thousand-dollar machine is a chunk of change."

As they were leaving the building, Holly turned again to Marilyn. "There is something I'm not sure I should mention..."

Marilyn's brow furrowed, and she waved a casual hand. "What's wrong? I'm not afraid of this Scott Bouchard, if that's what you mean. Isn't this matter over and done?"

"I'm sure it is, but I'm talking about something the boy said. That he had heard you arguing with a man a few weeks ago. That it was...violent." Was she being intrusive or just following up? Worrying a loose tooth? Should she even mention the envelope?

Glancing away, Marilyn stiffened. "I'm sorry, but I don't know that it's—"

Holly moderated her voice. "Not any of my business, you mean, but violence against women is *everyone's* business. When we first met, your eye looked..." Bonnie Martin's radar had been supersensitive to these "accidents", and she'd coaxed the abused women from denial. "Did Joel threaten you? You might feel better telling someone about it."

Leaning against the cinder-block wall for support, Marilyn swallowed heavily. Her knees seemed to weaken, and Holly gripped her arm as she took a seat on a bench backed by fragrant Nootka roses. "I'm sure he was exaggerating. It wasn't as bad as it sounds. I was too ashamed to tell you, to tell anyone. Joel was always a bully."

"And he was trying to get money from you? Big money, that is?"

"The lottery, what else? That's why he turned up in the first place. He'd seen the story in the paper halfway across the country. I gave him a down payment I'd set aside for the carpenter's supplies. It was so embarrassing. Maybe I could have had Joel prosecuted, but frankly I just wanted him to go away. It's an ugly thought, but the more money he had for dope, the more likely he was to be out of my life, one way or another."

"Never be afraid to come forward. Women don't have to take that any more."

Marilyn nodded, her lips firm. "I know that now."

"We saw a few hundred of what you gave him. Nothing more turned up in his backpack."

"It's possible that he spent it. Money always flowed through Joel's fingers, except it usually belonged to others, like Aunt Dee."

"There was an envelope he asked Pastor Pete to keep for him. He couldn't oblige, of course. It hasn't turned up. Perhaps that's where the other money went."

"I'm sorry to admit that I just wanted him to slip back down his snake hole, as long as it was off the island. He had a habit of ruining everything that was good."

"At any rate, it's over now," Holly said, mustering a smile. "You have your project ahead of you." And even Norman sometimes paid tradesmen in cash to get a lower price by cutting out the government. She wasn't working for Revenue Canada.

Holly thought hard about the situation all the way home. She had never met Joel Clavir alive, but she'd known many similar types. People like Pastor Pete loved reformed sinners. Holly hadn't the time, nor the resources, to invest in 24-7 reclamation of souls. The world was better off without them, though she'd never admit that professionally. In this case, a kind of rough justice had been done. But that damned envelope. As she passed Bailey Bridge, she remembered the geocaching concept. Hadn't Tim Jones said that there was a hiding place in the vicinity of Bailey Creek? Police work was 90% shoe leather and 10% inspiration. Maybe 2%. If nothing else, she'd get a pleasant walk. But first she had to do some research.

ELEVEN

That night after chili soy burgers, a lentil casserole with too much sage, and carrot cake, Holly left her father watching *Bob and Carol and Ted and Alice* and fired up her computer. The geocaching.com website was huge. Signing in with a free membership, she got the basic rights to hunt and seek. The site also sold clothing, geo-coins and metal travel bugs.

Logging onto the Google Earth map, she navigated to Vancouver Island, marvelling at the hundreds of caches peppering the south end. In Victoria they were often historical sites or even pubs. "Earth caches" meant a geological spot like the Oligocene fossil deposit on Muir Beach. She fine-tuned the map and found troves at Kemp Lake, and even at the small community hall in Shirley. The Bailey Creek cache was supposed to contain small plastic toys. According to the location log, it required only twenty minutes of uphill climbing from the parking area. Few people wanted to do extensive bushwhacking. "Codes" provided extra clues. You could choose whether to use automatic deciphering or solve the puzzle yourself. She chuckled to discover an alternate universe with the proverbial "fun for all ages".

Over ten people had logged the Bailey Creek site in the past year. Five who had failed had left frowny faces but said that the scenery was "cool". One obvious problem bothered her. It seemed imperative to have a GPS. Despite the clues, she couldn't stumble around blindly.

The next day, when Ann discovered Holly's interest, she said, "Hold on. Reg bought one of those gimmicks two years ago. Seemed silly at the time, but now it may come in handy." She put her spoon down beside her homemade bean soup.

After rummaging in one of the supply closets, Ann brought over a bulky Garmin GPS, peering at it like a strange animal and handing over a foreboding guidebook. "Haven't a clue how to use it myself, but if you need help, Sean's your man. He's mentioned this geocaching," she said, going to a drawer and pulling out fresh batteries. Ten-year-old Sean Carter was one of their special volunteers, too young for an official position, but always alert to "situations" in the neighbourhood such as abandoned cars and vandalism. He shepherded Ann around his local school on DARE (Drug Awareness Resistance Education) days. "He's been kind of blue lately. His older sister has childhood leukemia, and the family's been giving her all their attention, obviously. They're in Victoria at the General overnight sometimes. I've gone over to stay with him."

So Ann gave up some of her evenings on a couch to help others. "I hate when kids get sick. Damn, it's so unfair," Holly said.

Ann's voice was upbeat. "Her prognosis is good. She had a bone marrow transplant. Leukemia's not a death sentence any more, thank god."

Holly flipped through the guidebook. This was not her *métier*. And if kids had an expertise she didn't, why not let them loose? "Do you think he'd like to help me find that cache this weekend?"

"I'll set it up. The extra attention will mean everything to him. People say that kids shirk responsibility. That's bull. They thrive on it."

With "Gotta Fly Now" still pounding in her ears from her father's breakfast music, Holly met Sean at Bailey Bridge on Saturday at nine sharp. He had chained his mountain bike to a tree and was checking every tool on a gigantic Swiss army knife, blowing out dust and making sure the blades were shiny. His honorary RCMP patch, an old one Ann had found, was sewn onto his denim shirt. "Thanks for reporting, volunteer Sean," Holly said, giving him a crisp salute and keeping her face serious. She'd worn her uniform to add to the drama but was happy to omit the bulky vest.

"I brought a GPS," she added. Even two hours last night had left her no wiser about its functions.

Sean gave the Garmin dinosaur a polite look, but his scorn for out-of-date technology couldn't be hidden. "That's okay. I have my own," he said, patting a slim unit on his belt. "Got it for Christmas. It's a lot...smaller and lighter than that one you have." As a second thought, he added with an earnest nod, "But yours is good, too."

Holly tucked the device into a small packsack she'd brought along with some drinks. "Hope you like root beer," she said.

"Cool. Anyway, I ran off the Bailey Creek cache like Corporal Ann asked," Sean said, showing her the printouts. "So we start at the parking lot. Uh, should I call you Officer or Corporal Holly?"

"Just Holly is fine, since we're officially off duty," she said, hiding a grin. "Corporal Ann says you're quite the expert on geocaching." She watched his eager pink face swell with pride. His light brown hair was neatly combed around a stubborn cowlick. She fought the urge to smooth it down. Memories returned to her of her mother hauling out a handkerchief and spit-wiping a smudge.

"I've been doing it since I was a kid. Scored everything from here east to the city. My parents took me on the Grand Circle Tour when school let out. There's a whole bunch of neat stuff there. I bought a couple of travel bugs, too. We camped out and made fires in a pit. Lake Cowichan is awesome for swimming. My mom usually doesn't like me to go into the ocean here. I almost stepped on a jellyfish last time. That's dangerous." He added a mock shiver.

Holly was amazed at how fast Sean could talk. Once wound up, there was no stopping him. "Lead on," she said. "You're da man."

Walking slowly, they took the path up from the lot. A larger dirt track broken by quads ran up the right side, and a smaller creek path angled down the left. He frowned at the directions on the sheet as he squinted up through the leaf cover. "We can't get coordinates under the trees, so we'll have to do some guesswork. We want North 48 degrees 23.235, West 123 degrees 51.767."

Though the site had three stars out of four for moderate difficulty, this was harder than it looked. As Sean manipulated the unit, he was so focused that Holly felt like a total amateur. Operating a compass was her limit. Who said that kids had short attention spans? "Do we take the left or right fork?"

"It doesn't say. They don't want to make it too easy, like for babies. Let's try the right."

They tapped in and out of the satellite feed, checking in every fifty feet. "Closer, closer. It says we're a hundred feet away." Then Sean stopped and frowned. "What the heck? Now we're going away from it."

Holly tried to think of the angles, the road, the path, the creek. Two ravens danced overhead in avian harmony, dipping and diving in a game. "What now?" She tried not to sound impatient. How humiliating it would be if they had to give up. But Sean clamped his jaw and pointed ahead.

"We'll back up and take the left path instead. The clues talk about a mis...mistletoe. It was encrypted, but I figured it out. Only wusses hit the translate button," he said. "But what's a mistletoe?"

Her moment had arrived. "A cute little parasite that grows on trees. In England, the tradition about kissing under it started because it was one of the rare plants still green in winter. But in my knowledge of island botany, it's possible that the mistletoe idea is only figurative."

His face puzzled as he looked up at her. "Figurative?"

"Not the real thing."

They doubled back and took the other path, which led downward to the creek. Salal, false azalea and fragile red huckleberry branches brushed at their clothes. The massive thumb-thick branches of the Himalayan blackberry were emerging with thorns that could shred skin and blind an animal. Holly stumbled on a fir root arching its back onto the trail. "What kind of a cache would we be looking for? What size?" She hoped her computer research had given her some credentials.

"They start at micro, that's like an old film cannister or a medicine bottle, then small, then regular Tupperware or ammo cans, but in the city you're not supposed to use ammo cans or anything that looks dangerous."

"Makes sense. People could panic over a bomb scare." Ammo cans were ubiquitous in the boonies, where many households contained a shotgun.

"Then they go all the way up to large, like a five-gallon bucket."

Holly laughed and wiped her sweating brow. "Wish we were looking for that size."

"Ours is regular," Sean said with assurance. "Like you could use for leftovers from supper."

"Sounds easy enough to spot."

He shook his head. "Not really. A lot are covered with camouflage paint."

A blaze on a mother bigleaf maple so thick with moss that it housed at least six other biospheres of ferns in its crotches caught Holly's eye. Then they crossed the creek by skipping over rocks. In the wet season, it would have been a roaring, impassible torrent. On this humid day of activity, a few dunks cooled her sneakers. Back and forth they went like modern prospectors, taking readings, scanning near and far. Sean pointed up a high hill, crumbling at the top, a goat path if a path at all. "The first road we were on is beyond that, and we're about parallel now. The cliff is too steep. Something's not right. It's possible that the rains last winter washed the path away."

"Is it always this tough?" She stopped to rest her arms on her knees. Sean wasn't even breathing hard. Here was one kid with stamina. Inside his cargo shorts, his legs were skinny but muscular. Scabs on each knee proved his fortitude.

He walked a few more yards, checked the reading and gave a whoop. "I bet it's back across the creek. I think I see an opening by that tree."

They trip-tropped across stones onto a gravel delta and scrambled up the low bank, following what looked like an otter's slip. Sea otters were nearly extinct all the way to Alaska from two hundred years of trapping for the world's most sumptuous fur. River otters were smaller, and often quite comical, floating on their backs in the sun, even "holding hands" in one viral video. Then Holly took a few mental bearings and realized, despite the zigging and zagging, that they were in the vicinity of where Joel had died. A chill ran over her neck as Sean thrashed with a stick. From her pack she retrieved two thick pairs of gardening gloves.

"Put these on. And watch yourself grubbing in the brush. I'm sure you heard about the man we found here. He was a drug user." Suddenly she felt a sense of responsibility as the dangers of man overshadowed nature's.

"Here's the reading!" Sean said and hustled over to a rotted stump. "It has to be in here." He mucked around, tossing twigs and moss, rooting like a terrier. "Something's weird. This is the exact location, but where is it?"

Holly looked up. Fifty feet above, hardly noticeable in a western hemlock, was a small yellowish parasitic growth, branched and tufted. This "witch's broom" caused a distorted growth of the tree. A west-coast variety of its namesake. "Good eye. There's the mistletoe."

Sean whistled. "I never noticed that. Creepy stuff."

"So what do you think happened? Have you come across this before? Found the exact spot but not the treasure?"

They sat for a moment on soft moss clumps and divvied up the soda. "For sure. I hate that."

"It's not a very funny joke, making people come all this way."

"Owners are supposed to maintain the sites, refresh them, make sure they're not falling apart through the winter rains. And if they take them down, they're supposed to report back online. Keeping good records is important." It was obvious that this was a serious business to him. She found the idea endearing.

Far overhead, a pair of geese took their morning flight to the grassy fields at nearby Malahat Farm for a free lunch. Holly marvelled at the timing, but then she heard geese every day...and most nights. "Right. So people like us don't go on a wild goose chase."

As Auntie Stella said, she needed the patience of a deer. Giving up wasn't setting a good example for Sean. She stood up and assumed an official stance. "Look around, in and under everything.

We'll establish a logical perimeter. Could it be buried?"

"Uh-uh. You can't make people dig. No shovels allowed, no knives, nothing." Sean finished the soda, flattening the can on a rock for easier carrying.

Twenty minutes later, under a suspicious pile of rocks and broken roots, they found a Tupperware container wrapped in a new plastic bag from BC Liquors. A smear of dirt marred Sean's freckled brow. "This is pretty far away. Why did someone move it? No fair."

Together they knelt and took off the bag, revealing a plain plastic container with a watertight lid. "Wow," Sean said. Removing his gloves, he took out a couple of action figures. "Luke Skywalker, Princess Leia and Chewbacca. Cool." His eyes glowed. Joy in small things after a hard-won fight.

There was also a compact logbook, a cheap ballpoint and scribbled entries from people during the last year, all before Joel's death. This cache had been popular. She tried to put herself in his mind, addled by drugs. In all likelihood he didn't even know what he had found, probably some kid's pirate treasure. But in his craft and cunning, he'd changed the location.

A smudged white envelope lay on the bottom. While Sean was inspecting the toys, Holly opened it. Instead of the money she'd expected, it was a few folded pieces of lined paper from an old exam book, ripped out and ragged at the edge. The careful printing seemed to be the cast of a play and the description of a few scenes.

"What's that? Another log?" Sean asked, putting his small hand on her shoulder and peering. "A letter? Weird."

"It's...like a story." Was the paper as aged as it looked, or had it weathered in the damp?

"What's it about?"

"It's called..." She struggled to make out the blurred title.

178

"*Triumphe of Love: Godde Save Gloriana.*"

He squinted as he looked at the words. "Godde? That's not spelled right. Stupid."

A tiny smile broke out on her face. "I think it's meant to sound very old. They used to spell things differently."

His little eyes scanned the paper as he cocked his head in concentration. "Metchosin? Something or other of Renfrew? I know those places. What's it all mean? Are you supposed to, like, add to it?"

"I'm pretty sure not." Holly's right ear itched, and she scratched it thoughtfully. "There's no mention of this...story online, is there?"

"No, it just says the action figures."

"It's possible someone else left the envelope. Someone who didn't know about the game."

"You can take it," he said in an officious tone, "if it's not part of the cache. But what will you do with it? Does it have anything to do with that dead guy?"

"I'm not sure," she said, thinking about how she'd been about to give up the search. As for taking it, this was no crime scene. Or was it?

Sean looked at her, his cherubic face serious. "Can we update the log?"

"If that's the idea, why not?"

As they packed up, Sean added a tiny yoyo to the box, promising to log the cache online and post about the different location. "Never leave food," he said. "It gets stale and animals come around." They put the Tupperware into the liquor-store bag and tucked it under the log.

Going back down, Sean seemed to remember something. "Hey, I was gonna ask you about Scott Bouchard. Everyone's saying he's in deep shit..sorry, I mean trouble."

Word spread quickly in the small community. "It's against the law to deface public property, but he seems to have learned his lesson. No one wants a quad confiscated."

"For sure. I don't like him anyhow." He bit his small lip as his voice assumed the conviction of an older boy. "He's a big fat liar."

"A liar?" This interested her in the face of his accusations about Marilyn. She hadn't denied that they'd quarrelled, but she'd downplayed the level of violence.

"For sure. He couldn't tell the truth unless he thought he was lying." He laughed at the joke. "That's what my friend Pat says. He's in Grade Eight at the middle school in Sooke, same as Scott." Fossil Bay had only one school Sean's elementary one.

In their conversation, other noises were blocked out. Then Holly heard a sound that stopped her heart. It was a faint but determined huffing, coming closer. Then a scrabbling in the bush. A streak of black. "Sean," she said, "make noise. Lots of it." What a time to be caught without pepper spray. She'd left her duty belt at home.

He caught her hint. They started whistling and clapping their hands, and as she walked slowly back along the path, Sean sang, "Bear, bear, go away, come again some other day, go back in your den and stay, I don't really want to play."

Nothing pleased them more than the brushy sounds of retreat. Sometimes you eat the bear, sometimes the bear... Dramatic though it was to actually meet Bruna, either up a tree or nose to nose, it was better not to. Both species had made the wiser choice to head in the opposite direction. "That was a great song," she said as they stopped to catch their breath.

"Works every time. My grandpa taught it to me. But you have to stay calm. They can tell if you panic. They can smell your fear."

Back down at the trailhead, Sean unlocked his bike and saluted Holly. "Wait until my sister hears about this. We went on a real mission, didn't we?"

"Tell her you're our number one scout," Holly said.

Driving home, her heart rate returned to normal. This had to be the envelope Pastor Pete had mentioned. The proximity of the body was too coincidental. But why did Joel want it kept safe? This was no item of value. The writing was so small that she couldn't read some of it in the muted light of the rainforest.

*   *   *

At home that night at her desk, dictionary in hand, she was better able with a strong lamp and a magnifying glass to decipher the words. As for Joel, he had been farsighted, as Bill had said. If he could barely read it, how could it have any meaning to him?

On a piece of foolscap, she jotted the names. Lord Thomas, a ghost. The Duke of Metchosin. The... Earl of Renfrew. Eville Clarissa. Then the knights, whose names she couldn't decipher. A Page, Messengers. It seemed like a childhood fantasy exercise. Harry Potter in the middle ages. To what purpose?

This rough outline started with the Ghost's invocation. Hadn't there been something similar in *Hamlet*, which they read in Grade Twelve? Then came a scene in Hell with Ate and Lust. *Lust* she understood, but *Ate?* Act Two involved a kind of inquisition with comic relief from a Moorish servant and a cook. Act Three brought a test involving a temptation and an echo scene, whatever that was. In the last act the Eville Clarissa perished, having been cast from the ramparts. Ramparts? She thumbed the dictionary. Battlements in a castle. In a final scene, complete with a song, Gloriana was crowned during a celebratory masque. Masque? A dance, a pantomime. Was this a comedy or a tragedy, a little of both? Amateurish, though, even to her untutored eyes. English lit courses were as far from the practicality of criminal-justice courses as her father's profession was from her mother's.

This wasn't her father's area of expertise. But there was someone who could help. Sister Clementine at Notre Dame, Holly's old alma mater in Sooke, the private school where her father had sent her against her mother's wishes. Bonnie had felt that she should swim with the rest of the common folks, not paddle in an elite pool. Would the good sister still be working? Until they pried the chalk from her cold dead hands.

TWELVE

Chipper yawned and stood to stretch his tall frame. It was after five, but he was staying late to finish traffic stats, the downside of his job. Numbers of speeding tickets. Types of accidents with or without injuries. A routine seat-belt check at the Fossil Creek Bridge had yielded ten violations in one afternoon. One elderly woman claimed that the belt must have slipped open because she was "religious" about fastening it. When she saw the $167 fine, he thought he was going to have to radio for an ambulance. "Twenty-five dollars less if you pay in thirty days, ma'am," he said, touching the bill of his cap. Bean counting. If he'd liked that so much, why not become an accountant? Getting drunks off the roads pleased him most.

Holly had asked him to monitor the situation near Port Renfrew, where a landslide had washed out one lane. Only rudimentary repairs had been made. A visit down the road showed that the way was passable, but barely. More warning for motorists was needed. They'd need to call for official signage. Plastic cones alone weren't cutting it. And kids were stealing them. He had an idea about addressing the Port Renfrew grade school. If kids growing up formed a positive impression of the police...

For once, he was in no hurry to get home to his small room at the apartment. His grandmother was visiting from Durgapur, and since she was nearly deaf, the television had been blaring sitcoms every evening. His mother ruled the house, but she had to defer to her own mother. "When are you getting married, Chirakumar? Your cousins have all given me grandchildren. You will be an old bitter man and die of loneliness like the moneylender on our corner. Warn him, Gupta. He needs to hear it from his father," she'd say, wringing her small brown hands. Telling her his nickname had elicited a hiss worse than a cobra's. "What abomination is that? It sounds like a biscuit."

He rested his head on his hand and crossed off another day on his desk calendar. Six more before they took her to the airport. It was sweet of the old lady to make rosewater puddings for him, stuff him with parathas and pakora until he squeaked. But the apartment was too small for three, let alone four.

He was pondering whether it was "compliment" or "complement" to describe a group of officers when the phone rang. "Officer Singh? This is Mindy from the Sooke Animal Hospital," a melodic voice said. "You called earlier to ask about something you read online about Fentanyl being used to treat animals."

Someone else working overtime. He felt an instant camaraderie. "Thanks for calling back. We had a fatal overdose which involved that drug and have been trying to track down any local sources." He chastised himself for using the word "fatal" to make his business more important. Was it because he was talking to a girl? The last marriage prospect his parents had introduced was a cousin of some Victoria heart specialist, who'd seen his father for a check-up. A beauty on the plump side, she was as dumb as a box of rocks. And the way she'd fawned on him. Her jalabis were delicious, but sweets could be purchased. You didn't go to bed with them every night.

"I spoke with the doctor. We've used it a few times to treat severe pain, such as non-repairable hip breakdowns, spinal degeneration, older animals where the answer isn't an operation.

A temporary solution to make the patient comfortable in the final days. Palliative care, it's called."

Chipper perked up and made a fresh note. Holly would need to hear about this. But he needed more details. "Are we talking about pills? Powder? A liquid?"

Mindy excused herself to get the information. She sounded really friendly. But smart. Good vocabulary, too. Was she married? Did she like tall guys? What about officers? He hadn't been on a date since he'd transferred to the island.

"Here we are, constable."

He shook himself back to reality. It wouldn't look good to be flirting with someone he met on the job. But she wasn't directly involved in a case. What could a coffee hurt? "And please call me Chipper."

He heard a little giggle. "We use the transdermal patch."

"A patch? I've never seen anything like that. How does it work?"

"It's designed with a porous membrane for timed absorption. The animals seem to know that they're being helped and don't try to pull it off."

No patches in this case. "That doesn't fit our situation. Any other forms for this Fentanyl?"

"Ummm. There is a kind of lollipop animals can suck. The drug is applied lingually. Through the...mucous membranes." She cleared her throat.

A modest girl his mother might approve, even if she wasn't East Indian. His pulse quickened.

"Hello? Chipper?"

He blew out a frustrated breath. No patch or lollipop for Joel. "I see. Thanks, Mindy, for your help—" He hesitated to ring off, wondering if he could find a reason to see her in person. She didn't seem in any hurry to end the conversation.

A buzzer sounded in the background. "Oh, sorry. That's the dryer. I'm washing some of our crate blankets. But in one case, I remember now, the doctor prescribed the powder. To be used very, very judiciously for pain. One of our older dogs."

"How long ago?" *Snap.* There went the pencil's fine point.

"About a month ago. Ms...let's see...Clavir received the powder because her dog doesn't tolerate other options. The little girl was in very bad condition, but she had a will to live. It was a palliative care case, like I told you about."

His heart double-pumped at the connection. "Would that be Marilyn Clavir?" He tried to sound casual.

"Oh dear, I shouldn't have mentioned names."

"No problem. It's just a matter of research. You've been super to call me back so quickly."

Holly should hear about this. But it didn't make any sense. Joel had died almost instantaneously in the bush. Could he have taken it from her house? A few seconds passed, and Mindy was still on the line. That was a good sign.

Sitting up straight, he took a deep breath and asked her if she'd like to have a seven-sharp coffee the next morning before they both hit their shift. And she agreed. Then he had more sober thoughts. What did she look like? For all he knew, she was forty, but he could try Facebook. Damn. He didn't know her last name. He put on his iPod and switched on Iz, the supersized Hawaiian Elvis, singing "Over the Rainbow". It was only coffee, not a marriage proposal.

*   *   *

After spending the morning in Victoria, Holly headed for

Warren Street in Sooke in the late afternoon just after the last bus had gone. Despite the development chipping at its edges, here was one of the last working farms in the core. Surrounded by a greenbelt of forest, the acreage looked the same as it would have a hundred years ago. A dozen cows grazed on the sparse, rock-strewn ground. In former days, they might have had their spring forage boosted by eating the famous cow parsnip that lined the hedgerows. With its monster leaves and swollen stalk in the early spring, it soared seven feet into the air. Then past an aspen grove came the clearing with Notre Dame Academy. The huge red brick Romanesque building with white pointing had been constructed after World War Two for the daughters of the region's wealthiest families, owners of logging and fishing businesses. Forced to go co-ed by shrinking enrollment, the school found the key to rejuvenation. She parked in the visitor's lot.

Delicate Virginia creeper swept down the side of the building in an old-world fashion. Carved into the lintel was the school's motto: "Per aspera, ad astra." Through hardship to the stars. Hiking up the limestone steps, Holly muttered, "Abandon hope, all ye who enter here." She turned right in the main hall, noticing that a passing boy wore dark slacks and a white shirt while a girl had the same shirt, knee socks and a dark plaid kilt, easily rucked to a mini once outside the building.

Nodding acquaintance at a familiar mural which portrayed the timber industry as a doting grandfather, with logs piled like pencils, salmon leaping from crystal streams and children picnicking, she stepped into the office. A familiar polished oak bench circa 1930 still sat like a reproof under the regulator clock, where she'd spent many hours being disciplined. Skipping religion class to walk in the nearby woods, gaze up at the massive cedars and firs spared from the axe was a fair tradeoff.

187

"Officer, what can I do for you?" the secretary in casual jeans asked. "If you're looking for a teacher, we have only a few teaching summer school courses. I hope this isn't about any of our students." Her pale forehead creased with concern. Last year a graduating senior had drowned at Botanical Beach.

"Nothing like that. I'd like to talk with Sister Clementine. She hasn't retired, has she?" Holly explained that she had graduated from Notre Dame nearly fifteen years ago.

"Did you then? When it was all-girl. That was just before I came. We love to see our former students. ND is one big family. As for Sister C..." The woman shook her head as she laughed. "*Work* here? She *lives* here. The diocese provides a small apartment at the back of the school. At her...age, it seemed wiser than requiring her to make the commute from the mother house in Victoria or find suitable lodging nearby." The vacancy rate was below point-five per cent, even with illegal suites. The woman shouldered her purse and headed for the door. "I'm leaving now. If you'll follow me, I can show you—"

Holly waved her off with a friendly gesture. "I wore a path to the library...and to detention." Along with her buddy, Valerie Novince, one person she'd been happy to find in Sooke.

The high-ceilinged wainscotted library on the second floor had a million-dollar view of the small harbour. Holly noted with wry approval a number of "banned" books featured in a glassed display cabinet. *Huckleberry Finn. The Diviners. Catcher in the Rye.* Good strategy. Make something forbidden so that teens will read it. Sister C was an intellectual Jesuit far to the left of the infamous Torquemada, though a session at the rack for lazy students might have pleased her. "If you turn a blind eye to any information, you do yourself more harm. Knowledge is power," she always said, shaking a small, blue-veined fist. "Think for yourself. Let your conscience be your guide, as Jiminy says."

One large fan moved the still air. A figure in a white linen robe was staring out the window at a bevy of kayaks taking a group lesson in the cobalt-blue waters. They were headed for quieter coves in the interior basin because a slight chop was beginning to roil the waves as silver-edged clouds danced above. The woman stood with hands clasped behind a straight back as if giving posture lessons.

"The world is charged with the grandeur of God," the surprisingly strong voice said as if speaking on stage. One bony hand emerged from the robe, directing a choir.

"It will flame out," Holly added, moving forward. Sister had made them memorize a Hopkins poem in Grade Twelve literature. "Like the shining of shook foil." At the time she'd wondered how they had known about aluminum in the nineteenth century.

The sister didn't flinch, but her shoulders jiggled. "Look who's back," she said, turning. A small emerald winked at the end of a cross around her neck. Real or artificial? The girls had placed bets, and bold Valerie was designated to ask her. The answer had surprised them. "Let that remain a mystery to you, young ladies. We are none of us perfect. Sometimes a flaw is the best character trait." The senior students had speculated that she led a secret, luxurious life, and smiled at each other when she read the lines of Chaucer's Prioress. The starched white wimple left her brow creamy and innocent, elevating her above stress and strife.

Holly stuck out a hand in reflex like a student, but the old nun pulled her close and thumped her on the back in greeting. The woman had to be pushing seventy-five, wiry and strong as a greyhound. Holly imagined that she did isometrics in her cell... or her apartment. One year when the Sooke River had flooded, she had rolled up capacious sleeves and heaved alongside the sandbag brigade, singing "By the Waters of Babylon."

"And you're all grown up now. In the constabulary. And fully armed." Her tone was not judgmental, but Holly flushed. With all the technological devices on her belt, she felt weaponless looking at an elderly woman who used words like rocket launchers.

"Feels like yesterday that you made me stay late for a week to wash the blackboards on the entire second floor."

"Tea?" To be served in Sister's library was the height of honour. After school had ended, Holly had often helped her to shelve books and learned the difference between Darjeeling and jasmine. Herbal brews never touched those thin lips.

Balancing china cups of lapsang souchong, they sat in two padded leather armchairs as creased with experience as the nun's face. Sister thought that anyone who came to the library on serious business (as if there were any other kind) deserved comfort. Mindful of the budget, she'd snagged the furniture when the Greater Victoria Public Library had remodeled its reading room. And quiet was her middle name. The students learned to communicate by sign language, and only on her blind side. Notes passed were speared like minnows and displayed for all to read.

A decade passed in seconds. "I heard about your mother. Very tragic. Has there been any..." Her voice trailed off, which surprised Holly.

"Not so far." Holly managed to raise a tentative eyebrow. "But I'm back, so you never know."

"I have faith in you." Sister made a gesture of blessing.

Holly filled her in on the time that had passed since they'd met. The old woman nodded and smiled. "I was at a retreat in northern Alberta last year, or we might have met at the memorial service for Angie." Angie was the girl who had died at the beach.

"I'm on another kind of mission." Holly began to open a file folder. "I wanted to ask your opinion about this. Lit wasn't my strong suit...oh, not that I didn't like your classes..." She flushed crimson and wondered where to hide. Under a desk?

"Tut tut. I can read your face, my dear. It's fortunate that you didn't become a professional poker player." Sister's eyes narrowed like raisins in the sun.

"I found these pages under rather odd circumstances. It may mean nothing. I'd prefer if you didn't touch them." Holly spread out the sheets on a table and explained the details.

From a hidden pocket in the voluminous folds, the sister removed a pair of pince-nez, adjusting them on her aquiline nose. It smelled out trouble, she always told the girls.

"Torn out of an old exam book. A blue book, we would say, like the cover."

Holly saw herself hunched over a desk, sweating gallons as she fumbled to get thoughts on paper. She'd received a B in English, and how it stung, deserved or not. "I remember those. How far back did the schools use them?"

"Are you implying that I am that old?"

"'Venerable' is a better word. But you *are* a historian."

"Polymath. As all good students should be." For several minutes the nun gazed at the sheets. She read up and reread down, paused, pursed her creased lips, and repeated the action. Finally she looked up, her deep set eyes glinting with silver.

"Amateurish, but...there is some merit as pastiche. I myself wrote sonnets in all four styles as an exercise for Father O'Kelly at Concordia." She read:

Ghost: From my 'pointed vortex in the gale

> Across the running Styx where Charon makes
> His daily crossings with all damned souls,
> Ate, Lust, attend me now. Come forth!

For I have gnawing vengeance to perform.

Ate: My spleen has lately grown too fat for hell
    And I would fain expend this fretful ire
    On anyone your fiery tongue could tell."

Lust: And likewise do I answer at your call.
    To poison love with lust is my delighte."

Sister could have filled the Save-on Foods Centre by reading the phone book. And so it was A-te in two syllables, not like the past tense of eat. "Sounds like Shakespeare. But it can't be," Holly said.

"You do remember your iambic pentameter. But I know the canon and the Apocrypha. *The History of Cardenio. Sir John Oldcastle.* This is an amateur imitation. Reminds me of Chatterton and his 'discovered' odes. Imagine how a seventeen-year-old boy fooled people with those forgeries. Of course, education was superior in those days."

Holly suppressed a comment. Sister lived in a quiet, contemplative world removed from the exponential advances of science. "Anything you might have seen in your classes? The place names are local."

"True. But no student of mine could have done anything on such a grand scheme. Not the layout of an entire play. Mind you, there's no reason to think it went any further."

Holly sipped the fragrant tea. "What else can you tell me?"

"Two names lead the cast, but they are indecipherable with this mildew and brown spotting. The knight, *Br* something. And *Bel*, trailing off. There was a character called Bel Imperia in Kyd's *The Spanish Tragedy.* As for Gloriana, that's always been Queen Elizabeth the First. And the attempt at ye olde language is humourous. But it has merit, in its *sui generis* fashion."

Holly didn't dare ask Sister what that meant. She'd nearly

failed Latin and retained only a few helpful concepts like *qui bono* and *habeas corpus.*

Sister continued. "If we had the entire document we might know more."

"I doubt there is more." Holly spread her hands in a gesture of helplessness. "I found this near a dead man."

Sister flicked a dust speck from her immaculate white habit.

"Joel Clavir was his name. Did you ever teach anyone in that family?" Holly asked.

"Clavir? Not a chance. I'd remember such a unique name. So he tried to hide this for some reason. Then I understand your curiosity." She looked up with a question. "Where are your resources? What do they do on television? Analyze the writing? Shine a magic revealing light? Look at the fingerprints? Trace the bond of the paper?"

Apparently the sister wasn't as isolated as she pretended to be. "If I were in a CSI show and not real life." Holly shook her head. "I'd be laughed out of West Shore, where the detectives hang out. It's the content that will help us. And we're not going to find specialists in Elizabethan literature in RCMP detachments."

"Given the poor job prospects for English majors, I'm not so sure. May I make a copy of your pages?"

"Sorry. I'd rather you didn't. Regulations."

Sister nodded. "Then give me some time, and let us suppose, because of the place names, that this was written by someone in the *public* high school in Sooke. I have a few contacts with former teachers. Although this man in question..."

Something about her expression made Holly uneasy.

THIRTEEN

After setting his iPod on its charger, Chipper filled Holly in on what the vet tech had said about Fentanyl, his sharp eyebrows rising and falling with the narrative. They sat in the lunch room on a rare cloudy day. The tease of rain was reneging on the promise in its billowy silver-trimmed clouds, though Holly turned her head border collie-style, trying to detect the rumble of dry thunder reverberating across the strait from the purple hills. Blockbuster atmospherics were rare on the island. Dust-covered windows and cars and sneezes echoed on the streets as people coughed discreetly into their elbows. Drugstores were doing great business in allergy-relief pills and tissues for watery eyes.

"I discounted the patch and the lollipop delivery, but then came this." Chipper rubbed at the neatly trimmed beard. "Are you going to follow up?" His tone left her no choice, but the proposal tightened her stomach.

"Let's take stock of what we have." Holly ticked off a few points on her thinking pad. "A dead man. Marilyn admits that Joel visited her at home. If there was some of the drug left after Brittany died, did he take it with him? Is that why they fought? Or is the Bouchard kid lying to cause trouble? Remember what Sean said. I trust that little guy."

Chipper shook his head. "If she had trouble with him, why not get a restraining order?"

"Marilyn isn't a pushover, and I don't see her being shy about taking steps against a low-life brother. He came to the island to get money out of her after reading about that lottery win. Big money. Not petty cash like she suggested. Wins like this draw relatives like a magnet."

"And she gave him the large bills we found on his body."

She laced her fingers together and stretched. "Three hundred, she said. As for the Fentanyl, druggies are opportunists. Medicine cabinets are their favourite places for trolling. All you'd find at my house are Shogun's fish oil supplements and his applications for fleas and ticks."

Chipper got a gleam in his eye that spelled *brainstorm*. "Back up a minute, Guv. Did you mention the Fentanyl by name when you told her about her brother's death?"

Holly gave her head a mental scratch. "Honestly, I don't recall."

"Because if you did, she should have told you about her dog's meds and the opportunity he had to take the rest. And if you did and she didn't...or if you didn't..." He stabbed a long, tapered finger on the table.

Ben Rogers had said to take care of the little things, and the big things would take care of themselves. How sloppy had she been, working up the nerve to tell Marilyn the bad news? "Synthetic opiate? Maybe that's what I said. To be clearer to a layperson. It was only a factor inasmuch as we wanted to be on the lookout in case it appeared on the streets."

A knowing smile lit one corner of Chipper's mouth. "And it hasn't. Not outside of Vancouver. What does that tell you?"

"That it was an isolated incident, thank god."

Chipper leaned forward, wheels turning. "On the other hand, if Joel did steal the meds, it might make his sister feel guilty about his death, don't you think? What about that twist?" A dry breeze rustled the papers on the desk. A black and cerise cinnabar moth headed for a patch of tansy.

"I don't want to add to her misery. Frankly, I don't know what to think any more. Here's more fuel for our confusion." She handed him copies of the papers found in the Tupperware container. "I sent the originals off for ninhydrin treatment, but given the age and deterioration, I'm not holding my breath."

"Let's see what you turned up. When you told me what Pastor Pete said, I couldn't imagine what Joel might have wanted to hide." Chipper scanned the papers. "Bizarre, for sure. Some old play or something. What the hell would that be doing in a cache?"

She told him about her research on the hobby and its rising popularity. "I'm thinking Joel chanced on that cache and decided to use it for his own valuables. The envelope."

Chipper blew out a contemptuous breath. "But safe from what? Who cares about this stuff? It's no treasure map."

"He must have cared. Look at the trouble he took. The question is why."

Chipper gave another glance at the sheet. "I can't make out this old-fashioned stuff."

Holly explained about Sister Clementine. "She'll get back to me once she contacts some teacher. One thing's sure. It wasn't there for long. In this climate, it would have disintegrated from the damp."

Ann came in waving the *Sooke News Mirror*. "Hey, look. Marilyn made the front page. Back in a minute. Have to go out for a can of coffee."

Chipper drained his mug, buttoning the top of his shirt, then headed for the washroom, rolling his shoulders. Holly liked the way he was taking hold of this puzzle, brainstorming at her side, putting in long hours without a complaint. Other than seeing a few films, he'd never mentioned much of a personal life. She recalled how busy she'd been learning the ropes as a rookie.

The lead story in the free local weekly had a colour picture of the complex, featuring Marilyn in a rainbow African-print caftan, arms uplifted in welcome. Behind her, blurred in the background, were a main lodge and several smaller buildings, then the rising hills of the San Juans. Large trees had been logged before World War One as the acreage turned to pasture. Recently the aspen taking its place on the edges had been dozed into brushing rows waiting for the rainy season to be torched safely.

"The House of Alma, a wellness spa designed to minister to the needs of the body, mind, and soul, will open at the end of September, according to the owner, Marilyn Clavir of Fossil Bay. Ms Clavir took her training in Vancouver and San Francisco and has operated a successful business in town for the past twenty years. In addition to the Osho rebalancing form of massage, alternate therapies such as reflexology, aromatherapy and cleansing of toxins will be available. Clients may enroll in classes on nutrition, vitamin supplements and cooking with natural ingredients in the "slow food" method. Local organic farms will supply fruits, vegetables, herbs and eggs along with designer island cheeses, wines and ciders. Though Ms Clavir hopes to reach an international clientele, special prices and discounts will be given to islanders."

Good PR, Holly thought.

Back from the store, Ann started her hourly workout on a small yoga mat she kept rolled in the closet. By now Holly knew the five-minute routine. With a characteristic lack of self-consciousness that testified to their comfortable relationship, Ann was busy with lazy pushups, then back stretches. Two inches shorter than Holly with the same one hundred and thirty-five pounds, she'd toned up on a new diet featuring whole grains, vegetables and fruit.

"Ooooo," Ann said, as she eased back into the chair. "If it hurts, it's working. If that isn't a paradox."

"I'm glad you found something that helped. Is it hot or cold yoga?" Remembering the tackle that had cost Ann an active career, no matter how much better she was, returning to that kind of duty could lead to nerve damage. The woman was a hero, disinclined to waste retirement years knitting, crocheting or even volunteering. Like the border collie born to its herding, Ann was bred to be a law officer.

"Depends on my mood and the temperature. But I'm better off hot, if you excuse the double meaning." Ann's grin looked good on her. Her face was losing that pinched and strained look. "I must be due for another massage, though. I hope Marilyn hasn't cut back on her appointments."

Holly thought a moment, still looking at the story in the paper. "Chipper and I have been looking into something. I'd like your input." She filled Ann in on the situation with Fentanyl.

"Yeah, that does seem like an interesting coinkidink, as my grandmother said."

"There's something she's not telling me, but my hands are tied. I'm not an inspector like Whitehouse." The obnoxious inspector from the Major Crimes unit in West Shore had been brought in on a murder investigation the previous year.

"That's the problem in a small detachment. They don't take us seriously. At least we're not one-man-bands up island in the middle of nowhere." Ann fiddled with a pencil sharpener, her grey eyes gleaming with interest. "Sometimes I wish..." Her voice trailed off.

Ann was no complainer. "Marilyn's a class act," Holly said.

"But something isn't right. I never liked the loose ends. If Joel stole that drug from her, she needs to know. Suppose she used it herself."

Ann put on her reading glasses but gave a scornful wave. "That's ridiculous. Think of her background. And besides, he said, she said, everything is hearsay."

Holly reminded herself that this was real life, where some mysteries might never be solved, maybe even her mother's. "How can we make sense of this play outline? What the hell was Joel doing with it? I don't fancy him the literary type."

"What's the timeline?" Ann asked, as if that should have been the first consideration. "Go back to the beginning. Maybe this is something from the past."

"Sure, but that paper couldn't have been in the cache that long. Not with our climate."

"Forget that for now. Let's deal with what we can verify."

"How old is Marilyn?"

Ann looked at the stain on the ceiling as she searched her brain. "She told me once when were discussing calcium supplements. Around fifty, give or take."

Holly pulled Joel's file from the cabinet. "Birth certificate put him at fifty-two. They grew up in Sooke."

"Weren't you around here then?"

"Not quite. Over in East Sooke, and for heaven's sake, I was barely born."

Ann gave a hearty laugh. "I didn't mean you. What about your par...your father?" She tiptoed around the sensitive subject of Holly's missing mother.

"My father the absent-minded professor wasn't paying attention to anything but his job. We need someone who has known her a long time. Neither her mother or father is alive. All she had was her brother." *Or was there something more Marilyn hadn't mentioned? Lying by omission was still lying.*

Ann leaned back in her chair but kept her back straight and her feet on the floor. "In those days, two or three children was normal. Even four. God, as a single mother, I could barely handle one."

Holly had never asked where or even who the father was. Particulars like that were Ann's business.

"Where did Joel and Marilyn go to high school?" Ann asked.

"Not Notre Dame. I already asked my old teacher. And Sister Clementine is following up with someone at the public high school."

"So you'll just have to—"

Holly snapped her fingers. "Hold on. There is an aunt. The one who raised her after her mother died."

Ann brightened. "Still living? She must have all the good genes in the family. What's her name?"

Holly drummed her finger on the desk. "Aunt Dee, or maybe it's D, as in short for something else. She's living in Eyre Manor. That much I recall."

A happy whistle was Ann's response. "Where Mother lives. Piece of cake. Let me handle her. I know how to talk to the old folks. Many remember Pearl Harbor better than this morning's breakfast. Something about the way the brain works. Cobwebs in the connections."

What could they expect from the aunt? Not everyone was as sharp as Stella Rice and Sister Clementine. Ann had mentioned her mother once or twice, but when it came to spilling her guts, she was as private as Marilyn. Here was the perfect assignment. "So you're there every week or—"

"I go there to have lunch with her on Sundays. That's about all I can take, but you'd have to know Phyllis to understand."

"Phyllis?" Holly couldn't imagine calling her mother by her first name. "Is she pretty...cognizant?"

"Like a cobra." Ann paused and polished her reading glasses with a tissue, holding them up to the light. "Aunt Dee, eh? My mother just moved there. I don't know many names. They come and go. The nurses' grim words, not mine."

Holly thought about her father's sudden vulnerability, quickly recovered or not. Was he only ten or fifteen years from this kind of life-changing event? "That must be tough."

Ann ran a hand through her short brown hair. "I was depressed at first, seeing Mother dependent, the old dragon. Sort of like a waiting room to the great beyond. Every month or so, an empty chair, a lonely pack of cards. Then I realized that these people had their own lives and personalities. There but for the grace of God. I guess it's a question of being satisfied with less and less after spending your life requiring more and more."

"A good way to put it."

"It's an excellent place for her. My appearance on a regular basis assures that better watch is kept, plus I make sure she gets seen if necessary when the doctor comes each week. Double-check her meds and monitor her clothes. Volunteers read to the seniors or just talk."

"I'm going to leave this in your capable hands. This isn't an official investigation. But find out what you can about the family. You're the soul of discretion." With a grin, Holly put a finger to her lips. Strange that Ann referred to her *mother,* more formal than *mom*, an indication that they hadn't been very close.

"That's the first time anyone's ever called me discreet. Are you flattering me?" Ann raised an eyebrow. "People clam up pretty fast if they think they're talking to a cop. But being too friendly isn't professional."

201

"Marilyn must have told Aunt Dee about Joel's death. And unless the woman's been gaga for years, she knows what a bad boy he was. Maybe this will shed light on whether those papers belonged to him. It's not like we have samples to examine."

"And it was printed," Ann added. "That changes everything. The handwriting class I took online last year says comparisons can't be made between printing and cursive. Totally different styles."

Ann's initiative reminded Holly that she hadn't done much lately to upgrade her own skills. "So that's why criminals cut letters from the paper or block print with a magic marker."

Fourteen

In her bright galley kitchen, Ann switched off CBC Radio shortly before noon and dished tuna into Bump's dish as the tortoise-shell cat twined around her ankles. Phyllis would be expecting her, probably tapping her watch. Supervised living had saved the day after she had fractured a hip falling in her classy apartment in Oak Bay last year. "Breaking a hip signals the end of life for many seniors," the doctor had said, speaking quietly in the waiting room after the operation. "Your mother is a tough old eagle with the bones of a sparrow." Home care wasn't practical for someone so frail and bent from osteoarthritis. She'd been a big cola drinker all her life, and it had come back to bite her. Exercise helped maintain bones, but that wasn't part of her generation's habits. And with occasional reflux, she wasn't a good candidate for the new phosphate drugs. The doctor had agreed that strontium couldn't hurt, and Ann had found a source at Popeye's in Victoria.

Ann's parents had been globetrotters even before his retirement from a career as a Canadian Tire executive. But then he'd slept late one final morning. Her face calm and her pinkie finger extended from a cup of tea, Phyllis had registered her usual sangfroid. "Fred's bought the farm," she had said when Ann rushed over. "I've called the police, the lawyer, the undertaker and the crematorium. Let's get things rolling. First up, sell the old Mercedes. Don't take less than five thousand. I never needed to drive, and at eighty, I'm not starting now. That's why God made taxis and children."

Ann was relieved to be able to move her mother to Sooke to keep a closer eye on her. "I don't understand why you want to associate with the worst in society, grub around in the gutter. You had such a way with people," her mother had said. "You could have been a teacher or a nurse." These professions were historically honourable for females during the Great Depression. "Or found a maaaan," she added, elongating the syllables. She'd badgered Ann so much about the mystery father that Ann had left for Vancouver six months pregnant and kept house for a friend until her son's birth. Her father Fred Troy had used his contacts to track her down and insisted on giving her a loan for the baby. Phyllis hadn't met her grandson until he was five. It had taken Ann years of working to raise her son before she could go to college then join the force.

Ann hopped into her sagging Cavalier, left her small condo behind Sooke Elementary and made a few turns into Eyre Manor. Conveniently located for shopping, doctors, dentists and restaurants, the handsome complex had been a successful and timely initiative. Short of blowing up the ferries, there was no way to stop the burgeoning numbers of retirees from frigid zones from tossing their long underwear and moving to Lalaland to play golf year round.

She was in no hurry to meet Phyllis. Their mutual abrasion was like two entwined trees rubbing wounds on each other. Ann spent a few minutes admiring the new landscaping. Rhodos, arbutus bushes, a mock orange, a row of cedars, even pear, plum and apple trees. Mobile residents were encouraged to get into action and help plant the annuals and trim the perennials. Beds of red and white petunias adorned the front. A few people with walkers strolled the grounds, and every now and then a wheelchair or motorized scooter, Canadian flag waving on a fibreglass pole, appeared around the corner. One narrow, enclosed vehicle was nearly the size of a Smart Car. Her mother had asked for one, but with that independent streak, she might tootle off to the beach, crossing thoroughfares at her own risk. Mother had always made the rules.

Three levels of living had geared-to-income costs: independent cottages, assisted apartments, and a care wing, aka nursing home. Entering the main lobby for the apartments to the tune of 101 Strings on the speakers, Ann headed for the dining room, steamy clouds of a hot meal meeting her nose. She paid for her own lunch on a monthly basis, though her mother thought she was treating her daughter. Ann left it that way. Her father had made bad investments, and the family fortune had been reduced by three-quarters the year after he died. Ann did the accounting, and when her mother asked how Nortel, General Motors and Katanga were faring, she replied, "Same as everything else these days." If Phyllis knew that she was being subsidized by her daughter, she might insist on moving in with her and driving them both nuts.

On the wall was a seasonal exhibit of arts and crafts by the elders. One watercolour caught Ann's attention, a picturesque cove with floating beds of kelp and seals basking on the rocks.

Her mother scuttled up behind her and tapped her on the shoulder none too gently with her malacca cane. Her head was bent as she peered beady parrot eyes at Ann. What she lost in height, she made up for in chutzpah. "You're three minutes late. Come on. It's fish today, and it's just plain disgusting when it's cold. So damn bland anyway. Why can't we have some real meat? Are they forcing us to turn vegetarian or just being cheap? Did you bring the Tabasco? That green kind. Doctor says no red for me."

Ann felt her chest tighten. Phyllis always made a food request, and this one had slipped her mind. Last week it had been Patum Peperium spread for her crackers. Anchovy paste. Talk about a salt lick. Try to find it outside of Victoria. "Sorry. I'll run some by on my way home."

"Gangway. Move aside," Phyllis said to a young server. Ann rolled her eyes sympathetically and got a nod. They made their way into the dining room and took a seat at a window table. With a ruthless perm that made her white hair even thinner, her mother had turned crabbiness to her advantage. She got her own way or made lives miserable. No one wanted to room with her, so a single became hers at the same price. Phyllis's icy pale-green eyes bored into Ann from head to toe. Powdered cheeks had the substance of pale lavender hydrangeas. "Are you gaining weight *again?* That's not good for your back, you know."

"I'm still at fighting trim. Haven't gained a pound," Ann replied.

"When I was your age, I weighed the same as when I was a girl of twenty. About what I weigh now," Phyllis said with a satisfied smirk.

Phyllis hadn't raised an honest sweat from hard work in her life, a trophy wife from day one with a weekly house cleaner and cook. She'd been a beauty and entertained on a rajah's level. Fred Troy's career had been boosted by the lavish dinner parties and salons. Their home wasn't so much a house as a theatre of manners and business. Ann had been glad to escape even though she'd gotten pregnant before twenty.

Ann's stomach was rumbling, and she shifted, afraid her mother would make a comment. A cheery, pink-cheeked volunteer waitress brought a basket of rolls, and, having missed breakfast, Ann reached for one. She saw her mother's narrowed glance and pulled back, brushing her hair with her fingers in a distracting gesture. Why couldn't she stand up to the old woman? She'd been afraid of her mother's viperous tongue for years, and now, when she could assert herself, it seemed mean-spirited. A retreat for charity's sake. People like Phyllis grew meaner as their abilities failed. Frustration turned against the world. To know all is to forgive all, Ann felt.

"So how's that job?" Phyllis asked. Her liver-spotted hand reached for one roll, then another, along with a wad of what looked like butter but was probably healthier and non-saturated. She put both on her side plate, tore into them like a velociraptor, and popped them into her mouth. Ann poured a glass of water from the carafe and sipped slowly. A slice of lemon showed the extra effort from the staff.

"Same old. Speeding tickets. A lost cat. We had an overdose in the homeless community. It's far from glamorous." Far from sympathizing, her mother had torn a strip off her when Ann had been injured stopping a felon. Whatever health complaint anyone had, Phyllis always had something more painful.

"It's no profession for decent women. In my day there were no homeless. People worked for a living or damn well died. We didn't even have socialized medicine, not that that's a bad thing. Abused by some is all. Rush to the emergency room for an ingrown toenail." Phyllis brushed a crumb from the floral shirtwaist. Women did not wear pants. Sending her clothes to the nearest dry cleaner in Langford was an extra expense for Ann. "Why didn't you become a teacher? I told you I'd babysit Nicky while you went to university." Having reopened as many wounds as possible, she shook her head in wonderment. As for charity, Phyllis claimed that she forgave, but she never forgot, so what was the benefit for the sinner?

A hot flash of suppressed ire creeping up her spine, Ann

boiled quietly, her best strategy and the way her father had coped. Maybe that's why he'd had a heart attack the year after he retired at sixty. "Take care of your mother. She thinks the world of Nicky. Sometimes love skips a generation," he'd said the last time they'd met. "And let her have her way. It's easier."

She smiled at the waitress as a plate of poached halibut, small potatoes and peas was placed in front of her. While the palates of the elderly demanded more flavour, stomach and gall bladder problems argued against it. Without thinking, Ann reached for the salt. Her mother's bread knife touched her hand in warning and left a small smear. "Stop that. Salt is a poison. We're addicted to it. Just break the habit on ten consecutive occasions, and you won't think about it any more. That's what *Prevention* magazine advises. You'll see, dear." She poured on ketchup until her fish was swimming in pink.

Ann milled pepper onto her food instead. Her stomach was cramping and to relax her muscles, she looked around the dining room. Effort had been made to make the place more homey and less institutional. Chintz curtains bordered the windows, and the tables and chairs were early American style. Easy-care linoleum on the floors simplified cleaning and facilitated wheels. The ratio of men to women seemed about one to five. The few males got star treatment and acted like pampered roosters.

Oblivious while she ate, her mother had cleaned her plate and taken another roll to mop up the juices, though her hand was shaking. Ann made a mental note to check her meds with the nurse. Then she pushed the last piece of fish aside and assumed a casual tone. "Do you know a woman called Dee? She lives here, or so I'm told."

"Dee?" her mother repeated, frowning. "That used to mean Dierdre. I don't know anyone called that. Not that I'm friends with everyone. There are some who..." Her voice trailed off with a humph.

One steely eyebrow arched to the ceiling, she turned to a woman on the left. "DO YOU KNOW A LADY CALLED DEE?" Ann flinched. Phyllis turned to her daughter and tapped her own ear. "Deef, you know."

The woman adjusted a hearing aid, pursing fuschia lips. "Dee. Dee. Let me see."

Phyllis roared out, "Something wrong with your mind? I said Dee. This isn't poetry class." As an entire table of diners looked over. Phyllis circled her temple in a "whacko" gesture.

"There *is* Dorthea. That's spelled D-O-R-T-H-E-A. Only one O."

Turning her back without a thanks, Phyllis resumed her conversation with Ann. "I remember that one. Very brash. She's in the left wing, perfect for her politics. Prefers meals in her room. Doesn't socialize at all. Reads mostly. Probably those trashy romances."

Ann balled up her serviette and rose. She motioned to the server who was bringing a tea pot. "Sorry to leave early. I have some business, Mother."

"What? You haven't finished your fish. No doggie bags here. Waste not want not. Where are you going? I want some ideas about Nicky's Christmas present." Phyllis's voice rose until the room became as quiet as a graveyard except for the clatter of dishes in the kitchen. "Ann? You come back right now, young lady. I'm..."

Without explaining further, Ann left her mother, her wizened mouth still open but her attention drawn to her teacup being filled and the heralded arrival of *petit fours*. She got quick directions from a familiar worker in rainbow scrubs and went down the bright hall to room 14. On the open door with the nameplate *Dorthea Roehl* was a collage of dried flowers and sea shells. Ann craned her head inside to see a very small lady at the window.

Dorthea carried herself like a duchess and probably had practiced posture with a book on her head. On the patio, she watched two hummingbirds duelling at the feeder. Then she moved to a cozy velvet chair, propping her legs on an ottoman. The room was small, but neat and clean, with a bed, dresser and side table. A handsome portrait of the young Queen mounted on a horse was on the wall. Down her back Dee wore a thick white French braid streaked with grey.

Ann came forward slowly in case the woman was hard of hearing. Introducing herself, she explained that her mother lived here and that she was volunteering to chat with some of the residents.

"Isn't that nice, dear, but you don't need to worry about me. I have my reading." The lady held up a large-print copy of Agatha Christie's *And Then There Were None*. "Talk to some of the others who need the company." She bent back to her book.

Ann twitched. How to get the conversation on track. A hook. "Someone said that you were Marilyn Clavir's aunt. I've gone to her for massage. A truly talented woman."

At this, a corner of Aunt Dee's mouth rose. "With her business, she doesn't have a lot of time to spare, but she visits once in awhile. Even took me to Fuse on my birthday." Fuse was an upscale restaurant with a gorgeous harbour view. The pride in her voice about this small grace touched Ann's heart, and she vowed to redouble her efforts to tolerate her mother.

Banking on the fact that older people loved to talk about the past, she added, "Marilyn said that she grew up in Sooke. It must have been different then. Much smaller. I arrived a few years ago."

"Oh, yes. People were so close in the community. Pioneer families. Eating the same apples from the same orchards as their great-grandparents. They helped each other and came together. All-Sooke Days. Our wonderful Fall Fair, over a hundred years old. Church, dances, there wasn't but one television station from the city. Bunny ears we had. My sister had the first colour set on our block."

"I understand that Marilyn's mother died very young. And her father, too."

"Tom went far too early. Those who say only the good die young had it right with that boy. Got home from a marathon race, went to sleep, and never woke up." She tapped her chest. "Congenital heart disease. Never knew what hit him." She gave Ann a softer glance and marked a page in her book. "Well, if you're staying, please sit down, for lord sakes. I've forgotten my manners."

Moving aside a copy of the *Times Colonist* and a *Maclean's* magazine, Ann took the only choice, the bed. It had a bright yellow afghan and a very realistic stuffed border collie. So far, so good. Dee had picked up on everything she'd offered and run with it. Perhaps she was lonelier than she let on. And she probably missed a dog. "Marilyn said that you raised her. She was very lucky to have a devoted aunt." *Careful with the fulsome praise. Dee's bullshit antenna would begin transmitting.*

"Kin do that, dear. Or they used to." Her milky blue gaze grew distant, and Ann could see that her jewelled cat's eye glasses had very thick lenses. Some drops sat on a nearby table. Glaucoma? "To be honest, my sister Clare was not my favourite person. She was downright mean when she had a few, and she never missed a day. Used to keep a glass of wine in the cupboard and nip at it, as if Tom weren't to know. Disposition of an asp, too. Marilyn was a very sensitive girl. More like myself way back when. In truth, she was better off with me, though I'd never confess that to a soul."

"It was kind of you." Ann summoned up a quizzical frown of concern. "What happened to Clare, if I may ask? I didn't want to pry." Using words like *pry* wasn't her style. Would it strike the right chord?

"Fell down the basement stairs. Now mind you, with the drink, I wasn't surprised. And the stairs were very steep in that old house they rented on Booster Avenue, Number 125, it was. No handrail. Poor lighting. And after Tom died, she'd hit the bottle full steam ahead."

Trying to sort out the timeline, Ann sat back in the chair. From down the hall, the smells of a strong disinfectant met her nose, and she heard the vague swish of a mop. "What a tragic and unusual accident. But I suppose with the older houses, codes weren't what they are today." Fred Troy had been a builder in the beginning and had taken his young daughter to a few sites.

Dee held up a crooked finger. The nails were clipped but nearly blue. "Not at all. Most accidents take place in the home, where you're off your guard. Bathtubs. Ladders, roofs, that's men's domain, but anyone can take a tumble down the stairs."

"Oh dear. Was it quick or did she...linger?" Ann squirmed inside at the approach, this womanly clucking. Proceeding one inch at a time, she wasn't sure how far she could go. Dee seemed like an intelligent woman.

"She went down every night after dinner for another bottle of her homemade wine. Made it a hundred bottles at a time. Disgusting stuff, not like our mother's elderberry, a tonic. You could set your watch by it. The stairs were not only steep, they were uneven." Dee smacked her fist into her hand. "Bang. Didn't stand a chance. Broke her neck. But to look at her, you'd never know. Serene as an angel in her casket. The head wound wasn't even visible. That was one blessing."

"What an awful accident." Ann made an effort to shiver.

Dee pulled her cardigan closer. Though it was stuffy in the room, the elderly had poor circulation. "I was right next door that night, helping the neighbour can peaches. She put up acres of them every summer. Marilyn was with me." She squeezed her eyes shut as if unwilling to remember.

Ann touched her hand, a bold risk. "Don't go on. It's clearly distressing."

But there was no stopping the woman. It was as if she had been waiting for years to tell her story. And perhaps she had. "We heard this dreadful cry, you see. Like a wounded animal, but muffled, like it was in the basement. And Marilyn rushed out. She got there first, poor girl. Found Clare at the bottom of the stairs. Not a spark of life in her."

"Wasn't there a brother in the family?"

Aunt Dee flushed with an unexpected rage. Her tiny hands balled up in fury as she growled an answer. "Don't talk to me of that devil. Clare let him get away with murder all his life, especially after his dad passed. He was seventeen when he came to me, Marilyn two years younger. Then I gave that little heathen some honest Christian rules. School, chores, prayers, sensible things."

"I have a son, so I know what you mean. It's tough raising a child alone."

"Indeed. And I had intended to stay single. Me and my dog and my job." She pointed to the stuffed animal. "That's Haggis. Minds his business."

"What a responsibility, though." Ann let a slight frown of womanly support cross her brow.

Dee waved a hand. "Clare left a very small insurance policy, and of course she had a tiny bit from Tom, though he'd been laid off from the shipyard in tough times. I was enough to help

213

Marilyn with her schooling after she graduated. I came down from Campbell River when Clare died and started a house cleaning service here. Easier to set my own hours."

Ann cast a surreptitious look at the clock. She needed to get back to work. On the hard chair without lumbar support, her back was beginning to throb. But things were progressing. "Go on."

"Anyway, one night after I grounded him for coming home drunk, Joel stole everything I had in my purse, about a hundred dollars, a week's salary in those days, and I never saw him again. Good thing I didn't believe in those newfangled charge cards, or it might have been worse. He took my little car and abandoned it in Medicine Hat or Moose Jaw or Swift Current. Can't ever keep those prairie places straight."

"And yet he turned up here just a few weeks ago." Ann cocked her head to judge the woman's response. She realized that she had given Dee a rather feeble explanation for her presence. Perhaps one of the facts of living here was people coming and going without stated reasons.

"That's no surprise. To get what he could out of Marilyn. Told her he read about her lottery win in the paper. He always was a sneaky little bastard." Dee's face was growing red with the exertion and excitement. "Can you get me some of that water on the table?"

"Did Clare work?" A few empty slots needed filling. A picture was beginning to emerge.

"In her mind, she did. Claimed to be an interior decorator. Ten-buck magazines up the wazoo. Took a course at Camosun. Not much came of it. Then she used her looks to hook up with an operator called Mitch Garson."

"Operator?" At the interesting new tack, she tried to keep surprise out of her voice.

"One smooth-talking snake. Investments in third-world mining companies. Probably a Ponzi scheme, like they call them today. He was moving to Toronto, and she was going with him. Had a few connections, or so he said." A contemptuous cough left no mystery about her opinion.

"That sounds like a serious adjustment for the children, going all the way across the country." Ann's son had staged a major rebellion when she'd been posted to Wawa with nothing to do but look at snow seven months a year. A threat to turn him over to the Children's Aid after he'd come home drunk sobered him up fast and set him on the right path.

"Joel was all for it. More action. No more sleepy island life. Marilyn was heartbroken. She didn't like leaving her...her friend Shannon." The old lady marked her page with a piece of yarn then closed her book and put it on a table next to her.

Ann took a breath full of hindsight, vowing to use neutral language. "They must have been very close."

"Inseparable. Even I remember sometimes. Passions run high in the young. In those days, well...not like now. Clare said it was a silly phase, and moving was the best answer. When Marilyn held her ground one night and threatened to run away, Clare slapped her silly. It was Christmas, and I was visiting. The girl came to me with a hell of a bruise. One eye was half-closed. I told Clare to smarten up, but she just laughed." She looked up at Ann. "Sometimes young people know when they belong together. After they finished their university studies, they moved in together in Fossil Bay. Shannon had her nursing job at the hospital. Marilyn started her massage business."

"Marilyn seems to have turned out very well. A credit to you."

"She was the light of my life. I can't imagine my own daughter being better. The girls had me to every holiday dinner all these long years. And visited regularly...until Shannon fell ill."

"That was very sad," Ann said.

The old lady was winding down, her words slower and slower, her eyes blinking. Small hands nestled together like sleepy puppies. "I'm very tired."

Ann rose slowly and moved to the door saying goodbye as the woman's head began to nod. She made a quick exit, avoiding the dining room. Mother would want to know everything that had happened.

Back in her car, she pulled out a pad of paper and jotted down what she remembered. She'd never even asked about that play and why Joel might have had the pages. Sounded like Marilyn had had a rough life with a bitch of a mother, a beloved father and partner who had died too young. She felt as if she were spying on a decent person. The tension made her back throb. When she got home, it was going to take an entire bottle of red wine to relax.

FIFTEEN

Don Yates, former English teacher at Edward Milne High School, lived in nearby Shirley. Yates had been Marilyn's English teacher in Grade Ten, Sister had said on the phone. "*Entre nous*, of course, now that you are an adult and with law enforcement, I must tell you that Mr. Yates was urged from his career by the discovery of his predilection for young men. Not that such might have a bearing on his testimony on other matters."

"Was he prosecuted?" Holly asked.

A bitter chuckle answered without words. "Those were very different days. And he was extremely careful. An errant hand. A close whisper. On the third offense, the principal took him aside and suggested in no uncertain terms that he was due for a very early retirement. He cleaned out his classroom that Christmas and marched down the steps. He was only forty but had a cushion from his parents' investments."

A small frown crept across Holly's brow. "I feel uncomfortable that you're telling me this. So he's been living in the community for decades? I've never seen his name on a list."

"For good reason. It was my understanding from the principal that the warning was sufficient. He was forbidden to have any contact with young people, and he's not a stupid man."

A candidate for using undcrage porn sites, Holly thought. Maybe she should run a check. "Do you think I can trust his word?"

"Donald was never a liar, just in the wrong profession. Far too many temptations. He was his own worst enemy. He's probably never forgiven himself. The worst sin of all."

That Friday Holly kept the arranged appointment with Don Yates, preferring a face-to-face meeting, for obvious reasons. Calls to the detachments in Sooke and in Langford had turned up nothing new. Apparently the man was minding his business and didn't even have Internet access.

At Invermuir Road, she made a right towards the ocean. The rugged dirt road coiled through second-growth forest until it ended at the historic Shirley lighthouse. Now on an automatic system, the site was maintained by a faithful support group that raised money selling shirts and mugs. Holly noted the bulldozing devastation of yet another new housing development connected all the way to Seaside Road at French Beach.

Then she turned down a drive of overlapping cedars with a sign long fallen into a tangle of berry bushes. It read "Manderley". The Prelude's front-wheel drive lapped up the steep, winding hill. She stopped at an unprepossessing bungalow. Its wooden roof was scrofulous with miniature ecosystems of moss and sprigs of future saplings. The stucco was stained and chipped, the place merging with happy slugs in the deep and dark.

Don was seated in a single pool of sunlight, looking out at the waves. Haloed by the sun, he was a frail man, his chino pants almost empty on his crane-like legs. His head rode forward on his neck and thin shoulders as though from osteoporosis. Far away, a freighter full of logs plied the choppy strait. Despite its steep cliff instead of beachfront, the property was worth a fortune. The taxes would be enormous.

"Welcome," he said, reaching for a tray with a sweating pitcher, his sharp elbows jutting from sleeves of a linen shirt with bow

218

tie. "Corporal Martin, is it? Please sit. I put out some lemonade for you. I don't often get visitors."

With a thanks, she settled into the uneasy depths of a Muskoka chair. The tart lemonade slipped down well. She suspected he had a mind to match, judging from the *Harper's Magazine* and *Atlantic Monthly* beside him. A faint English accent favoured by radio announcers tinged his speech, not unusual in a place "more English than England".

"Sister said you were interested in a former pupil of mine. Is there a question of a crime?"

She didn't know how much to explain. That depended on what he told her. "I'm not really sure." That sounded sinister.

His rheumy eyes sparkled. With evil or mischief? "Did you bring this document she spoke of?"

"Yes, but please don't touch it." She opened an envelope, and with tweezers, set it on the table.

He picked up a large magnifying glass. "Sherlock Holmes style," he said with a wry grin.

After no more than a few minutes, he glanced back at her. "Of course I recognize it. The eccentric handwriting's a dead giveaway. It's Marilyn's work. Marilyn Clavir."

"I see." Or did she? Holly scratched her chin, where a mosquito was tickling. In the dense forest, away from the sea air, the bugs reclaimed their territory. "What can you tell me about Marilyn and Shannon? You knew them in high school. What does this all mean?"

He sputtered with phlegm then pounded his birdlike chest with a liver-spotted hand. "Arcadia."

"Pardon?"

"It was a world they created. An escape from reality. The concept thrived long before Sir Phillip Sidney and his opus.

Every society looks back, however purblind, to a Golden Age."

"I know Marilyn's life was hard. She lost both parents. What about Shannon?"

"Shannon's father was a minister, what some would call a talibangelical today."

"Tali...oh, I understand." The man had a sense of humour. Perhaps a charm of sorts, but she hadn't forgotten his predilections. Sociopaths were excellent conversationalists.

"A wee joke. Anyway, he was a remote and demanding man. Her mother bowed to his wishes, and Shannon was an only daughter. In a small school, you get to know this."

"Was the play, or this plan, an assignment?"

"Yes," he said. "For creative writing. They were very precocious, you see. Always reading ahead of their age. At the time all we had were the old classics, *Wizard of Oz*, the Narnia series. Tolkien. Very male-oriented. The idea of a female knight intrigued them. Galvanized their thoughts. That's how they latched onto Spenser's *Fairie Queene*. It wasn't the historical politics of the poem at all."

"Today they might be as obsessed about vampires or sorcery."

Don found this amusing. His shoulders jiggled, and he stifled a cough. "Oh, my dear. No animal torturing or spells. Merely the epic struggle of good and evil that has fascinated mankind."

"Evil. So who was the villain?" At the word *villain*, did she see his brow rise?

"Villainess, actually. Throughout Spenser's saga, Duessa, the false one, takes on many beautiful shapes and forms, but she lurks everywhere. She enlists the Blatant Beast with his lies and slander, much like the tabloids today. Now the Salvage Man—"

"Salvage?" This man spoke a language long forgotten, and for good reason.

"A variant of savage. Untutored and entirely amoral. Like

220

Nature, I suppose. Then there's my favourite. Talus, the iron man, gave rise to those heroes in films who have a psychopathic sidekick to do the heavy lifting. Nothing is new under this old sun."

"I took English lit, but it wasn't my best subject. And I don't remember Spenser at all." The way he related the themes to the modern age made it come alive again.

"Indeed, it's a formidable work even for graduate students. I read it through once a year. But those girls devoured it like candy. Total immersion. The Garden of Adonis vs. the Bower of Blisse. The lovely mutability which orders that winter must follow summer as opposed to the brittle and unchangeable fabrications of man. A flower cast of metal. Beautiful but sterile."

She looked at the scrap again and the cast. "But is *The Fairie Queene* a play?"

"An epic poem. Don't look for that genre in Canada later than E. J. Pratt's *Titanic*. The girls chose a play for the narrative possibilities. Simple iambic pentameter, not those tedious Spenserian stanzas. I suspect they planned to stage a few scenes for the class. Plays are not for reading. They are for experiencing."

"Is this all there was?"

"Spenser's work was never completed either. He had planned to cover all the ten virtues, twenty, some say." He shrugged with a sad expression that urged his jowls downward. "Even on their smaller scale, the girls never completed theirs, other than the first three acts. But after they graduated, who knows?"

"Most of us leave our high-school days behind. I presume their interests changed."

A dry laugh sounded from the folds of lizard-skin on his throat. "Nothing was beyond them, with their steely focus, but events caught up to them. It happened so fast. Marilyn's mother died in the late fall. And I went on...sick leave after Christmas.

And then I retired...early. I suppose you know all about that." His gaze sent her a challenge that she ignored.

"Did you keep in touch with the girls?"

"I saw Marilyn in the Sooke library from time to time. Shannon became a nurse, I hear."

Holly looked the old man in the eye. "The Duke has her father's name, Thomas. The ghost's invocation. What does that signify?"

"Ghosts are always appearing in Renaissance plays to give advice and warning, or charge the main character to make a pledge. Helps start things off with a bang. Catch the attention of the groundlings. You *did* read *Hamlet,* didn't you?"

She gave an noncommittal monosyllabic answer. "Who are these two characters listed first?"

He held the magnifying glass over the words. "Faded, but you can make out the letters if you know what you're looking for. Britomart and Belphoebe. They are key characters in Spenser's poem. Britomart has an entire book to herself. A female knight the equal of Arthur himself. Belphoebe was raised by Diana. She's a heroine of chastity and may represent Queen Elizabeth on another level."

Marilyn and Shannon had committed themselves to a long-term relationship. "Surely Spenser didn't intend...they weren't..."

"Spenser was very conventional." Don leaned back in his chair and assumed a lecturer's voice. "The lady knight Britomart was in love with Artegal. Arthur's equal, you see. Belphoebe was a huntress, riding through the woods. In the true courtly love tradition, the lover admires from afar. It derived from medieval times when lords were away fighting in distant lands, and their ladies, complete with chastity belts, had younger admirers writing songs for them."

"And..."

"And look at the name of the play, *The Triumphe of Love.* Anyone who might threaten to part such destined souls..."

"Like Clare Clavir." She found herself whispering, "Clarissa."

"A fall down her basement stairs. Steep, those old houses. There were rumours that she..." He tipped a glass for effect. "I felt sorry for Marilyn. Once the mother came to a parent teacher conference. She was like a dog in heat. Ripe in more ways than one." His long nose wrinkled in distaste. "Reeking of cheap perfume and hormones. Short skirts and plenty of cleavage. Scarcely the motherly type. You'd never have known they were related."

Holly told him about Joel's life and death. "This fragment was found hidden near his body. As if he had some purpose for it."

He looked sidelong at her. "Joel was in the bonehead English class, not mine. They read short stories and other trash. He was such a contrast to Marilyn. But it takes all kinds, doesn't it? And if he were the blackguard you say he was, I leave you to conclude what he was doing with this evidence from the distant past."

Holly collected her papers and stood as the brief sun flickered out behind a cloudbank. "Your information has been helpful, but we don't operate on pure speculation, no matter how tempting. My discoveries keep leading me deeper into the forest."

He waggled a bony finger. "Your images sound like Dante and his dark woods, or nearer to home, Robert Frost on that snowy evening. We are all of us lost at times. That makes life interesting. The object is to make the right choices at the crossroads."

"Suppose there aren't any more crossroads?"

SIXTEEN

Holly had dinner with her father, beginning with cocktail wieners and bacon-wrapped water chestnuts and pineapple, then spinach salad and chicken baked in mushroom soup with Minute Rice. A Jello poke cake made her fake a smile. Norman had put *Animal House* on the DVD player, but she begged off.

"Your mood ring is jet black. No wonder you're so crabby tonight," he observed.

"I'm still cold from that walk to the beach with Shogun," she said, taking off the ring and placing it on the table. "This isn't rocket science. It reacts to body heat." As "The Way We Were" played, she thought of the girls and their alter egos. So much time had passed. If there had been a crime, where did it begin and end? At the old family home Marilyn had mentioned.

"I'm going into Sooke," she said. "Gotta check something out."

"Take Shogun. He loves car rides."

Fifteen minutes later, she was in the town core. Turning at the stoplight, she passed rows of older bungalows on a geological plate. Rhodenite, Quartz, Pyrite and Talc streets spread out against a distant backdrop of steeper hills and valleys which "smoked" when warm air met cold. Marilyn's former house at 125 Booster Avenue looked vaguely Victorian, as if it had stood there since the Spanish-American War, daring civilization to approach. On one side, a mammoth housing development was gnawing at its edges, the vegetation sheared off and erosion washing red soil from the nude hills. Next door, working overtime, a noisy backhoe with a diesel engine puffing black diesel clouds was moving its slow thighs to clear a final patch of land.

With two acres of gnarly and neglected fruit trees and slumped bee hives, the Clavir home had been one of the holdouts. Holly hopped out, leaving Shogun in the car, and began a methodical assessment. Three stories with an attic on top and dormer windows. A roofing job sometime after asphalt shingles had replaced cedar shakes. A dark basement with a storm door more practical for Kansas tornadoes.

All first-floor windows had been boarded, presumably to prevent access. In human form, the house would have begged for euthanasia. Yet overgrown lilac and spirea bushes, indefatigable red and white peonies and a pink rose climbing a lurching trellis showed a loving hand gone to the grave before Holly's birth. Out back were a whimsical playhouse turned chicken coop and a rusted swing set, its bones creaking in the wind as one seat moved.

An ancient Douglas fir with large conjuring arms held split and greying boards from what Marilyn had described as Joel's tree fort. Holly had taken many a tumble in her own climbs. Life wasn't much fun wrapped in cotton batting with monkey bars now forbidden on playgrounds. Sometimes, like wood-duck chicks, you had to trust in luck and leap from the nest.

Mounting a set of cement steps, she tried the large front door with its round ringer in the middle of the panel. Locked. Then the back door to the kitchen. Both seemed firmly locked. On the overgrown lawn, a faded realty sign had fallen to the ground like a tired tombstone. A snail had left a trail of shiny slime on its mossy plane.

Perhaps someone with more nerve and fewer civic morals might have found a way to break in. Holly took stock of her information and her choices. Joel's body had been found under suspicious circumstances, Chipper's information about the Fentanyl, Ann's talk with Dee, her own intuition, for what that was worth. Maybe old Dee was confused. And certainly Don had his own credibility problems and a past he wished buried. Hampered by her lowly status as a corporal, Holly needed all her stuffed cats in a row before throwing the carnival baseball. It was an entertainment cliché that the police arrested people on spurious causes, proving their case later. What could the sad house tell her?

It was eight p.m., but in high summer during the real-estate rush and the wealth of light, Valerie Novince was cruising 24-7. Feast or famine in her risky business. She answered on the first ring. "Holly-O?" The middle name of Oldham came from her great-grandfather in Devonshire. Only Valerie knew about it, and for good reason. With schoolyard tongues and taunts, Holly would have been called Old Ham.

"Lemme pull over and still my heart. Back for friggin' months, and you're finally calling me to get together? I was beginning to think you didn't like me any more. Or do you want to buy a house? The market's full of bargains for first-timers, and you don't even have to sell yours. Tired of living with your father? He's a doll, but a girl needs her independence and—"

Valerie could talk the pants off of the prime minister, an unnerving concept. "Slow down and breathe, you. I need to see a house."

"Reeeeeeeeally? Getting married, are we? Tell Val."

"Give me a break. As if I have time to date, keeping you safe. Call it research." Holly felt almost embarrassed at being tossed back to adolescence. Val had been her one friend, heading straight from high school to a stint in the army before growing up. Now she had a seven-year-old and a handsome Norwegian husband who ran a specialty woodworking business.

A loud guffaw ensued, and Holly pulled back the phone. "So you are *cereal...*or *serial.* What was that joke we used to—"

"Get serious for once. I need your help." With a friend like Valerie, a decade could pass like an hour.

"Not one customer in two weeks. Only poor sods who want to sell. And only four closings since Christmas. I was thinking of trolling the pubs. Now, what kind of—"

When Holly described the property, Valerie's voice dropped a few decibels, along with her enthusiasm. "God, the old Mattoon place? That's been on the market for dog's years. Rental in between minimal cleanups. More run down each time, like an old whore without lipstick or powder. I was surprised it didn't burn to the ground some Hallowe'en, the kids these days, my dear daughter aside."

Holly laughed. "You're sounding your age, which is mine."

"So true, girlfriend. You always knew me best. Didn't we do detention together every week? Wait a sec. Lemme get my Blackberry. Don't know what I did without it."

There was a sudden quiet. "Some people look at houses for free entertainment. Have me drive them all over on Sundays blowing gas bills out my butt then never make an offer. Sheesh."

"So can you come through for me?"

"I'll need to call the listing realtor at ReMax and get the key. Let's say tomorrow morning. Ten sharp. Suit you?"

"Meet you at the Stick."

*   *   *

Chipper took his cap from the closet as Holly came in the next

227

morning. "Gotta head out to Bletcher Road. Grass fire started when some idiot tossed a cigarette. The roadside's like tinder now."

"What about the Fire Department?"

"Already there, but they need traffic control. Just pray the wind turns, or those new houses might go up. They're just shells with heaps of scrap lumber around."

"Jesus. When are people going to learn?" As he turned to go, Holly added, "Take that face mask in the closet. Smoke's no fun, especially from toxic building materials."

He put on his duty belt and snagged the Impala keys from the hook. "I remember when a barn of pot went up near Prince Albert. It was like one big doobie. I didn't come down for a week."

"One of our perks."

Chipper examined the mask like a fashion accessory. "This won't do much good except keep off sparks."

"That baby face will thank me. And be careful." She gave his shoulder a friendly prod.

*   *   *

At ten over in Sooke at the Stick, Valerie was sharp as ever in a tailored butter-leather jacket over beige slacks, a silk blouse and lizard print low-heeled boots. Her hair had left the bottle for a softer ash brown, a natural improvement. The curly tangles were corralled in a scrunchy.

After munching a warm brie-on-brioche, Valerie led the way to a flashy Lexus SUV. She patted the hood, planting an air kiss on it with her plump pink lips. "It's a hybrid, so don't sneer. Last year I made a fortune. Now we're eating home-made beans. And it's leased anyway. Soon you might see me driving an antique like yours." She elbowed Holly in her usual madcap style.

"Hey, beans are back in style. Good carbs." Holly hoped Val wouldn't wallow on about the steep drop in house sales as the North American economy faltered. Government services would be next. Would they lose an officer or transfer Chipper? Suppose they shut down the detachment and sent her to Fort St. John just as she was starting to investigate her mother's disappearance?

"Don't cry for me, Capital Region. This will purge our ranks of part-timers who made bundles when ordinary houses hit the half-million mark. You're looking at a *survivor*." Valerie thrust out her ample chest. "Allow me," she said, opening the door to a leather living room. A CD labelled *Timeless Classical Melodie*s sat on the console. "Some Mozart? Sets a classy mood for the clients. Though, make no mistake, I'd sell a mobile home in a flash. Pardon me, I mean a manufactured home."

"They'd probably prefer the Dixie Chicks. Victoria is too snooty for country." Holly struck a society pose then buckled up.

They climbed the hill to the top of Booster Avenue and parked. After they got out, Valerie beeped the car, triggering a whirring answer from a raucous Stellar's jay in the high branches of a huge maple. "Why *exactly* do you want to see this poor old white elephant? The truth, now," she asked with a suspicious look.

"It's a very interesting building," Holly said, ignoring the frown. "I hear it's been empty for years."

Val nodded, giving a snap to her Juicy Fruit, and opening a notebook with pictures. Born to the profession and as tenacious as a pit bull, she maintained a thorough dossier on every place she showed. "Once it was a proud palace. Built at the turn of the century, not the last one either. By Henrick Mattoon, a brewery magnate from Rosedale. That's in Toronto."

"As ritzy as it sounds. I visited Toronto once and took a walking tour of the city."

"But it's a mixed-up baby." She waved her arm at a turret. "One of our interns from head office had an architectural background. Told me most of these styles don't fit. Hard to imagine the house in her prime, the white paint clean and sharp instead of that mould and moss. Columned porches, Pal...ladium or something windows, multiple gables, half-timbering. Crap, I'm no historian. That top floor with the tiny window would have been a servant's quarters or perfect for a mad aunt in the attic."

Holly looked up at three chimneys, crumbling as the Virginia creeper advanced on sticky pads. "Hell to heat, too, even with all the fir you want, or coal from when we still had mines up island. They must have spent all day hauling fuel to the top floors." Missing shingles testified to water seepage from the roof, a sign of approaching life support.

Valerie shrugged. "After the owners died in the Forties, the place passed to relatives in California. They arranged for rentals, but it got shabbier and shabbier. Finally it was condemned after a kid broke his leg climbing in a window."

"Why wasn't it torn down?"

"Guess they were sitting on it waiting for the migrations of retirees who couldn't afford Victoria. After that accident, the owners boarded it up and waited for urban sprawl to do the job."

"Maybe the time is now." In addition to the homes at Sun River, the arrival of sewers had spurred development. Even sidewalks were arriving.

"This parcel of three acres could be zoned for a dozen micro lots. Look out your back door to twenty other identical yards with barking dogs. No challenge to selling that shit."

"Ouch. We're crowded enough on one-third acre."

"Let's go inside. Sooner or later, you're gonna come clean with me about your interest. So tell." They climbed to the generous gap-toothed porch, behind them the strait view obscured by bigleaf maples and alders with a century head start.

"Never could keep anything from you." Holly locked eyes with Valerie as the woman's French-tipped fingers fiddled with the keys. "Someone...died here."

A small smile flitted on Valerie's expressive lips, but her sangfroid hadn't mellowed. "Baloney. Enough years, and every house has a ghost. People have to die somewhere. But maybe you're not talking about natural causes."

They entered the foyer, and a dusty crystal chandelier tinkled in the stagnant air currents. Surprisingly intact, it was inaccessible without a twenty-foot ladder. Several crystals were missing, and one lay smashed on the scuffed hardwood floor. To one side was a parlour, as Val called it, and on the other a dining room. No furniture remained, and someone had used the fireplace for a urinal. Empty beer cans lay in a pile along with fast food wrappers. "A real firetrap. And catch that reek," Holly said.

"Exactly. That's why it's boarded up."

A tour of the upstairs led to four bedrooms and only one bathroom with the black-and-white octagonal tile of bygone years. The tub was lion's claw, the enamel chipped and the brass fittings worn. A portable rubber hose was affixed to the tap, the kind used to rinse hair before showers were invented. Valerie lifted the toilet seat.

"What are you doing?"

"Just a habit." The bowl looked as if a bloody massacre had occurred. "See this rust? It's from their drilled well. One hell of an iron problem, and in the old days, they didn't have expensive filters. I always check the toilets and take a drink from the sink of every place I list."

"You must have one hell of an immune system."

Dust motes rising in the air made them sneeze. Valerie asked, fanning the air, "So what else did you want to see?" Her diamond eyes slitted in suspicion.

As they descended to the main floor, Holly looked at the scratched fir boards, trying to imagine the honeyed tones from a weekly waxing. "The person who died here fell down the stairs."

Valerie looked at the steep banister, ending in a pineapple-shaped newel post designed to bruise a coccyx. "Here?" She jumped back and hugged herself.

"No, the cellar stairs. That's what I want to look at." She tried to imagine Marilyn and Joel as teenagers in the Seventies, the tie-dyed era. Their father's sudden death. The proposed move to Ontario. Then the place Aunt Dee rented and this house left behind with such violent memories.

Valerie kept peering around as if spirits might pop out of the wall. "You always were a weird one. Helping banana slugs cross the road. Making goddamn leaf collections. My lord, girl. Didn't you ever have a Barbie doll?"

"You drew a tattoo on the chest of your GI Joe." Holly gave her an even look. "Dollies weren't my thing, either."

They passed through the kitchen, a giant area with pale-green, glass-paned cupboards. Judging from the ugly orange fake-brick linoleum, it had been updated by a colour-blind designer. Valerie considered several doors, opening a pantry. "Handy," she said. "Wonder why they're so rare now?"

"Except for my father, nobody cooks any more. The TV room's the centre of the house."

Another small closet held brooms, a bucket and cleaning supplies. Both of them froze at the scurry of tiny feet then laughed to see a robin scuttling on the windowsill. "That must be the basement."

Holly opened the door as an eerie wave of cold filtered up as if from a tomb, and they stared down a steep stairway. Stone walls framed each side, and a handrail was broken. The wooden steps looked firm enough, but the light was bad. Flicking switches at the top did no good. The power was off. Holly took out her Maglite.

"Careful," Valerie said. "The firm's liable for your injuries. In fact, do you *have* to go down there? It stinks. Maybe there are rats. And snakes to eat them."

"Haven't changed at all, have you? Harmless garter snakes are the only variety on the island, and they wouldn't be down there anyway. They're looking for frogs."

"Spiders, then. A pal of mine got a wicked infection from a brown recluse bite. Came off some bananas from Honduras."

Holly continued, stepping carefully and reaching the bottom with a relieved sigh. The basement floor was poured concrete, cracked and patched from the shift of the land in occasional earthquakes undersea. Long before cozy basement rec rooms and pink styrofoam, here was mere space for sagging clotheslines to hang dank washing during the rainy winters or cold storage for root vegetables. Cupboards held rows of empty, dusty bottles, both for canning and wine. This must have been where Clare kept her supply. A naked bulb dangled from the rafters, and a mouse scuttled somewhere. Not a rat, Holly thought, training her beam like an impotent laser light.

With every corner covered, Holly turned to go. What had she expected to find other than a steep staircase where a fall could have caused death five ways?

"Come on, you're creeping me out," Valerie called. Her cell phone twittered with the theme from *Batman*. "Yes, I'm in the friggin' bowels of some goddamned house my nutbar friend wanted to see. Catch you at Wink's in ten minutes. Order me a Potholes Poutine, double gravy. No onions." She looked down the stairs with a plea in her whisky-tenor voice. "We *are* leaving now, right?"

Holly came up each wooden stair, inspecting them from side to side. Dee had said that Clare had hit her head. Surely not merely on the wooden stairs, which she might have survived. Yet falling head first didn't jibe with an ordinary drunk, who might land on her bum.

Valerie was tapping her foot. "Let's go. You promised."

Then at the top of the stairs, Holly thought she saw something. "Wait a minute."

"What now?"

Holly knelt and rubbed her fingers over the darkened wood. On one side, then another. There was the slightest colour difference. Like a small round hole had been drilled or punched by a nail on each side, then filled in and sanded smooth. "Very interesting."

"What? I don't see anything."

"Exactly." Holly took a penknife from her pocket and began chipping, placing the sample in a paper envelope.

Valerie looked on. "What the hell? Are you digging for gold?"

Holly said, "You said the place is headed for demolition. I need to take a sample of this. And don't you have a camera in your car? Can you get it? Please?"

"Bossy. What did your last servant die of? You owe me." She gave Holly a mock salute and turned on her heel.

Holly called to her disappearing back, "Dinner at the Nut Pop Thai."

While she waited, the radio on Holly's shoulder crackled. Ann's voice was tense. "Chipper's been taken to the General."

SEVENTEEN

Police work not glamorous enough for you?" Holly sat by Chipper's bed at the hospital. They were keeping him for observation and oxygen therapy combined with prophylactic antibiotics for his lungs. Many people became hypersensitive after a smoke event. He'd been lucky to have received only minor burns on his forehead and hands. No scarring was expected.

He looked pale, and his face was slick with ointment, but his coughing spasms had slowed. "Maybe if I smoked, I'd have some resistance," he said, his face contorted behind the tubing which ran up his small nose. With his height, his toes were dangling off the bed. Her red and white carnations in a vase on the table warred with the smell of disinfectant.

"Tell you what," she said, touching his shoulder under the thin gown, the cotton equalizer which made everyone a mooner in hospital. "Enjoy your time off, though it's a tough way to get a vacation."

He pointed to the mask on a table along with his wallet and some magazines. "Better take that back. Looked stupid as hell, but they say it saved my life. Do you know how fast a brush fire can move with a forty klick wind? It shifted directions in a second."

"Even a racehorse couldn't outrun it," she said, tucking it away in her jacket pocket.

They both jumped when the phone rang. Holly picked up the receiver and handed it to him. "Oh, it's you, Mindy," he said.

Standing in the doorway, Holly raised an assessing eyebrow and he blushed. "How did... Ann told you?"

He listened for a few minutes, saying only "yes" and "go on."

Holly looked at her watch and made motions that she was leaving, but he shook his head and waved her back. "Thanks for calling. I really appreciate it. And I'll...that sounds great." He hung up, looking suspiciously like a guilty tomcat.

"New girlfriend?" she asked with merriment in her eyes.

The vet tech had called with more information, he said. "Remember that typhoon last year?" Thousands of fallen trees had crippled the area. Roads were closed. Power was off for a week or more.

"Sure."

"Someone broke in and robbed the vet's office. They smashed into the narcotics cabinet and took everything. Fentanyl was only one of the drugs. They got away with PCP, too. That's an animal tranquilizer."

So someone else in the community had the drug. Holly's theories were shaken. "I hope they have a no-fail alarm system now."

"Big bucks. With its own backup battery."

"That was months before Joel came to town. But we haven't heard anything about it."

"Right, so now what are—"

A scurry in the hallway brought an older couple through the door. They hurried to the bedside with worried faces. The woman carried a package of food redolent of curry and coconut and wore a gold and emerald sari. "My baby boy! My angel! Are you all right? Have you eaten? You look pale as a ghost." She threw her chubby arms around him and squeezed. Holly stood back and nodded to the father. From Chipper's conversation, she felt as if they had already been introduced.

"Ma! Cut it out. This is Holly, my boss." The cords in his neck strained in embarrassment at the embrace. "I'm going to smell like your perfume." Clouds of jasmine warred with the flowers and disinfectant.

Hands were shaken all around, and Holly left Chipper smothered by maternal love. As he stood against the wall out of the way, Gopal gave her a nod.

* * *

The next morning over their toast, Norman turned to his daughter with a wan smile. "What's wrong, Dad?"

He stuck out his lower lip in the way he always did when assigned a particularly noxious cleaning chore by her mother. "It's time to clean out the rat traps before fall. That's when they nest."

"Those chickens next door and their feed. That's the attraction. So what's the procedure?" She gave a shudder.

"Your mother got a bucket and filled it with hot water, dish soap and a half cup of bleach."

Since he had done the shopping and cooking, she had handled the other chores. Letting the man even approach a lawnmower was a big mistake. He could break anything in a minute.

"Then use the rubber gloves and take the traps out of the pump-house. Clean them in the solution, as hot as possible, mind, then leave them in the sun. Spring the traps first, of course."

"I'm not stupid enough to pick up a set trap." Norway rats were fond of maritime coasts. They drove any weaker rats away. One mating pair with a reliable food supply could produce six hundred and forty babies in one year, and calling them kittens didn't make the idea any cozier.

Having gathered her gear, she went with trepidation to the small, vinyl-sided pumphouse, turned the nail which secured it, and as the creaky insulated door opened, nearly vomited. A giant female, gravid by the size of its belly, lay in the trap, its head smashed and blood leaking from its mouth. None too fresh either. "Can't you stay in your house and out of mine? Can't we all just get along?" she asked as she bagged the body and cleaned up. But it was just being a rat.

While she was there, she rapped on the large black water-storage tank. Instead of the crystal clear aquifer fare from their shallow well, recently there had been a brownish tint. The tank gave a hollow response. She got out the eight-foot ladder and climbed to the top, lifting the lid and peering. Nearly dry. The pipes were sucking mud from the well.

After finishing and washing her hands against bubonic plague, she said, "Call the water guy. We're nearly out."

Her father's frugal nature sent a crease across his broad freckled brow. "That's impossible. We've never run out yet. A timely rain always fills the tank."

"This is the driest summer in decades. Anyway, I pay the utilities, so what's the problem?" What was a hundred and ten bucks when you needed to flush and shower?

"Huh." He headed for the phone. Potable water tankers circled the town perimeters from June to October.

That night he was unusually quiet. He accepted her compliments about the dinner but didn't deliver his usual running commentary, quizzing her every five minutes on films, television shows and fads. After dinner, he took his decaf to the solarium, turned "Eleanor Rigby" to a bare murmur, and sipped pensively as he marked papers. On the deck outside, a few sparrows and red-capped finches sparred for crumbs fallen from the barbecue.

Holly opened a copy of Jane Hall's book *The Red Wall*, describing her experiences in 1977 as one of the first women in the RCMP. Her graduating class had been issued pillbox hats, skirts and purses. For their guns?

Her father clicked his ball point. "Final exams. No pride in their work. You should see the spelling. I don't know why I waste my time teaching. And this summer course is even worse. I see all the people I failed."

"Maybe you should teach report writing for law enforcement. They'd take you seriously. We have to be letter perfect." She spoke tongue-in-cheek, knowing that such a practical discipline would never interest him.

Every now and then, the cocoon of his Ivory Tower wore thin. She had noticed this first after her mother had disappeared. Without Bonnie as a counter-balance, the black dog had held him so fast in its clutches that Holly'd been on the brink of recommending anti-depressants. She debated now giving him the lava lamp as a very early Christmas present.

He barked out a laugh to let her know he was trying to cheer up, tucked away the papers, then returned to *Jonathan Livingstone Seagull,* slumping in his recliner.

Later as she came to his bedroom to say goodnight, he was standing and staring at his wedding picture on the bureau. *Déjà vu, memento mori,* and all points in between. He wore a bell-bottomed suit Seventies style, and Bonnie wore a batik dress with her shiny ebony hair flowing like velvet to her shoulders. Looped in colourful leis, they stood on a beach on the Big Island, its volcanos in the distance. His parents gathered around, beaming. Margaret and William Martin had been buried years ago in Sudbury, where he'd grown up.

Instead of pink belly up and legs splayed on the bed, Shogun was lying in the corner as if banished. She could hear his border-collie grumbles. "What's the matter, Dad? We *had* to order the water. It should do us until the rains start."

This time his voice had a slight edge. "It's not the money. Just something I'm working on. I'll tell you in a few days."

"This sounds sinister. Tell me now."

"No big deal. Really, I need to turn in. I'm bushed." As a hint, he hung up his dressing gown and pulled back the bedcovers.

The jut of his jaw and his tone made her retreat. Clearly something was bothering him, but for now she chose to let him tell her on his own schedule.

EIGHTEEN

I'll be late tonight, Dad. Maybe eleven. Don't wait. Of course I won't skip dinner." Holly hung up after leaving the message. Hamburger Helper wasn't one of her faves anyway.

Quarterly reports were due, and she'd left them until the last minute. But thanks to Ann staying overtime without pay, they had everything wrapped by nine. Ann had brought in hot turkey sandwiches, and they'd made a picnic clogging their arteries.

"Chipper usually does this. I'll see that he pays," Holly said as they sealed the material into a manila envelope for the courier. The doctor had prescribed a few days of rest at home for him until his lungs were absolutely clear. Last time Holly had seen, though, he had locked eyes with a cute nurse. To her surprise, Holly felt proprietorial about her handsome co-worker. But what about poor Mindy?

Arriving home around ten, she was surprised not to see Norman's car. No barking erupted as she came in the back door. The lights were burning in the lower part of the house. The stereo was playing "Down on the Corner". A dinner plate and cutlery sat rinsed by the sink as on the abandoned *Marie Celeste*. And no note. Had he taken Shogun for a walk? Surely not in the dark, since the flashlights remained in the cupboard.

Calling Madeleine brought only worrisome information. "Sorry, I haven't seen him since I went by with the dogs late this afternoon. He was in a very pensive mood. Distracted."

"He gets that way sometimes but usually fights it off. It's very strange that he's not here, nor Shogun."

A tinge of concern crept into Madeleine's voice. "I asked him over for coffee and Tosca cake after dinner, and he said he had an appointment."

"An appointment at night?" Insurance? Investments? Drafting a new will? Another woman?

"He said nothing more. I didn't like to pry."

Upstairs in her father's study, she found his usual clutter and piles of papers. *"I am sorry that according to the grading protocols, fifty is the lowest mark I can give you. Your proofreading is an absolute disgrace. Take some pride in your work,"* red ink proclaimed on the top essay. To maintain students in a time of dropping enrollment, the university had gradually adopted more quantifying schemes which saved a few. Was that what was bothering him?

Then back in the kitchen, she noticed the answering machine still glowing. A message had been played but not erased. With a trembling hand, she pressed the button. A gravelly voice said between coughs, "Fan Tan Alley. Ten o'clock. Go to the end. And don't be late. Bring the money. Twenties and fifties. Nothing bigger."

A cold chill of a nightmare ran down her back. At intervals, Norman had placed a newspaper ad seeking information about Bonnie. Some insect was bound to crawl out of the woodwork. Tonight, knowing that she wouldn't be home until very late, he had gone off playing detective.

In a few minutes, in a lather, she was tooling down West Coast Road, then Sooke Road, then winding her way through Luxton, Langford and catching the busy TransCanada to downtown Victoria. Even at night in the core, tourist traffic was brutal. The poorly-lit crosswalks every half block along Douglas Street didn't help, especially when people wore fashionable black. She cut over to Government Street, braking at Chatham for a smooching couple.

Fan Tan Alley. Once the entrance to a maze of convoluted passageways, courtyards, opium dens, and gambling clubs, the warren had gotten its name from a popular game. At the time of the construction of the Parliament Buildings and the Empress Hotel, which still anchored the Inner Harbour, Chinatown was a thriving community of several thousand souls. Now only a few buildings, restaurants, and the elaborate Gates of Harmonious Interest remained to harbour ghosts. Yet their people had endured.

The alley snaked between Fisgard and Pandora. Holly pulled into a pay lot, amazed to see the little blue car, circling the block like a persistent beetle, looking for a meter with two minutes left, no doubt. He'd probably forgotten that parking was free at night. She waved both arms, and her father pulled over. Slowly the window rolled down.

"Next time if you don't want to be found, erase your tracks. Where the hell do you think you're going? I was worried out of my mind," she said, her pulse beating in her temple. Shogun was dog-belted into the passenger seat.

"Watch your language, young lady." Norman gripped the wheel, clearing his throat in embarrassment. "I have this all set up. If you butt in, he might—"

"Butt in? Pardon me? Who might what?" She spoke in a hiss. "A sleazebag could leave you unconscious in an alley...or worse! I can't *believe* you did this behind my back."

"He has information. And besides, here's my guard dog." He cocked a thumb towards Shogun, sitting at attention with an insouciant look.

"Shogun's not a pit bull. Anyone could dropkick his forty-pound pedigree over the Gorge to Esquimalt. Now stay here until I get back, or I swear I'll take you to the cells myself. You need to cool off."

"On what charge, if I may dare ask?"

She pulled up the first words she could find. "Obstructing justice."

"I'm trying to see that justice is done!" He pounded the dash, and Shogun gave a nervous yip.

"Stay, Dad, and I mean it." She emphasized her message with a gesture. Never before had she found herself in the position of dictating to him. It wasn't pleasant. In some ways he was even more truculent than her mother.

Dressed in a blue trench coat on a night cooler than usual, she still wore her uniform. Serious trouble was unlikely, but she unfastened the holster and nestled her hand on the gun like a little friend. Gang wars were relegated to the other side of the Georgia Strait in Vancouver. Victoria had two murders a year. But who wanted to beat the odds?

The clouds parted to reveal a full moon streaked with grey. From down the street tourists exited an upscale nightclub. With the heavy Maglite for her truncheon, she made her way down the dark alley, passing closed stores, an old-fashioned barbershop, a craft store. At a rusty iron gate near the end, she turned into a putrid square obviously used as a bathroom, the underbelly of the City of Gardens. The squalid space was deserted, except for a person of indeterminate sex slumped on a piece of cardboard in a corner. She walked forward quietly and toed the bundle with her boot. "About time. Did you bring..." the slurred voice asked, and then stopped as he looked up. "Hey, who the fuck are you? I ain't doing nothing. Leave me alone." The homeless knew that they were less likely to be hassled than a jaywalker.

"Exactly what information do you have?"

"What the hell is this?" The skinny man rose to his feet with a scowl, then noticed the open holster.

"You tell me," she said in as low a voice as she could muster. "Now put your hands against the wall, spread your legs. DO IT!"

She patted him down, giving him a final trip. He fell with a thud onto his cardboard and turned away. "Move your face into the light. I want to see your pretty mug," she commanded.

"Fuck off, asshole." He blinked as the beam shone in his chinless face, smug in the fact that it was no crime to swear at the law.

Holly pulled her coat aside to reveal the taser. Her badge glinted in a small shard of light. "Maybe a tiny nip from this would help."

"Whoa! I don't want no trouble. This is a big mistake."

She tapped the taser, not good policy but effective with vermin. "Now what were you going to tell the man? What were you going to tell my father?"

"Your..." His hollow mouth showed a row of dull rodent teeth. "All right. So I got nothing. Gonna charge me with extortion? You haven't got jack shit in proof."

"What were you planning? A little robbery in the night? Roll the professor? Give me your ID. Now!"

He shrugged, his grubby jacket pulled aside. Baggy jeans and a dirty t-shirt. "It sounded like easy money. Tell him some bullshit. Can't blame a guy for trying."

He handed over a thin wallet, and in the glow of a street light she read the name, then handed it back. There was no way she could take him in. This wasn't even her jurisdiction. "If I ever see or hear from you again, you'll be riding in a squad car some cold winter day and left on a logging road in the bush. That's the way we operate in the Western Communities."

It was an ugly and preposterous threat, but he said nothing, merely rolled back on the mat, picked up a mickey and drank. The smell of cheap rum drifted up.

As she walked away, she wished that she had been wrong. That he had information worth the price. No sum would be too much.

She returned to the car to find Norman biting his lip, hands gripping the steering wheel. "At least you didn't lose any money over this, just pride," she said. "How much did he want?"

"A few thousand. Nothing."

For a penny pincher, that was major. "What did he say he knew?"

"Something about seeing the Bronco up by Campbell River. And your mother with another man."

"That's all? He could have found information like that from newspaper morgues. The library's down the street. He could have used the search engines for the archives." As for the *other man*, they both knew about Larry Gall, her boyfriend. He'd been cleared completely and seemed to miss her as much as they did.

"You can do that? I didn't imagine." Except for trolling for nostalgia items, the most he did on a computer was check for plagiarism." He felt that Wikipedia should be shut down for ignorance and oversight.

"And next time," she said, leaning into the car and rubbing Shogun's ears, "pick Dragon Alley. It's upscale and a hell of a lot cleaner."

NINETEEN

That afternoon, after strings had been pulled all the way to the Vancouver labs thanks to Boone, the substance analysis from the stairs of the house on Booster Ave came back. Munching flaky kuchen from the Little Vienna Bakery, Holly sat with Ann in the easy chairs in the lunchroom. Things had been so quiet that morning that they'd both nearly fallen asleep. "Plastic wood," she said, showing her the print-out.

"Kids in Wawa used to sniff that," Ann said. "How long has the stuff been around?"

"Home Hardware guy said since the Forties."

"And your theory is..."

"It's obvious to someone looking closely. There was a trip string or wire on the second stair from the top. Two nail holes, an accident waiting for a victim. You don't need much with a staggering drunk. If Clare Clavir had survived, she wouldn't have known what happened. I saw a guy once who'd cut off his hand with a chainsaw. So drunk he was feeling no pain, or maybe it was the body's defenses. Lucky his buddy knew about tourniquets."

Ann crossed her legs and got into a more comfortable position. "Dee said that she and Marilyn were next door helping a woman can fruit when they heard the scream. Marilyn ran over there like a shot."

"Joel was asleep in his room. That's the strange part. Why didn't he wake up?"

Ann's eyes crinkled at the edges. "You've never been a mother. Teenagers sleep until noon like they're unconscious. My son did."

"So she yanked the nails then later, in the confusion, filled the holes with plastic wood. Maybe a quick sand." Her voice slowed in contemplation. "You'd need tools. Sounds like a plan. She must have hated her mother, and from what I've learned, no wonder."

"It looked like an accident. Paramedics tried to revive her, but she died instantly, the coroner said. No one considered it a crime scene." Ann put down the old report Boone had also faxed over. "I still can't believe it. Marilyn is the last person I'd suspect of violence."

"I know what you mean. And, Ann, she couldn't even have been sure Clare would be killed."

Ann blew out a breath, then finished her tea. "But she'd sure as hell be incapacitated for a long time. Enough to delay or even prevent the move. Clare's boyfriend didn't sound like the kind to wait. Con men depend on timing."

"What happened to Mitch Garson? You were going to run a check," Holly said, wondering if he could be another slimy piece of this ugly puzzle. Joel had surfaced after over thirty years like a filthy penny. Why not this piece of trash? Except that he'd be in his eighties.

Ann put her arms behind her and stretched. "Did two years less a day in Milton for lottery fraud twenty years ago. Then he turned up in an obituary in the Calgary papers last summer."

"What makes you think Joel had no role in his mother's death?" Holly patted crumbs from her mouth, then tossed the serviette into a wastebasket.

"Hell, Dee claimed that Clare gave him everything he wanted, and he was happy to be moving to the big city with more scope for his schemes. No motive." Ann gave Holly an even look. "We're omitting one person. Shannon. What did she know? Nothing? Everything?"

"Or something in between. Nowhere to go on that."

"Like in 'two people can keep a secret if one of them is dead.' So what now?"

"Let me mull it over."

"Mulling is good." Ann smiled.

As Ann returned to her work, Holly finished the dregs of some coffee as noxious as her thoughts. The big dogs at headquarters were no more likely to consider this piece of history any more than they'd examine the Shroud of Turin for trace. Joel and Shannon were dead. Unless she got a confession from Marilyn, this was merely an exercise. And if the woman refused to cave, what then? Avoid her for the next few years and hope to be transferred? Face it, she thought. All over the world are cases in which the law knows the person is guilty but can't do a damn thing about it. Still, as in her mother's fate, she wanted to know. The truth was the thing. Painful or not.

What about Marilyn's conscience? Was she waiting for the truth to free her? The cliché had legs. How many times on the *First 48* had a detective reduced even a hardened suspect to tears, forced him to admit what had been gnawing his soul? One minute the thug was talking tough or pulling his arms inside a hoodie in a gesture of guilty withdrawal. Then came the magic words. Asked to "man up," tears would stream down his face, and the "baby daddy" would ask to see his three-year-old. Marilyn had been only fifteen. What about a reduced charge? Manslaughter. Reckless endangerment. If she claimed to have been abused as a child...all bets were off. But what proof remained of that? Only her word? And Aunt Dee's.

She forced herself to call Serenity. The answering machine

gave a reprieve: "I'll be out of town until Wednesday...sorry for the...if this is an emergency..." Holly tried her cell, but the line went straight to Telus voice messaging.

"There's only one choice left. I'm going to talk to Aunt Dee," she said to Ann, who gave her an ok sign.

Ten minutes later, she crossed the threshold of Eyre Manor, holding the door for a man exiting on a scooter and narrowly missing a bruised knee. The staff was cooperative, but curious. Holly explained that she was closing out an accidental death case involving Dee's nephew. "She's in her room writing down her mother's recipe for bean soup. Dee has made a special project out of improving our meals," an aide said.

Holly had never been in a nursing home and considered it as depressing as a hospital, but the place seemed cozy and friendly. A man with an accordion was playing "Lady of Spain" as dozen people in armchairs and wheelchairs clapped to the rhythm. En route to Dee's wing, she found herself buying tickets on a log cabin design quilt from a fireplug of a lady with a chipmunk voice.

Dee looked up from her notebook and didn't seem surprised to see her. Holly noticed the family resemblance in her classic features and strong cheekbone structure as she introduced herself. "I wondered about that other woman and her questions. Now it makes sense. Just because we're old doesn't mean we're stupid." Dee levelled knowing eyes at her. One visit was understandable. A second meant serious business.

Holly closed the door as Dee asked and drew up a chair. After giving Dee some background, she related the information about the stairs.

Dee spent a moment collecting her thoughts. She did not seem at all surprised. Then she reached for the comfort of Haggis and settled the large stuffed dog on her lap. Holly thought of children and the teddy bears many cruisers carried. "Over the years since...Clare's been gone...seeing the girls grow up, I wondered. Not that I really wanted to know. The mill of God and all that baloney. I can't tell you more. Marilyn can decide for herself." She gazed out the window at a sparrow hopping for seed at a feeder. "What might happen to her? Can you arrest her after all this time? I've heard that—"

"There's no statute of limitations on murder. If Marilyn set that trap on the stairs, if she doctored Joel's drugs, she has to face those facts." Holly looked into the faded sand-dune eyes. "No matter what I find, no matter what I can or can't do with the information, I won't turn back. And Joel's death happened on my patch."

Dee dabbed at her eyes with a tissue. "She's at the House of Alma. They're putting in the gas for the stoves and for the fireplaces. Those big propane containers. Bringing in a crane, I imagine." She seemed resigned.

"So close to realizing her dream. No points for atonement in this life. That doesn't make this easier for me either."

"The scales of justice must balance. I understand. As for blame? You won't find this old lady pointing a finger." Dee extended a paper-dry hand to Holly and squeezed for all her life. "He was an opportunistic little bastard. Took after his mother. No tears from me for his worthless life."

"Where is it, then? Where's the House of Alma?"

*   *   *

Back at the station, it was nearly five. Ann was straightening her desk prior to leaving. Holly went to a large topo map of the southern shoreline all the way to Port Renfrew. Marilyn's property was west, in the San Juan foothills, a few kilometres into the heights. From a time when the island grew its own food, this area would have been hayfields supporting cattle and horses, even a few sheep. Since then, it had been a church camp. Any roads would be rutted and winding, part of the charm.

"I need the Suburban for some back-country work. What's its status?"

"Apple pie order. Chipper just had it into Tri-City for its 300,000 kilometre checkup. Even filled up now that gas costs less than champagne." Ann tossed the keys to Holly, who caught them in one hand.

"Call me a bloody fool. I'm going out to the House of Alma to talk to Marilyn." She told Ann about Dee's reaction. "If I can get her to confess…"

Ann scored a three-pointer in the corner waste basket. "I thought you might decide to talk to her. But seriously, do you really think that she'll admit to killing her mother and Joel? Everything is so circumstantial. A fall decades ago. A drug overdose long overdue. He was no fool. She couldn't have injected him, so how—"

"But killing a parent. I don't understand."

"Yours loved you and defined your upbringing. All Marilyn had was Shannon, and that relationship was being threatened. Passions run high."

Holly turned at the door. "Wish me luck."

An uneasy look came over Ann's square face. "What about back-up?"

"Don't be so dramatic. Marilyn is no low-life."

"Maybe so. But that's bad country once off the main roads. And as for radio contact, you might as well send up smoke signals." Ann gestured to the computer screen, gone to sleep

252

with its wandering shapes. "Something more disturbing. The Weather Network said that winds from the south are expected to reach over sixty kmh by early this evening. Bad news for those fighting forest fires. The Otter Point dispatch called up reserve staff and asked for volunteers."

Holly went to the closet. "I'll be fine. This won't take long. If she stonewalls me, there's nothing I can do. No prosecutor would go to court on this." As she put on her jacket, she felt something in the pocket. The mask she'd given Chipper. Then she went back to her desk for one last item.

Giving a guttural groan, the old Suburban roared into action. Without a functioning air conditioner, hot blasts rushed through the open windows like the punishing mistral winds. As she accelerated up the first hill, dollars blew through the exhaust. Maybe Tri-City had rebuilt the carburetor, but the response was jerky. She passed Point No Point resort, then the former logging flats of Jordan River and China Beach. The fog across the strait had blown north, enveloping the land and disorienting her. Washington State to the south might have been as near as Asia. Finally she headed up an old logging road into part of the Jordan River watershed. Nearby in the hills, a massive steel pipeline snaked down.

Someone had started upgrading, Holly noted as the tank-like vehicle shuddered forward on the washboard. Tracks showed where a grader had passed, followed by pit-run gravel dumps to level dips. People spending hundreds for a spa weekend wouldn't appreciate leaving a muffler behind. When the tires spun, she stopped and switched to Four-Low gear for more traction. Stress clamped her jaw. She was coming to accuse a woman she liked of murder. Denial could keep Marilyn safe, but would her body language betray her?

Now that she could see how far she was from the main road,

253

being out of contact added a second worry. The island's problematic CREST emergency radio system, constructed at a cost of seventeen million dollars in 2003 to unite police, fire, ambulance, military and transit agencies didn't work west of Fossil Bay.

At the top of the ridge, as a rising wind rustled the undergrowth, she gazed across the strait at the changing view. Huge cumulus clouds brooded over the blackened waters with not a boat in sight. Ann had been right about the dangerous weather. Then she headed north as the dirt road smoothed between wide brown meadows of former grazing land. Old-fashioned split-rail cedar fences stood after a hundred years. Heavy lug marks indicated that a large truck had passed. Probably delivering propane tanks, followed by a gas truck for the fills.

She heard a solid wall of crackling, ear-splitting cicadas in a group mating effort. *Pick me, pick me,* their whirring wings seemed to plead.

As she drove, the wind increased, and tumbleweeds of tangled brush blew across the road. Ringing the property like rolls of barbed wire were burn piles of second-growth aspen cleared to improve the view. The grass was golden and dry, wild shafts of timothy hip-high like a Kansas wheatfield. At a padlocked gate, she stopped the vehicle, her lips parched. Sweat poured down her brow, wicked off by the wind, and she felt like removing her confining vest. Had she been wrong to come without backup? In a three-person detachment with one out of commission? This wasn't a drug bust of Hells Angels. But she needed to remember that life often had a blackberry custard pie up its sleeve.

After parking, she stepped over the heavy chain meant to keep out motorcycles and ATVs. The crack of thunder in the distance made her jump as she smelled faint ozone. Roiling clouds launched themselves across the strait as if Woden himself

254

was orchestrating the Ring cycle, tossing lightning bolts for emphasis. Like a dark grey velvet curtain concluding a final act, the sky was darkening, even at five thirty in the afternoon. She felt exposed in the face of nature, especially since that typhoon last year. Spruces and firs six feet in diameter had crashed to the ground like toothpicks, their rootballs groping twelve feet into the sky. After a year of clean-up, many monsters still lay in the deep woods back of town, mute witness to a century storm which took no prisoners.

New hydro poles marched to the complex. A main log house and several outbuildings appeared, their wood refreshed with varnish. A handsome sign, "The House of Alma", featured a dove nestled in strong, welcoming hands. Holly'd learned online that in *The Faerie Queene,* Alma's castle represented the balanced body under command of the rational soul. *Mens sana in corpore sano,* Sister would have said. Banks of white feathered pampas grass led down the drive, with freshly mulched beds planted with drought-resistant agaves, yuccas and heather. Scottish highlands met the desert. A series of barks overhead startled her, and she looked up at a single bird, fighting the winds as if floating in place. A rare snow goose, not the usual grey Canada version or smaller, darker short-necked cackling relative. Its cries were more raucous. Warning or announcing? As she trod the dusty track, her boots complained and her toes ached.

As the sky turned black and sheet lightning flashed, Holly expected to feel raindrops, but none came. "Hello," she cried, but the words blew back in her face. She continued to the main house, noticing only Marilyn's Audi. The workmen must be gone for the day. Beside the house and another large building which might have been a cookhouse and mess hall, two enormous propane tanks on cement pads hunched like bloated toads.

Noting the new red metal roof, she stepped up to the full-length porch with fresh-milled boards and a handrail for security. An attractive rustic swing set, chairs and side table gave a cozy welcome. Huge wooden shutters were lowered across the front of the house, though a can of paint and brush sat waiting. Then she knocked.

"Is that you, Mike? Why so formal? Just come on..."

Then the door opened, and Marilyn stood in a faded denim jumpsuit, smear of paint on her nose. "Holly, what a surprise. You're the last person I was expecting. I thought it was the carpenter come back to pick up a load of shingles for the dump. You can see we're almost ready to go. And the propane people were here earlier with our tanks. Then the delivery came to fill them. That was a punch to the pocket. You'll have to try our water. They went down four hundred feet, and it's sweet as—"

She seemed to be talking uncommonly fast, perhaps swept up in the thrill of the moment. Holly felt like she was delivering a deadly telegram or a letter edged in black. "I'm sorry, but—"

"Oh, you're not intruding at all. I was about to break for dinner. Please come in. As you can see," Marilyn's arms swept the room with pride, "it's painting time. Something easy I can do myself. Sweat equity, they call it." A large grin illuminated her face as Holly came in from the blast outside.

Marilyn closed the door and latched it, giving a little shudder. "What a wind. Sweeps up the hills like the wrath of God, doesn't it? But not a raindrop yet."

She ushered Holly down a short hall across the burnished, wide-planked firwood floor to a wicker chair in front of a large picture window in the rear. It overlooked a ravine down to a creek, trees as far as the eye could see, with the San Juan Range in the distance.

"How about some iced green tea? I'm ready to quit. There's fruit, cheese, bread, all the necessities of life," Marilyn said, and Holly postponed the moment of truth. Something dark and sour snaked up her esophagus. The woman took Holly's silence for acquiescence and excused herself.

It was nearly pitch outside, as if it dusk had fallen. Holly's eardrums thrummed with pressure, real or imagined. The idea that something terrible was about to happen made her heart batter its ivory cage. She willed herself to calm down, but an unresponsive primitive brain held sway. Should destroying Marilyn's life to discover a buried truth be left to a higher power? Why had this information been given to her like a solemn burden?

A tinkling sounded, and Marilyn returned from a side room with a tray, pitcher and two glasses of ice cubes. As they both sat snug against the blast, shutters banging in the wind, she raised her tea in a silent toast, and to her own discomfort, Holly obliged.

"So it's settled. You can stay, I hope. Get ready for a loonie-special tour," Marilyn said as a crack rent the air outside. "That was close. We need the rain desperately. I can't even risk burning the building debris. No permits are being issued. Mike will have to lug everything to the dump."

Holly ran a hand through her hair as she reached into her core of strength and lifted as if she were bench-pressing twice her weight. "I don't know how to say this..."

Marilyn caught the look, and something alien flickered in her grey eyes. Once they had seemed soft, but now the colour resembled tempered steel. She lifted her chin, clasping her hands. "You sound so serious. What is it? I thought your father had recovered."

A second passed. "It's about *your* mother."

The words aged Marilyn a hundred years, shot in a vital spot like an elephant sinking to its knees.

"What...about her? She died many years ago. I told you that." Her voice was even, but underpinning it was a treble bar.

Forced to bluff, Holly reached for the oldest line in the world, a roll of the dice, an insult to an intelligent woman. But intelligence was not wisdom. "I know what you did." Aware that her every motion could be read, she crossed one leg and sat back in the chair. Keeping her face impassive would be a heavy task.

"Go on." Marilyn matched her, motion for motion, sisters in a mirror.

So far she had admitted nothing. Where could Holly go now? Interrogations were like a chess game. The accused could hang himself with his own words, but if he stayed silent, the onus was on the interviewer. Would Marilyn ask for an attorney? The Canadian version of Miranda was on the back page of every pocket notebook, nothing more than reassurance of a fair and speedy process.

Suddenly another crash outside made them both jump. Marilyn shook her head. "Even closer."

Seconds ticked, and a third crash rattled the room, and from the kitchen, glassware on shelves tinkled. But they were both frozen in a tableau.

Her throat dry from stress, Holly took a drink and held the glass against her forehead. Her hand was close to quivering, as if she suffered from familial tremor. "I—"

Marilyn's shoulders sank, and her resolve melted faster than the disappearing cubes in her sweating glass. "Oh, my dear. I never was any good at this kind of game. It all started so long ago in a parallel universe. I was a different person. Can you believe that?"

"Arcadia." Holly's vision drifted to a large book on a table.

Handmade, it had a velvet cover with that word.

"Arcadia was a child's dream. This is different. The House of Alma will be perfectly pure and good. Tell me, because I am curious. How did you learn about Arcadia?"

Another crash, but with the tension of the moment, outside noises were as easy to ignore as an errant mosquito. "Joel had a few old papers. The master plan of the play." She explained how she had found it in the cache. "That was the beginning."

A dark looked passed across Marilyn's stately eyebrows. "I suspected as much. He took it from my desk drawer that night. An old draft. I can't throw away even fragments. This precious book never leaves my side." She picked up the treasure and clasped it to her breast like an infant. "A world apart. I used to read it every night, but the pages are so fragile. Once more won't hurt. Come see."

Holly leaned forward at the opened page. "The calligraphy is beautiful. A medieval effect. It must have taken months."

"Two years. We wrote the story together. I was Britomart. And Shannon was Belphoebe. It was a way to escape. And then *she* was going to take me away. To Toronto. Before it was finished. So I had to...we had to..." She closed the book with reverence. "There was no choice."

"Tell me your side of the story. Was Joel blackmailing you?" Leading the witness by giving them self-serving options. Would she never learn the techniques? But how different in a textbook and in the flesh and neurons of reality. On one side, decency. On the other, Clare and her dangerous son. She was rationalizing, resorting to the means-to-an-end fallacy. That some people deserved to die. A fatal option for a law officer.

Marilyn nodded, then rubbed her temples as if to press away pain. "He wasn't content with a reasonable sum. Twenty thousand, even thirty. He wanted to destroy this place, make

259

me liquidate everything. All of the lottery money had been committed. Shannon and I had put our hearts into it. And it *will* be a success. A monument to her and the worthwhile lives we made together. We help people. You do understand."

"Finding out about your supply of Fentanyl. Discovering the cache. Timing wasn't on your side, much less fate itself. Ask yourself why." *Will it be a success?* The future tense gave her a window to Marilyn's mind.

"Convergence of the twain. The *Titanic* in search of an iceberg." Marilyn gave a bitter laugh. "Joel wasn't stupid. He learned fast on the streets, but he had a feral cunning. When he saw the manuscript at my home, it all became clear to him. He had shed no tears for Clare. All he cared about was that it meant he wasn't going to get to move to Toronto."

"I can see why you did it." Did what? She left the question open. Was she setting snares for herself?

"Suppose I told you that Joel had abused me. That he was the twin of my mother. Once I stole a few pennies for candy, and she burned my hands on the stove." She held them out, flexing her joints. "It's ironic, but I don't have clear fingerprints. Luckily there is feeling."

The pads were blurred. Marilyn wasn't lying. But why *suppose I told you?* "Was there no one to help you? Aunt Dee?"

Marilyn's laughter was bitter and short. "This isn't today, where a whisper can bring down a child care centre. Dee was only visiting that day. She lived up in Campbell River before Clare died."

Clare, not Mother. "I can't pretend to—"

"How *can* you know? Your father is a prince, like mine was, but you never lost him."

But I lost my mother. This was no time to contest Marilyn's claim. The woman needed validation to draw out the poison.

Marilyn stood slowly and walked to the mantel, pointing to a silver-framed graduation picture of Shannon. An old-fashioned nursing cap framed her face like the angel of mercy she had been. Marilyn lifted it like the holy grail. "Was it worth it?" Then she turned. "She felt no pain. I am quite sure she felt no pain."

Holly blinked and took a deep breath. The atmosphere was close, like a vacuum. If she didn't get some air... "Shannon?" And then in Marilyn's pooling eyes, she saw another depth like a mirror reflecting mirrors. "You mean your mother. Clare."

Marilyn's fist pounded the chair back, and tears of rage lit her eyes. "Other people's misery was his happiness. A user with no conscience. Then...later...he took off, leaving poor Judy in the lurch. Thank god he never got his hands on that son of his."

Marilyn could have blamed Joel. Dead men make the best villains. "So you killed him."

Marilyn tossed her head back like a warhorse summoning its last strength. Her wild curls rearranged themselves in defiance, and the veins in her neck stood out. "He took that Fentanyl himself. It *was* in the medicine cabinet. That's the first place addicts look."

Or did you put it in the 007 case that night he stayed over and wait for his addiction to take its course? "A bit of luck for you."

Marilyn's voice rose. "It was about time. Joel deserved what he got. Death by his own selfish hand. I'm *not* sorry it happened."

"But listen to yourself. Years of atonement show that you must regret what happened to your mother."

Marilyn folded her arms as her muscles went rigid. "You *say* you know. Let me call your bluff."

"I saw the nail holes on the stairs. Had the filler analyzed. I took pictures. Explain that away."

"She was dead drunk every night. Animals have more caring

261

mothers. And besides, the house is gone. Pictures won't prove anything. It could be anywhere."

"What?" The room was stifling. Something smoky met her nostrils, and she thought she heard an ominous crackling despite the roaring winds.

"Demolition finished today. They set charges to defeat those old fir beams. It collapsed like a pancake. For a moment I felt like applauding. All these years it's sat there like a reproach. A tombstone. I sang our anthem."

"Your anthem?"

Marilyn began in a clear soprano. "Stronger than Spain and France, Queen of the Renaissance. God save the Queen. Long may her banners wave, o'er nobleman and knave, but never passion's slave..." Her voice trailed off.

In the middle of an opera, Holly felt a surge of heat rush through her spine and into her chest. She touched her pocket where the tiny recorder hummed, picking up human voices. "I still have the play fragment back at the office. And this tape."

The fragile skin around the corners of Marilyn's eyes revealed her age, despite her musculature. No matter how hard the deed, she was still soft inside. The fact that she and Shannon had dedicated themselves to a life of service proved that. Holly was already trying the case. A kind of self-defense. With the mitigation of her youth. Only fifteen.

Suddenly the lick of a wild grass fire streaked across the picture window and lit up the room. Embroiled in a brutal conversation, they had been oblivious to what was happening outside.

Marilyn ran to the front door, opened it as a wave of heat pounded in and slammed it. The yard was on fire. "A lightning strike. We can't go this way," she said with a hint of panic in her voice.

White blaze surrounded them as they exited a side door to meet a vortex of vampiric winds. Holly shouted, "The debris around your property is going up like tinder. We're trapped in a fire ring."

Marilyn wiped her forehead. Faced with losing everything, she seemed preternaturally calm. "Bobber Creek. There's a boat. A canoe."

"Then for God's sake, move." Holly shoved her shoulder, and they took off running down a narrow path. Behind them trailed the hissing of the fire and the snap of vegetation exploding. Looking back made no sense. Why stare death in the face until the last moment?

Marilyn's arms pumped as they sprinted to the edge of the ravine, then skidded down what looked like a game trail. It had been years since anyone had chopped at the creek access, and a thicket of brambles, willows and scrub bushes impeded them. Creatures normally unseen in their camouflaged habitat burst forth in a primitive urge to escape their fates. A rabbit screamed as it bolted for the creek. Songbirds darted upward from the flames, and above, a raven soared straight through the boiling smoke, its shrill awk-awk a clarion call. The winds that hurried the flames also dispersed the choking clouds so that sometimes breathing was safe, sometimes impossible. In her hurry, Holly lost her hat to a gust which carried it over the creek into a tree. She yanked the mask from her pocket and pulled it over her head, leaving her nose free for the moment. She needed all the oxygen she could get.

Coated with dust, their faces streaked with soot, they reached a narrow run of water about a foot deep. In shallow places, it dabbled over rocks in a boulder garden. Holly had been naïve to think that they could have charged into the boat and floated to safety downstream like in a Grade D movie. While she could, she took huge gulps of air fast disappearing as the flames sucked oxygen. Marilyn dropped to her knees, her face contorted with fear.

"We can wade across, Marilyn, but what's the purpose? In these winds, the flames will leap from crown to crown. This isn't substantial enough to be a fire break in the dry season." Why did she imagine that Marilyn would think straight after facing a desperate past? She had allowed herself to be led into death's hot mouth. Remaining in the house might have been a better idea. Grass and brush fires burned themselves out fast. With its huge logs, the house might have withstood death's whispers.

Marilyn stood and turned slowly. They looked at each other like ruined lovers as a holocaust of flames roared up behind them in curtains of fiery lace. "The water's a foot deep. There's a small aluminum canoe for the rainy season when the water is high. We can overturn it and stay below until the blast passes."

Holly was wringing wet from perspiration and exertion. Her thighs were screaming from lactic acid. "That doesn't sound much like a chance," she yelled.

"It's the only one we have. You can't outrun a fire."

At the bottom of the ravine, the shrunken creek was about twenty feet wide with overhanging alders and bigleaf maples. Marilyn pointed to a metal prow, and with mutual grunts, they pulled the old aluminum bathtub of a boat, crusty with decades of green mould like any stationary object in the temperate rainforest. "We'll haul it out, hunker down, and hope for the best," she said. Was this the way stupid people died, Holly wondered? But she had never imagined the speed and quixotic nature of a forest fire spawned by unlucky blasts of lightning.

Together they urged the light craft toward the water. The tape recorder dropped from Holly's pocket, tramped by her boot in the shallows. Her brain spun at warp speed, estimating time and space. Vegetation was sparse. Marilyn's assessment might be right. The water wouldn't evaporate. The flames would pass over or die, depending on the capricious wind. At any minute it could shift and leave them safe.

Just as they prepared to drop to their knees in the water under the craft, Marilyn stopped and groaned. Determination overtook the look of stress as a blue vein pulsed in her temple. "Our book. I have to go back. It's all that's left of Arcadia. I can never...I would never—"

"That's crazy," Holly screamed as her face flushed with the heat of the advancing flames. "You have no choice."

"Oh, but I do. Use the canoe. Save yourself." Marilyn dropped the boat and splashed to the edge of the stream, stumbling twice but rising as if jolted with adrenaline. Each step seemed to give her renewed strength. "And if I'm not..." she added and gave a salute. It was the bravest gesture Holly had ever seen.

"Come back. It's suicide!" As Holly struggled to hold onto the boat, the woman disappeared into the burning alders as if parting the Red Sea. Flames licked at her soaked clothes as her head disappeared over the ridge. Would that moisture give her momentary protection? It was a fool's wager.

Holly shivered in the cold water, despite the rising heat and stifling air. No sane person would follow that exit. Marilyn had judged herself and passed sentence. With a resigned sob, Holly sank into a sitting position and urged the small boat over her head, turning the prow alongside the negligible current, allowing the water to slide by. It was dark beneath with only the light diffused from the water. Bracing herself on the strut like doing pull-ups and submerging herself to her nose, she waited for eternity to knock. The boat wouldn't melt at this temperature, but if it got too hot, it would resemble an oven.

A roar and a rush moved her metal carapace. The frets grew warm, then hard to hold, even with the cold water. She could hear the hissing of steam as vegetation fell into the creek. How many cubic feet of breathable oxygen did she have? Her lungs were beginning to ache. Was this the beginning of the end? Had she done those things which she ought not to have done and left undone those things which she should have done?

Suddenly there was a giant boom, and the canoe shook like a dying dog. The aluminum was scorching her fingers. She exchanged one hand for another to hold on and keep her shell in place. Panic shot through her like an arrow. She was going to roast alive. If one animal was a worse totem than the deer, it was a turtle. She coughed a grim laugh. Then another explosion rattled the canoe like the knock of death. The end of the world. Soon she'd pass out, drop the canoe and drift into history. Who could explain to her father why she had abandoned him just as they had become a family again, just as the enigma of her mother began to reveal itself? "Noooooooooo," she called, only to have her ears blasted by the hollowness. Despite her will, she began to hyperventilate, exhausting what little air remained.

Marilyn would not return. Even with her soaked clothes, if she'd reached the house and her lost dream, even if by some miracle the wind had shifted...the propane tanks had exploded. At one with the boat, Holly felt something fall overhead. A small flutter echoed in her ears. Pat, pat, patter, pat. The tiny casket cooled. The rain had arrived. Her breathing slowed.

TWENTY

H er watch had conked out in the creek. What time had elapsed Holly couldn't guess, but it was getting stuffy and cloying in her prison. She weighed her options, knowing little about physics. Perhaps the remaining hot air would suck out the canoe itself, leaving her scorched and her lungs fried, if she didn't die from smoke inhalation. But slowly she felt the heat dissipating. Where it had been unnaturally bright for a moment through the reflections of the water, it was now darker. Had the fire passed?

She dared a peek and saw only cooling smoke blowing back toward the sea. The wind had turned. Coughing, she shoved aside the canoe and looked around. As quickly as it had rampaged, the fire had left only smouldering bushes and grass. Her face felt greasy, and she wondered if her hair and eyelashes had singed. She pulled off the mask and squinted through stinging tears. A path led down the creek, perhaps bypassing the worst of the fire. Marilyn had chosen her fate. No one could have survived that blast. Holly shivered from relief as well as cold. It wasn't just raining. It was pouring. This coast held the record for most rain in Canada in a twenty-four hour period.

Holly edged her way along the creek. The flames hadn't reached this area, and where erosion had spilled down the banks, the vegetation was sparse. In a few hundred yards, she was able to crest the hill. As she had expected, the durable log house had escaped the fire damage, but one wall had been destroyed in the blast. Pieces of the propane tanks had scattered like shrapnel into the other buildings. A still, bloody form, clothes tattered but intact, lay in the burned grass stubs. Though the woman was long beyond help, Holly trudged forward, her boots hot from the ground, steaming from the rain. She couldn't feel her palms, but she knew they would hurt later.

Marilyn was fifty feet from the house, facing toward the creek, as if felled in completing her mission. Many things could have killed her. Smoke inhalation, the flak from the exploding tanks. She lay on her stomach, fists clenched but her clothes barely scorched and her hair flecked with ashes. She seemed to be protecting something beneath her. Did the book mean more than life itself?

At a painful trot, Holly headed back down the lane toward the fence where she had left the Suburban. The wind from the south had carried the lightning strike towards the house. This area was untouched. Nature had toyed with the scene, like the patches of Hawaiian jungle left by lava flows which oozed around them and into the sea.

In the truck, she tried the radio. No luck. In the distance a helicopter droned forward as if on reconnaissance. She flailed her arms in the usual distress gesture and watched it swoop down in an untouched part of the field to the south. A man in a grey uniform got out and walked toward her. He carried a small pack.

"All right, officer? We just got word on the fire from a passing tourist who called us from Rennie." He looked her up and down, then at the car. "Were you back there in the fire? You should have been dead, from the looks of this."

She shook her head and blinked back salty tears. "There was a fatality. The lady who owns the property." Why get more complicated than that? "The propane blew."

He rubbed his rough jaw, probably on call for the last twenty-four hours. "Holy crap. It looks like a bomb hit. How in hell did you make it out?"

She explained the scheme with the creek as he handed her a bottle of water. "You were lucky," he said.

While the pilot radioed back to headquarters to send an ambulance, Holly sat in the Suburban. Her eyes were raw coals of pain, and she felt feverish, as if she had sustained a serious sunburn on her face and hands. The officer brought their first aid kit and dabbed an antiseptic lotion on her exposed skin. His hands were gentle. For some reason she felt cold and went behind the vehicle to retch what was left of her lunch.

Assuring the officer that she was well enough to remain, she waited for the ambulance. It took a mere half hour from Vic General, a record time for the area. Boone Mason stepped out, his trademark hobble easy to recognize from afar.

The furious force of the rains had passed, leaving the fields black and smoking. In only a few weeks, grass would spring up where char had been. The force through the green fuse would be obeyed. Across the strait, the sun was surrendering in the west amid diffusing clouds and particulate. An apricot haze was streaked with crimson and purple. The day was going down on Marilyn's dream. Holly hoped that she had passed quickly and joined her one love.

Gauging her emotions, Boone made few observations, just patted her back with his ham-hock hand and got to work with Marilyn's remains. Then he called in the stretcher bearers with their heavy plastic body bag.

She could hear them muttering discreetly over their task. Mason came over with a silver flask. "Drink up," he said. "Settles my stomach."

She took a deep draught of the rye and wiped her mouth old-west style. "Thanks," she said.

He looked at her with skepticism. "How come you're still here talking to this old man?"

"It's a long story. Got a few hours?"

Mason stuck his corn-cob pipe into his mouth and sucked audibly. They were doing their duties with tenderness and dispatch. As the men slipped on latex gloves and began to move Marilyn, one said, "Hey, look at this."

"Yeah, some kind of a fancy book."

Holly moved forward. "I'll take it. It was hers."

"And she gave her life to save it? Was it, like, rare or something?"

"You might say that. One of a kind."

It was charred and still warm. As she opened the pages, they began flaking, carried away by the wind. The words *folie à deux* came to mind. Clare Clavir had paid dearly for trampling the dreams of impressionable and sensitive young spirits. Marilyn seemed to show little if any remorse for having taken a life. Shannon was a cypher, her thoughts lost in death. They had kept their secret so well. Was there atonement in delivering thirty-five useful years? The question was now academic, little point in even revisiting the unprovable crime. Holly wondered if her own sheltered upbringing had prevented her from understanding the depths and heights of human motivation. She could but try.

Epilogue

Holly sat with Great Auntie Stella as the parade began to kick off the Indigenous Games in Duncan. Down Canada Avenue over 4500 young athletes marched proudly with banners. From all over the country and even part of the States, twenty-three teams representing at least that many tribes had come to compete with the best and brightest. Before passing through the symbolic red gates at the Si'Em Le'lum Field, the leader of each team asked permission from Cowichan Tribes Chief Lydia Hwitsum in order to enter the territory. This was the seventh event in a tradition started in Edmonton in 1990.

Stella had brought lawn chairs and a cooler of iced drinks, and they sat close to the field, thanks to her position of respect in the small community. A crowd of about twenty thousand waited for the festivities to start. This was the first time that a tribe, the Cowichan, had hosted the event instead of a city. Spirit drummers sounded from every direction. Even the Premier of British Columbia appeared at the festive opening ceremonies.

"Look at our spirit pole," Stella said as it was raised in pride with the same significance as the Olympic torch. It had travelled all over the province, and over ten thousand people had helped symbolically with its carving. A frog, salmon, wolf and eagle took their places on the fabled log of traditional Douglas fir.

Holly rose in salute to a common purpose and proud heritage. The fact that the crowd was demonstrably multi-ethnic made her even happier. Everyone was sharing in the spirit of friendship and accomplishment. Several of her distant relatives, second and third cousins, were participating in the lacrosse match. One was expected to win the archery contest. Canoe racing and rifle shooting were among the hottest tickets. Best of all for her, strong young women were taking places of pride, something her mother would have championed.

"Feel at home?" Stella asked, giving Holly's arm a squeeze. "You have returned for a purpose, you know, not just to catch up on old times and fool around with your cousins or to have some of my stseeltun baked on a cedar plank." Along with the trademark salmon, Stella had promised a magnificent feast of traditional dishes, including duck, venison and sea asparagus.

"I haven't learned anything else about Mom's disappearance," Holly said. "Terry Hart won't be back until next week. He might have the information on that flight to the interior. It's taking so long."

"Hasty as usual, little deer. Watch for predators before you move. The journey has just begun."

As they looked up, a doe broke from a thicket, crossed the street and bounded off. With a grin spreading over her apple-doll face, Stella nudged her. "You're on your way."

Lou Allin was born in Toronto but raised in Ohio. Armed with a Ph.D. in English Renaissance literature, Lou headed north, ending up teaching at Cambrian College in Sudbury, Ontario.

Her first Belle Palmer mystery, *Northern Winters Are Murder,* was published in 2000, followed by *Blackflies Are Murder, Bush Poodles Are Murder, Murder Eh?* and *Memories Are Murder. Blackflies Are Murder* was shortlisted for an Arthur Ellis Award.

Lou has moved from the bush to the beach: the village of Sooke on Vancouver Island, the inspiration for the Holly Martin mysteries, the first of which was *And on the Surface Die.*

Her website is www.louallin.com